PLAGUE

ARC copy

Julie Anderson

CLARET PRESS

Copyright ©Julie Anderson
The moral right of the author has been asserted.

Cover and Interior Design by Petya Tsankova

ISBN paperback: 978-1-910461-46-4
ISBN ebook: 978-1-910461-47-1

A CIP catalogue record for this book is available from the British Library.

This paperback can be ordered from all bookstores as well as from Amazon, and the ebook is available on online platforms such as Amazon and iBooks.

www.claretpress.com

Claret Press

PLAGUE

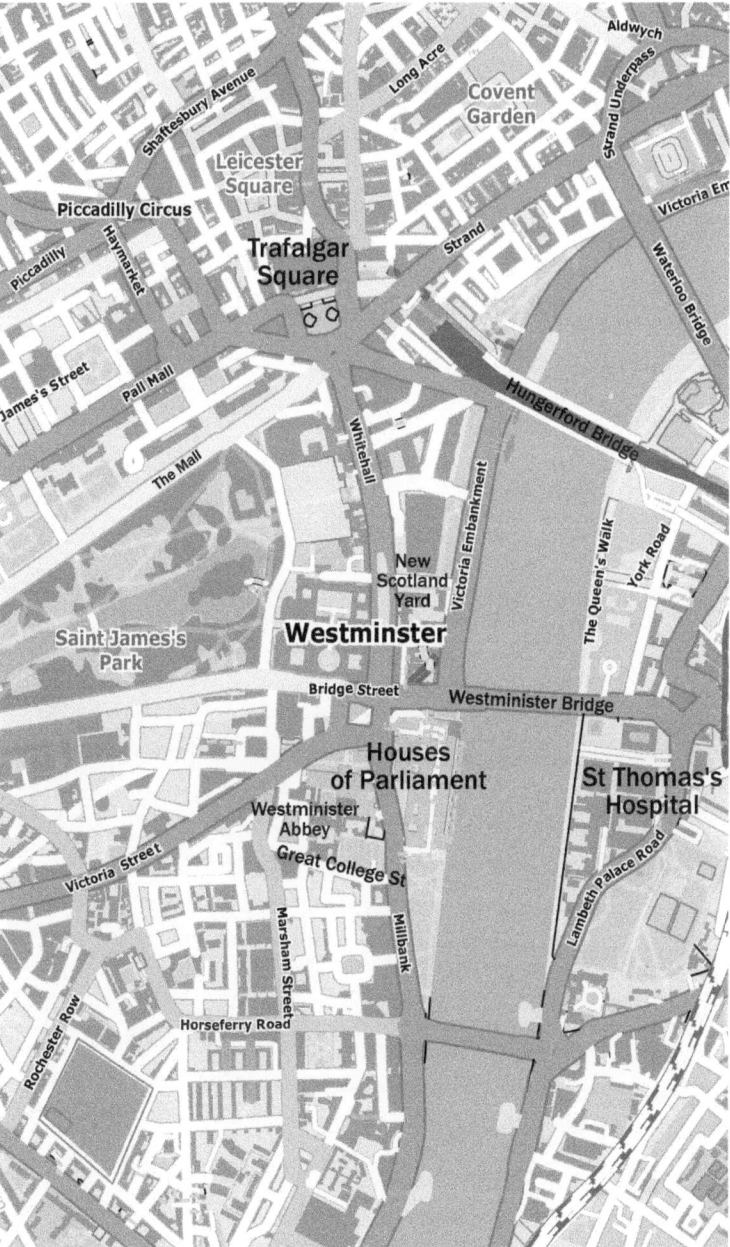

C O N T E N T S

PROLOGUE

A lattice of shadow and coloured light fell upon the two women standing at the front of the chapel. A tall, broad-shouldered man in a business suit stood further back.

'We commit this child of God to be cremated.'

The chaplain intoned the final words of the brief funeral service and pressed the button marked 'Christian Trad.' at the lectern. The curtains behind him drew closed and the coffin disappeared from view as organ music played. He snapped shut the prayer book and stepped off the shallow step into the aisle between the rows of plastic chairs.

'Vicar.' One of the women caught his eye. 'This is Ms Skarlsgard from the Danish Embassy.'

'How do you do?' the Dane said as she offered her hand. 'Unfortunately, we have not been able to identify the dead boy. A university signet ring was just not enough to go on.'

'OK. We'll keep the ashes for a year then scatter them in our Garden of Remembrance,' the chaplain said. 'If he's identified in future, relatives will have a place to visit and pay their respects.'

'That will be acceptable.'

'Charge the Tower Hamlets account,' the other woman said.

The two women followed the chaplain down the aisle.

'And you are...?' he asked the solitary man.

'Detective Inspector Rowlands. I'm in charge of the case.'

'Good of you to come.'

'Not at all.'

His presence was a mark of respect the boy had not been afforded in life; it was the least he could do. The policeman followed the others out into a sunlit municipal cemetery of neat, marble-chip graves and well-mown grass.

The Danish boy's bloated body had been found entangled in a pleasure boat's anchor chain, to the distress of the partygoers on board. He was the latest addition to a growing case file of young and vulnerable victims found raped and sometimes tortured to death. There were seven now, seven young lives cut short. Some were identified and their families informed. The unnamed had a public health funeral, like the one in Tower Hamlets, and no one was much the wiser.

They had been targeted, he suspected, because their disappearances wouldn't raise an alarm. All seemed forsaken and far from home. There was no outcry, no one had been charged with their murder, nor was there a single suspect. DI Rowlands had hesitated before adding the Danish boy to the list. The body was disfigured, but it seemed his wrists and ankles had been bound and his throat may have been cut, like the others.

The neglected killings offended Rowlands on a personal as well as a professional level. They insulted his sense of justice, so he pursued any links or clues to the youngsters' fate, often in his own time. There would be no plaudits for doing so, but he was determined to find and expose whoever was responsible.

He turned into the high road and headed towards the underground.

MONDAY

◊ ONE

'Customer information: due to construction works at this station there is no direct access to South Molton Street. Customers wishing to visit South Molton Street should exit on to Oxford Street and turn right into New Bond Street.'

The announcement sounding in her ears, Cassandra rose with the escalator, gliding into daylight. It was the construction works she was there to see. The glossy tiles and mirrored surfaces of Bond Street Underground station threw her hazy reflection back at her as she headed towards the exit. Now she had to find the building site.

Difficult to miss.

The horizontal jibs of giant cranes swayed sideways against counterweights, their towers looming over tall wooden hoardings. Unseen machinery rumbled and bleeped. In a gap in the perimeter stood a bearded man, who wore a hardhat and hi-vis vest. He carried a clipboard.

That must be the way in.

Her name was checked off his list and she was directed to a row of temporary cabins. Bulky men in hardhats strode past, dust rising from their heavy boots. They shouted, purposefully, to each other in different languages, ignoring her presence completely.

In the cabin designated 'Reception', a young woman sat behind a cheap desk.

'Ms Fortune,' she read the name from another list. 'Please leave any personal belongings in the final cabin along; it's quite secure. Here is your hat and your pass. You'll find shoes, dust masks and safety glasses in the cabin. They're waiting to go down; you're the last.'

Cassie winced at the earsplitting rat-a-tat of a jackhammer starting up nearby. In the furthest cabin people were still changing, fellow civil servants whom she greeted wordlessly as she put on hard-toed overshoes and safety equipment. Together they crossed the site to a single storey building destined to become the new rear entrance to the station, where the other members of the Project Board waited.

Outside, a thickset man spoke rapidly into a walkie-talkie. 'OK, all here now. On our way down.' He made a show of clicking the 'off' button and beckoned them forward into the building. 'Everyone come please.

My name is Bogdan and I am the foreman. I will take you.'

They clomped down a set of stationary escalators and the clanking of machinery grew fainter. Then down another level to the platforms, where the curving walls of the tunnel were completely bare of tiling or decoration and the concrete exposed. Like an older woman caught without her makeup, Cassie thought, unready to be seen by the world.

'Follow me, please.' The foreman climbed down a wide ladder into the central trench where the rails would run. 'Take care where you walk.'

Naked light bulbs drooped from cables hung from the tunnel walls and shadows loomed then shrank as they walked along the trench. A generator hummed nearby and there was a metallic taste to the air. The ground became uneven.

Ahead Cassie could see building workers gathered by a side opening. Bogdan called out a question and one of them replied. Another began to complain. The foreman cut him short by turning to face the visiting party.

'Ladies and gentlemen,' he said. 'We are now approximately two hundred feet below South Molton Street. We discovered the cave you are about to enter at the end of last week. It is a burial chamber. Please stay near the entrance, so as to respect the graves. The archaeologist is already here and can answer your questions.'

He led them through the opening into a cavern.

About twenty feet wide, its rough floor stretched back forty feet or so. It was about the size of a tennis court. Arc lamps showed shards of broken masonry scattered among large, upright pieces of grey stone. Grave markers, Cassie thought. The white electric light created slender shadows in the shallow inscriptions cut into the stones. These must have belonged to a much older London.

'Oh!' The woman beside her caught hold of Cassie's arm in surprise as a figure rose from behind a gravestone

'Hello. Sorry, I didn't mean to startle you.'

The man grinned.

Sorry? You're enjoying yourself.

'My name is Dr Holle Maartens and I'm an archaeologist with the Museum of London. With discoveries of this kind, construction work must cease to allow for archaeological exploration.' He rested one trail-booted foot atop a pile of stones.

'How long will the project be delayed?' someone asked.

'That depends. The investigation could be over and the site reopened in a week. On the other hand, if we find anything of significance, we'll have to remove it, which, given the fragile state of some of this, might take much longer.'

Not fragile enough to stop you posing on it.

'How old are the graves?' she asked.

'Anything from three to five hundred years old. London's population expanded hugely between 1500 and 1650 and existing churchyards couldn't cope, so overspill burial grounds were created, outside the old city limits. I think this is one of those.'

'Are they quite common, then?' someone else asked.

'Yes, but there's something of greater interest here. I discovered it late last night.' The archaeologist chuckled. 'Let me show you.'

They followed Dr Maartens to the back of the cavern where he connected up a light. Cassie gasped as it clicked on.

Bones. Human bones.

They lay in heaps. Skulls, femurs, ulnas, finger and collar bones, all mixed up with shattered slivers. Some were large and heavy looking, others tiny, children's bones.

'It looks like they've been dumped, not even given a proper burial,' a man observed.

'I think that's exactly what happened to them,' Dr Maartens replied. 'And I think we'll find more of them below, a whole pit of them, I suspect.'

'A pit? What kind of pit? Like a plague pit?' There was a tremor of excitement in the man's voice.

For a few seconds, Cassie heard only the faraway hum of the generator. Then people began to murmur.

Plague. *Ciuma. Pest. Plaga.* In any language, a word of power and fear.

This was news to the workmen, she realised. They hadn't known about the plague pit.

Most of them wouldn't have been in London when the last plague pit was found, almost thirty years before. With shocked and angry faces, they surrounded the foreman. Others, hearing their protestations, came to join them. Space and oxygen contracted as men jostled at the entrance of the cavern.

Cassie sensed the rising panic. Fear, as contagious as any virus, was spreading invisibly from one to another, infecting them all. The hairs on the back of her neck rose. A few moments longer and they'd be stampeding along the narrow, half-lit passageway.

People were going to get hurt.

She looked over at the archaeologist. Maartens was watching the workmen, open mouthed. Gone was the easy showmanship, replaced by astonishment. Meanwhile the hubbub of fear grew, voices jumbled and the noise level rose.

Do something, say something.

A chunk of sculpted masonry, part of a fallen mausoleum, lay propped against the cavern wall. Stretching to get a handhold, Cassie clambered on top of it, her head almost up against the roof. She shielded her eyes from the glare of the lamps.

'Wait!' she shouted. 'Listen to me!' Faces turned towards her and she heard the faint fizzing of the arc lamps in the sudden silence. 'It's not contagious, or dangerous. The bacillus dies with its host. It's safe – *sigur, bezpieczny, saker... seguro*. We know this because we've found plague pits before.' She glared at the archaeologist. 'Haven't we.'

'Er, yes, that's right,' he confirmed. 'That's why I'm happy to work here. You won't catch anything here more dangerous than a cold.'

There was a general muttering, though the men seemed to accept what he said, temporarily at least. Cassie noticed one or two civil servants still casting anxious glances at the bones and hopeful ones towards the tunnel.

'There's no need to worry at all,' she reiterated, brooking no denial. 'There's no danger.'

As she spoke she felt the stone move beneath her feet and instinctively bent her knees and raised her arms for balance. The structure was shifting. A deep growl of noise began and pieces of rock and clay showered her from above. She lost sight of the people in the chamber as the light dimmed, then was snuffed out.

The cavern wall was collapsing and the roof was falling with it.

'Lady! Jump!' she heard the foreman yell.

Against all her instincts, she leapt from her stone perch.

◊ TWO

She stumbled as her legs hit the ground. Sprawling, she gasped for air. What was happening? Soil and rock fell around her, an underground avalanche. Was the whole cavern subsiding?

Get out. Move!

She thrust herself upward, a kneeling sprinter starting a race. She was trapped in slow motion as the ground slid from beneath her feet, but, legs and arms pumping, muscles taut, she drove against the yielding soil and stones. She was almost free of the earthfall when she collided with someone.

The archaeologist - he had been standing close by her vantage point when the collapse began. Each grabbed the other and they staggered towards the opening of the cave. There the ground was solid beneath her feet and Cassie stopped, chest heaving.

'You OK?' Bogdan asked. He scrutinised her face. 'Death is very bad publicity.'

Cassie couldn't help but smile at him. A joke, even a bad one, was welcome. Floating particles of dirt caught in her throat and she coughed, her eyes watering.

'Yeah,' she croaked. 'Thanks – and thanks for the warning.'

It might have saved her life. Even with a hard hat, one falling rock could have stunned her and she would have been buried beneath the earth. It wouldn't have taken long for her vital functions to fail.

Don't think about it.

She straightened her shoulders and began to brush down her clothes, discreetly wiping the tears away. Stepping out of her shoes she emptied them of earth and pebbles.

'How about everyone else?' she asked.

'We just got dirty. You and the doctor got the worst of it,' he answered, then grinned. 'Some ran back into the tunnel, very quickly.'

Cassie turned to look back at the place where she had been standing when the collapse began. The ruined mausoleum had disappeared beneath a mound of earth and rock. The cavern wall had fallen in, soil spilling across the old burial ground to reach more than halfway to the tunnel.

It seemed to have settled. Workmen were already tamping down loose dirt. Beams of light veered around the chamber as they hauled on cables to tug lights free of the rubble. The plague pit was now completely covered over.

'What's that?' She pointed to a dark opening at the top of the new slope.

'It's another chamber,' Dr Maartens replied, curious. He took a heavy torch from his pocket and directed its beam into the darkness. 'We must have disturbed its wall. I wonder what's in there?'

'Dangerous,' Bogdan said. 'Enough for today. Everyone is going back to the surface.'

'Let me take a quick look,' the archaeologist said. 'I've lost my plague pit, after all.'

The foreman hesitated.

'Please, just a few minutes,' Maartens pleaded. 'I'm going to have to go in there anyway. This might save some time for the project, right?'

'Looks like it's OK,' a workman said. 'Probably.'

'Well... a few minutes only,' Bogdan reluctantly agreed. 'And I come with you.'

'Me too,' said Cassie. She wasn't going to be left behind. 'I want to know what's up there; it could have killed me. May I borrow...?' The workman gave her his torch.

Climbing the mound was like walking up sand dunes. Ahead of her, Bogdan reached the top and turned to offer her a hand.

'Is rock here,' he said, stamping.

In a few sinking strides Cassie reached the ledge, about ten feet above the floor of the first chamber.

'It *is* another cavern,' Maartens called from inside.

Cassie shone her torch across the floor immediately in front of her. It looked more like rough concrete than rock. She joined the archaeologist who was stepping forward very slowly and carefully, shining his torch.

'Careful, stay behind me,' he said, holding out his arm. 'Mustn't inadvertently - oh! Fuck!'

'What?' Bogdan called. 'What is it?' He pushed past them both. '*Stranje!* Everybody back!'

'A body,' Maartens' voice quivered. 'It's a body.'

Cassie stepped forward. On the bare floor she saw a naked young man, his pale skin waxy in the torchlight. Lying face down, his arms reached out towards them, unmoving.

Bogdan tried to usher them back to the opening.

'If he's dead then this is a possible crime scene,' Cassie said to him, quietly. 'Make sure no one else comes up here. I've done this sort of thing before.'

Almost true.

'And call the police, but do it discreetly. Call Scotland Yard. They won't want word of this getting out until they know what they're dealing with.'

The foreman swallowed hard.

'Death is very bad publicity'. Well, now it's unavoidable.

He nodded and started back down the slope.

Cassie knelt to examine the body. She didn't want to touch the pallid skin but she had to be certain that the boy was dead.

'Don't,' the archaeologist said, as she reached forward. 'You don't need to. He's dead alright. Look at the side of his neck.'

She peered more closely and saw the end of a distinctive red-brown slash slicing round his neck. The ground beneath it was stained dark. Someone had cut his throat.

How old is he? Twenty? Maybe younger?

His muscular arms were bruised purple and brown, almost obscuring a tattoo. It was an anchor, no, a *kotwica*, a Polish symbol.

She raised her torch to look beyond the body.

What is this place?

Skulls grinned at her and skeletal hands clawed the air. Part of the chamber wall was packed tight with bones. A snake slithered from an eye socket.

No, not a snake. Of course not, only a trickle of dirt.

A heavy metal ring reflected in the torchlight. It was fixed into the wall of skeletons and streaked with slivers of silver where the rust had been rubbed away. Someone had recently been tied or chained to that ring.

Cassie glanced down at the boy's wrists. Their skin was red and raw.

Exactly what happened here?

'Maartens?' Cassie said. 'What are these bones? Are they part of the plague pit?'

'What?' he glanced over at the wall of skeletons and straightened up. 'Not necessarily. Once a place was known as a burial site it was often reused.'

He swung the beam of his torch around the chamber, revealing stone walls and large puddles of what looked like solidified candle wax. The cavern had been lit by candlelight.

Cassie heard someone breathing hard as they climbed the slope. It was Bogdan, returning.

'Police are coming,' he said, panting, as he reached the top. 'Nobody leaves. Wait for them in the cabins. I stay here and make sure it's not disturbed.' Cassie exchanged looks with Maartens. She retreated towards the cavern but stopped as she drew level with the foreman.

'Do you know what a *kotwica* is, Bogdan?'

'Polish for anchor,' he answered, promptly.

'Yes, it is.' She started down the earth slope.

◊ THREE

Bright sunshine and blue sky.

Cassie's mood lifted after her gruesome find beneath the earth. She dropped the safety equipment in the cabin and wandered towards the site entrance, now closed off, considering who would have to be informed about this latest development.

The police had already commandeered the other cabins. She could see the back of a man's head through the window of the first of them, a civil servant speaking with someone seated further inside. The door of the Reception cabin was open, revealing a uniformed PC now sat at the desk. Workmen came and went, giving their details and having their documents checked, she assumed.

Was the dead boy a construction worker?

Even if he was, how had he come to be naked in the underground chamber? Had he been killed there? The bloodstains would suggest so. Or was it where his body had been dumped? Forensics would answer that question. There had to be another way in.

It's not your problem. Leave it alone. You've left all that behind.

'Ms Cassandra Fortune?' a sharp-faced woman in her late thirties called to her from the door of the cabin. The man she had noticed was walking away.

Cassie followed her inside as the woman held out her hand, 'I'm Detective Serjeant Daljit Patel. This is Detective Inspector Andrew Rowlands.'

A tall man placed two mugs of dark brown liquid on a desk and then offered his hand. His expression was professionally neutral.

'Coffee?' he asked.

The inspector's making the drinks, so these two are a team.

'No thanks. Though some water would be good. It was rather dusty underground.'

Serjeant Patel reached into a small cabinet behind the desk and produced a bottle of mineral water. Cassie took it and drank. It was wonderful.

'You're a civil servant, an assistant director, I believe, deputising –' the Detective Serjeant began.

'For my boss, Duncan Macfarlane, Deputy Prime Minister's Office,' Cassie cut in. 'This was supposed to be a routine field visit to better understand why there was a delay in the project. I didn't know about the plague pit – I don't think anyone did, certainly not the people who were working down there.'

'We were told that you stopped a panic,' said Inspector Rowlands. 'That was quick thinking.'

Cassie said nothing.

'It was handy, your knowledge of languages.' He left the sentence hanging.

Fishing for information?

'A rusty knowledge,' she said. 'At least no one got hurt. Except the boy of course, the Polish boy.'

'Why do you say he was Polish?' The serjeant leaned her forearms on the desk, sitting forward.

'He has a tattoo on his right bicep,' Cassie explained. 'It's an anchor, but of a specific type, a *kotwica*: a symbol used by the Poles in Second World War. It may simply be a fashion statement now, but to me it suggests that he's Polish. His body is covered in bruises and lacerations so I assume he was hurt before his throat was cut.

Before you ask, it was necessary to check he was dead, so I looked.'

Neither of her inquisitors said anything.

'Have the reporters arrived yet?' Cassie asked.

'We're keeping them outside the site for now,' DS Patel said, exchanging glances with her boss.

'Yes, I imagine the presence of a DI might excite speculation. Though they'll expect a statement when the Department of Transport press officer arrives.'

Cassie waited. The police need not say anything to the press. They could allow the press officer to do it, putting the focus on the historical details and the delays to the project.

They're fools if they turn that down.

DS Patel looked as if someone had just announced that Christmas was coming early. The inspector's face registered nothing; no surprise, no emotion.

'You're not, of course, suggesting that the death go unreported,' he said.

'It looks like murder and I'm surmising, perhaps wrongly, that you'll want to find out how that boy got there before you make matters public,' Cassie said. 'There must be another way into that chamber and you don't want journalists and thrill-seekers finding it before you do and ruining any evidence. The press officer can make a statement in good faith without saying anything about the more recent corpse.'

A digger restarted. The grind of industrial noise was oddly comforting to Cassie.

'I'll speak with the press officer,' Rowlands said. He rose. She was being dismissed.

DS Patel gave her a tight smile. 'Thank you for your cooperation.'

Cassie was ushered out of the cabin and she heard its door close behind her.

Let the professionals get on with their job, she thought as she walked back to the other cabin. It's their case.

◊ FOUR

Cassie closed her eyes and turned her face towards the jet of steaming water. She kneaded shampoo into her hair and scalp, the soft foam dribbling on to her shoulders. Her skin tingled as the water ran in rivulets down her body. At her feet, the dirt and grime ran into a brown whirlpool before disappearing down the plughole.

Clean. At last. So good.

She turned off the shower, slicked the water from her head and reached for a towel. Wrapped in a heavy cotton robe she wandered through to her bedroom, pulling a brush through her hair.

Sunlight shone through the garden doors on to familiar things, the king-sized bed and the rococo mirror above the dressing table. Both had come with her from her previous home, so were too big for the bedroom in the flat. She sat before the mirror to dry her hair without seeing her reflection. Other images flooded her mind: the archaeologist lecturing them, the jumbled bones in the plague pit, the wall of skeletons and, above all, the naked, white body of the boy with his russet necklace. Beaten, his body abandoned. She wondered if he had been abused.

Put it out of your mind. You don't do this anymore.

She had spent eleven years at Government Communication Headquarters, making connections, detecting crimes and identifying betrayals. She'd been very good at it, with reputation enough to command the attention of the highest in government. Her job had brought her access, knowledge and power. And she had loved it.

Then it had all gone wrong. Now she oversaw minor procurement projects.

She had pined for her old job like a grieving widow, scanning the news, watching for signs of cases broken or resolved, trying to read between the lines. She lurked on departmental discussion boards to catch the scent of something familiar and feel a shiver of excitement. At those moments, she had the sense that, if she could only gain entry, she'd find a secret self who'd never left. She raged at her exclusion. Once the anger was burned out, a shame crept in, a curdled brew of hostility and confusion. She realised she was becoming an embarrassment to herself.

That was over three years ago. When she allowed herself to feel anything, she had to admit that the ache of loss and longing hadn't gone away.

In the glass dish on the dressing table lay her wedding ring. Her marriage had ended amid anger and recriminations and her husband had slipped away from her, exhausted and spent, as she clung to the shipwreck of her career. He'd been a good man, a friend as well as a partner, and she'd hoped she'd been the same for him, though he'd assured her otherwise. Their divorce caused little more than a ripple on the surface of others' lives.

Half of the proceeds from the sale of their home provided the deposit on a flat in south London. It was her own space, even if small and she was determined to enjoy it, to decorate and garden. Then there were the pleasures of living in the city: the theatre, art galleries, walks in the park, the cinema. Her job held no interest for her, in comparison, weekend matinees were a pleasure. A pleasure, she told herself. My life is a pleasure.

Spiggott the cat leapt up on to the dressing table with a meow, tail perpendicular. She stretched her neck and closed her eyes against the hairdryer's blast, blowing through her long black and white fur.

'Down you get.' Cassie switched off the dryer and placed the cat on to the carpet. 'Let's go and see if we're on the news.'

In the living room she and Spiggott curled up on the sofa. Cassie's eye was caught by early evening commuters returning home to the tree-lined street of Victorian terraces. The leaves of the roses around the bay window were no longer glossy. It had been a long summer.

She switched on the TV. The newsreader had reached the final item.

'Work stopped again this week on the long overdue London Crossrail project. Over to Bond Street.'

The screen filled with a picture of a London correspondent standing by the Bond Street Underground sign.

'Workers have downed tools, amid much speculation about this latest delay,' he said, contrived excitement in his voice. 'Two hours ago, an announcement was made by a Transport spokesperson.'

The picture cut to a press officer, smartly suited, surrounded by a thicket of microphones. A small group of workmen and project people stood behind him and Cassie caught sight of herself in the background, brown with dirt.

No wonder I got some funny looks coming home.

'The tube extension work has halted because of the discovery yesterday of an ancient burial ground. Archaeologists from the Museum of London are already on site and we anticipate that the site will be examined and resealed within the week,' he was saying, his voice competent and professional. 'Work can then recommence. In the meantime, work elsewhere on the line will continue so the overall schedule of the project should not be impacted. Thank you.'

'Is it true that a plague pit has been discovered?'

'Is there any danger of the plague spreading?'

'Just to be clear,' the press officer responded. 'An old plague pit *was* discovered within the burial ground but there is no possibility of the plague surviving. I stress, there is no danger of plague. It's quite safe. If you have any more questions please direct them to the London Crossrail Press Office. Thank you.'

The picture cut back to the studio and the weather.

Cassie pressed the off button and resumed stroking the cat who had snuggled up close. She let her mind wander until the ring of her phone drew her back to reality. It was Duncan, her boss.

'So you had quite a time this morning,' he said in a soft Scottish burr. 'Even made the local TV news.'

Duncan MacFarlane was in his fifties, very upright and steady. He had come down to London thirty years before and, like many who saw their stay in 'the smoke' as temporary, had never left. Cassie rather liked him.

'You could say that. I was going to phone you.'

'Well, I got in first. Simon Joliffe, Secretary of State for Transport, wants to thank you. Someone's told him about the panic and the cavern wall collapsing. There's a reception going on at the Palace of Westminster this evening, we've both been invited. You can speak with him then. And it's a chance to raise your profile.'

As if there's any point in that.

It didn't feel right to be going to a flashy reception when only that morning she had discovered the body of the boy, but she didn't really have a choice.

'What time?' she asked and they arranged to meet. She looked at her watch when the Scot had rung off.

Time to get moving.

Sighing, she tipped Spiggott on to the floor.

In the bedroom she took a simple, pale dress from the wardrobe and hung it on the back of the door. She'd better make an effort, if only so as not to let Duncan down. The minister had asked to see her. It was an opportunity to impress, to signal ambition and energy. It might help her career, which was clearly what Duncan thought. Cassie knew she should be grateful. Duncan was doing his best for her.

She sighed. Her career had been destroyed and there was no way of getting it back.

'I better look keen,' she said to the cat and began to dress. 'However I feel.'

◊ FIVE

Cassie stood in the middle of Central Lobby, at the very heart of the Palace of Westminster. The Palace was home to the Houses of Parliament, where political power in the United Kingdom of Great Britain and Northern Ireland lay. Voices and people whirled about her as she looked up beyond the glittering wall mosaics to the high-vaulted ceiling. Impervious to the desires and ambitions of today's politicians, the marble statesmen of yesteryear stood on their plinths around the periphery of the octagonal chamber.

The space was filling with guests arriving for the reception and Cassie moved out of the crush to stand by some temporary barriers at one side. Behind them, overall-wearing workmen were recreating the elaborate design of the encaustic tiled floor. She watched their painstaking work as the crowd grew.

Many of the visitors were newcomers to the Palace of Westminster. They clutched invitations and visitor passes and gazed around, awestruck, at the history and power of the place. Cassie glanced down at the two passes hanging around her neck and removed her own general access pass, slipping it into her handbag. The visitor's pass she left in place. Now she blended in.

Old habits die hard.

She recognised senior corporate executives as well as civil servants among the arrivals. The commercial people were there to impress the decision makers involved in the Thames Estates Programme, the billion pound redevelopment of prime Thames-side government real estate. There were contracts to be had and money to be made and the reception was to mark the start of the programme.

Duncan was approaching from St Stephen's Hall and Cassie stepped out into the flow so he could see her. Returning her wave, he fell in beside her as they both turned into the Peers Corridor.

'Do you know how the minister's reacted to the news statement?' she asked him.

'He's content, as far as I know,' Duncan replied. 'Have you ever met him? Simon Joliffe?'

'No.'

They turned left through double doors into another long corridor and the green of the Commons side of the Palace was immediately replaced by the red of the Lords side.

'I have,' Duncan said. 'He's standard issue - clever enough, personable and ambitious.'

The hubbub of voices and laughter grew louder, but the sounds changed once they were on the Terrace, the party din dissipating in the open air. Black-clad waiting staff wove amid the guests, carrying trays of canapés and glasses of wine or water. Flashes of colour, of women's summer garments, were sprinkled among the predominant greys and blues of business suits.

Eyes were darting. Everyone was watching everyone else. Who was talking to whom? What alliances were being forged? What groundwork was being done for future contracts? How could the competition be outmanoeuvred?

The civil servants were no less sharp-eyed than the commercial people. Cassie spotted colleagues from the Deputy Prime Minister's Office. Sir Terence Spencer, the Permanent Secretary and head of the department was there, a garrulous man of middle height who was in his element, wheeler-dealing and paying court. At his side stood a tall and spindly figure with a beak of a nose, Charles Morecombe, the Deputy Prime Minister, the second most powerful man in government and the highest-ranking politician at the gathering. Technically, he was her boss but he probably wouldn't know who she was. He barely spoke but, from his great height, observed everything. His eyes missed nothing. As Deputy Prime Minister, there wasn't a lot which Charles Morecombe didn't know about, Cassie guessed.

This was my world, once...

'There's Joliffe,' Duncan said and launched himself into the throng, Cassie following in his wake.

Simon Joliffe, Secretary of State for Transport, noticed their approach. His face was flushed, because of the warmth or because of the wine, Cassie couldn't tell. Slightly corpulent, with brown but greying curls, he smiled. 'Duncan Macfarlane, isn't it. And this must be the heroine of the hour?'

'May I introduce Cassandra Fortune,' Duncan said.

'Minister,' Cassie nodded.

'I hear you've been saving lives this morning.'

'Not really,' she replied, forcing herself to return his smile.

'I must mention it to Charles,' the Minister looked around. 'He's around here somewhere. Ah, William...let me introduce you to William.'

A tall man with a long, tanned face and a high-bridged nose joined them. Cassie guessed he was in his late forties but his old-fashioned cream linen suit and patrician features made him seem older. He looked as if he ought to be at Lord's Cricket Ground or the Garrick Club.

'William, Lord Priess, may I present Duncan Macfarlane and Cassandra Fortune. Cassandra is the woman who saved the day.'

The aristocrat smiled, his eyes twinkling, and offered his hand. 'I saw it on the news. Very brave. Well done.'

'Yes,' Joliffe said and drew himself more upright, ready to move on. 'William, we need to talk about the Oversight Committee, if you would excuse us.' He nodded to Cassie. 'Well done.'

This was the signal for the civil servants to step away. Joliffe had bestowed his thanks and promised to mention her name to the Deputy Prime Minister. That was all she could expect. In this world, it was enough.

She could go home now. Or she could work the room, impress people and make sure they'd remember her and her name, when positions had to be filled, or promotions advertised.

'Always nice to hear,' Duncan murmured, as he scanned the gathering.

'Now, who else do I need to speak with? Come on, there are plenty of important procurement folk here, let me introduce you to some of them.'

For the next hour Cassie asked and answered the appropriate questions but became less and less willing to demonstrate an eagerness she did not feel. Procurement wasn't her chosen field, *that* was closed to her and she found it difficult to dredge up any enthusiasm.

Others were less reluctant. There were new jobs attaching to the Thames Estates Programme and some determined efforts were being made to climb the greasy pole. She looked on with detached amusement and increasing cynicism.

Who am I to judge? Better get out of here before I say something inappropriate.

'I'll make a move, I think,' she said to Duncan, during a lull in conversation. 'I want to look in at the office before I go home and I'm not feeling so great.'

'If you're sure you won't stay longer...' Duncan's face registered a mixture of concern and disappointment. She could imagine his thinking: why wasn't she grasping the opportunity to raise her profile, to help work her way up the ladder?

Not for me, not any more.

'Well, have a safe journey home and well done for today. It was quick thinking and quick acting too, just as well for the folk who were there and for the project. See you tomorrow.'

Praise is pleasant. Just don't take it too seriously. It's only words.

She returned to the terrace doors and scanned the crowd for the last time.

Duncan was now chatting with a dark-haired man in a well-tailored suit, probably a lobbyist, who wore a sour expression. At the periphery of another group, Lord Priess noticed her departure and raised his glass to her with a smile. She returned the gesture, enjoying his courtesy.

By the balustrade, Simon Joliffe was regaling a ring of officials with what seemed to be an anecdote. Sycophantic laughter rang across the Terrace.

She put down her glass and stepped through the doors into the Palace.

TUESDAY

◊ SIX

The mood on the morning bus was relaxed. The summer weather promised to go on for a few more weeks and the holiday feeling lingered, but Cassie felt an undertow of tiredness. Her dreams had been disturbed by images of the dead boy, the wall of skeletons and the reception. She had awoken Spiggott at three in the morning when she wandered into the kitchen to get a glass of water.

I'll shake it off once I get into work.

The bus halted and a number of passengers got off, Cassie among them, to join the tide of people walking into a large, glass-fronted building. She fished in her handbag for her pass.

Where is it?

She moved aside, allowing the people behind her through the electronic turnstiles. At the front desk she turned out the contents of her bag. No pass. Texting her secretary, Siobhan, to come down and sign her in, Cassie accepted that she would be teased about it all day. How could she have forgotten it?

The round-faced, red-haired young woman exited the lift minutes later and came through the gates, grinning.

'Good morning. All this gallivanting gone to your head has it? I saw you on the news last night. Rang my Mum to tell her to watch.'

'Thanks.' Cassie took a visitor's pass once Siobhan had signed the entry book. She thought about reporting her own pass missing but decided against it: it would be at home. 'Anything urgent?'

'Not immediately, though Duncan wants a word in his office.'

'OK. While I'm gone can you do some research for me?' Cassie spoke softly, as they arrived at their floor. 'There were a lot of old plague pits in central London, apparently. Find out their locations, please, in case I'm asked for a follow up.'

'Will do. Have you seen social media this morning? It's gone potty about the plague. Hashtag Plague is trending on Twitter. It's gone viral.' She laughed. 'Bubonic plague still exists, you know and sometimes people die from it, even today. There are lots of tweets about bacteria surviving for centuries and causing modern epidemics.'

'People will believe anything these days. I'll go and see what Duncan wants.'

She strode across the office.

'Hi there,' Cassie greeted Duncan's secretary at her desk. 'Duncan wants to see me?'

'He does, though he's got someone in with him now. Take a seat. You had quite a day yesterday, I hear. And best bib and tucker on the Terrace, last night, too. You shall go to the ball, Cinderella.'

Cassie sighed. She'd never enjoyed the gossipy aspect of Whitehall but it was part of the job.

The door to Duncan's office opened.

'Ah, Cassie. Perfect,' the Scot said as he came out. 'Could you find me another room for half an hour please,' he asked the secretary. He looked back over his shoulder and spoke to someone inside. 'You can use this office.'

What? Duncan's giving up his office?

Cassie stood.

'Someone to see you,' he said to her.

Eh?

'I suggest you go in.'

Mystified, Cassie entered his office.

By the window, Detective Inspector Rowlands rose from the sofa as the door shut behind her.

'Detective Inspector?'

'Ms Fortune.'

'What is this about?' Cassie said, sharply. She moderated her tone. 'I'm happy to help the police with their enquiries, but I hadn't expected you to turn up at my place of work. Serjeant Patel has my details.'

'She tried to telephone you earlier this morning but your phone was switched off.'

Cassie always switched her phone on when she rose at seven. She fished the phone from her pocket and realised that she must have been so tired that morning that she hadn't turned it on. Missed call and voicemail message icons flashed as she did so.

What's so important?

The inspector remained standing.

'At approximately six o'clock this morning, a London Underground worker arriving at a Bakerloo line depot found the corpse of a young man. His throat had been cut in exactly the same manner as that of the body which you and Dr Maartens found yesterday.'

'What's that got to do with me?'

'When we examined the body we found something inside his jacket pocket,' the inspector said. He held up a sealed transparent evidence bag. 'This.'

Inside it was a bright chequered ribbon and a rectangle of plastic. Cassie's face stared out at her.

It was her own government access pass.

◊ SEVEN

Cassie took a couple of steps forward and reached for the bag. She examined the pass without opening the seal. There was no mistake.

Abruptly, she sat down on the sofa.

When had she last seen her pass? Outside of work it lived in the zipped pouch of her handbag. Otherwise she wore it all the time during the week. She hadn't been anywhere near the Bakerloo line.

'Where is the Bakerloo line depot?' she asked.

'London Road between Blackfriars Road and Elephant and Castle.' Rowlands resumed his seat. 'Were you in that vicinity at any time after leaving the Bond Street site yesterday afternoon?'

'No,' Cassie shook her head. 'I took the tube back to Clapham, cleaned up and changed, then came into Westminster on the Number 88 bus, via Vauxhall.'

The inspector said nothing. He was watching her reactions closely, she realised, as she would have done had she been the investigating officer.

'I doubt that anyone can corroborate that,' she added. 'I was in the Palace of Westminster by six thirty, with Duncan Macfarlane. I attended a reception there.' She gave a grim smile. 'I didn't stay late. It'd been a long day and I wasn't in the mood. The parliamentary security system will show arrival and departure times.'

'It does.'

So they'd already checked.

'Did you go straight home?'

'No, I came here first. The reception staff will be able to confirm that. I picked up some papers from the front desk, my secretary had left them for me.'

'How did you get home?'

'Bus.'

'Did you see anyone who knows you, either in transit or after you got home?'

'No, I don't think so. It was too late for the usual commuter crowd. Isn't there CCTV from the bus?'

'Did you go anywhere near London Road?'

'No. Nowhere near it. Besides, someone might have noticed me if I tried to get into the depot. I was hardly dressed for breaking and entering.'

'You could have gone home, changed and come out later to meet the victim.'

'It's possible, but I didn't. Once I got home, I stayed at home. I went to bed at about eleven after setting my alarm. The system record will show that I didn't go out after that. Look, am I a suspect?'

'This is a murder enquiry. Your office pass was found on the victim. What do you think?'

Of course I'm a suspect. The inspector's only doing his job. Yet…

She sensed that he didn't really believe her capable of the killings. Did he know her background?

Cassie glared at the policeman. He returned her look with a level stare.

'I would like you to accompany me to London Road depot.'

'Why?'

'You are clearly linked in some way to the victim, even if you don't know how. The scene of the crime might prompt some further thoughts.'

'Very well,' she rose. 'I'll just have to–'

'I have already appraised Mr Macfarlane.'

'–let my secretary know when I'll be back. I will be coming back won't I?'

'Yes, I imagine so.' The inspector's lips twitched. 'I have, as yet, no plans to arrest you.'

Was that a smile? Arrogant bastard.

'Good. Follow me.'

Cassie led Inspector Rowlands through the building, noting the interest of her colleagues, the surreptitious glances and the brazen stares. There would doubtless be speculation as to who he was and why he was there. It didn't help that he was good looking, in a square-jawed, masculine sort of way. People would remember him. Siobhan was certainly impressed, her eyes sliding sideways as Cassie explained that she had to go out for a while.

'Shall I call you a cab?' the secretary asked.

'No, we can hail one,' Cassie said as she collected her bag. 'I shouldn't be more than... a couple of hours?' The inspector assented, wordlessly. 'See you later.'

The lift was full, so nothing more was said until they were out of the building and walking down Marsham Street.

'Why do I merit a visit from you, Inspector?' Cassie asked. It would, she thought, have perhaps been more usual to send the Detective Serjeant.

'You were helpful yesterday with the *kotwica* and the press statement, Ms Fortune.'

'And you've done some research?'

'Yes. You didn't mention yesterday that you were an investigator at GCHQ and in Whitehall,' the inspector looked at her with a speculative glint in his eye. 'I have a senior police officer's security clearance but I can't find out what you worked on, which suggests it was both secret and sensitive.'

Cassie said nothing.

'I need to know if it might have any bearing on this case?'

A legitimate question.

'No, or at least, I don't believe so. It was a long time ago, so it's very unlikely.' Cassie had no intention of saying anything more on the subject. 'Do you know who the boy at the burial site was?'

'Not yet, there were no indications on the body. We're trying Polish Community Centres.'

'What about today's unfortunate discovery?'

'Again, nothing on the body.' He hesitated for a second before continuing. 'There was a stroke of luck, however. A wallet was found elsewhere on the site with ID belonging to the dead man, José Galan Ortega, a Spaniard living in Elephant & Castle. It also contained a card for a company called Coldbridge Services Ltd aka CSL.'

Cassie looked up sharply.

'Do you know it?'

'I recognise the name, but I don't know where from.' She paused, waiting to see if her brain would supply her with the detail. 'It'll come back to me. Anything else?'

'Not yet. We're speaking with the Spanish embassy.'

The inspector looked past her to hail an approaching cab.

Twenty minutes later the taxi drew up alongside a two-storey Victorian building which stood beside a small traffic roundabout. Its windows were boarded over and its brickwork was in need of repair. This was all that remained of the original entrance to the railway depot.

Cassie followed the inspector to an iron gateway which opened on to a rubbish-strewn alleyway by the side of the building. He pushed a button on the gate and, with a buzz, it opened. At the far end she saw a figure, it was DS Patel. The serjeant smiled in greeting.

'Body's been taken to the mortuary,' she said. 'Forensics have gone.'

The inspector acknowledged her. 'This way,' he said to Cassie.

Behind the depot entrance the site opened out into a triangle of land, with the entrance building at its apex. It was the old railway yard, stretching from the rear of the shops and houses on the left to the large old engine sheds of blackened brick on the right. Railway tracks ran from the depot building to disappear beneath a bridge into a tunnel at the furthest point of the site.

Disused places like this are usually the haunts of addicts and itinerants. Witnesses perhaps?

Amid the engine sheds stood a dilapidated low-rise 1930s London Underground station. A uniformed police officer stood outside it.

'He was found inside?' Cassie asked.

'Yes,' Rowlands replied. 'It might not look like it but this is still a working yard. A security firm does a regular sweep, to keep out the dossers and junkies. Mind your step.'

She followed him down winding tiled stairs into an engine shed. A series of trenches where rails had once run ran out into the yard, ending in metal buffers. Weak daylight filtered through grimy windows high above.

At the far side, a square tent had been erected. The inspector entered through an open flap and Cassie and the DS followed. Inside, the cream floor tiles were discoloured by a large rusty-brown smear. Blood.

'This is where the body was found,' the inspector said, his voice dispassionate. 'As I said before, his throat was cut, not a common way of killing. The details of the first murder haven't yet been made public, so that rules out a copycat. It's likely that whoever killed that young man is responsible for this murder too.'

A serial killer?

'Cause of death is one link, you are the other. Do you know how the victim could have obtained your pass?'

Again, Cassie racked her brain. She had worn it all yesterday. Did she remove it when she was given a Palace day pass? She thought so but couldn't recall putting it away when she reached home.

'No. I wish I did.'

The inspector changed tack.

'Yesterday when you entered the second chamber, who saw the body?'

Cassie thought back to finding the Polish boy.

'Myself, Dr Maartens, Bogdan the foreman, then all the people who attend such scenes. Was the chamber cordoned off?'

'Yes,' DS Patel answered.

'Have you found the other entrance to the chamber yet? There has to be one.'

'Yes.' The inspector added no more.

She bit back her next question. He was making it very clear that it wasn't her business.

'The only clue we currently have,' he said, 'aside from the second victim's wallet, is your access pass. And you discovered the other body yesterday. It seems you're our only suspect, Ms Fortune.'

Her pass had been found on the corpse but there was no other evidence, no motive, no witnesses.

This is ridiculous.

Cassie glared at him, ready to argue, but realised that the inspector was goading her, trying to prompt a reaction. Well, she wouldn't rise to it. She clamped her lips closed.

The sound of traffic from Lambeth Road could be heard in the pause that followed. Eventually the inspector spoke to the serjeant.

'Concentrate on finding out everything you can about the dead man,' he instructed. 'His family, friends, habits. And check if we've identified the Pole. Ms Fortune and I will go on to the mortuary.' He turned to Cassie. 'If you're up to it?'

Cassie gave him a curt nod and followed him back up the stairs.

◊ EIGHT

'Yesterday wasn't the first time you've seen a new cadaver, was it?' the inspector asked, his voice echoing in the basement corridor of the Westminster Mortuary.

'No.'

Cassie didn't elaborate. She could be as close mouthed as he was.

'Here we are.'

The white-tiled room was lit by a series of lights hanging low above a line of metal tables. There was only one window, very high up. Cassie smelled antiseptic.

'Andrew!' A bespectacled and balding man exclaimed as he looked up from examining a cadaver. 'I thought you might be along.'

'Bill,' the inspector acknowledged the other man. 'Dr William Pottinger, forensic pathologist, Ms Cassandra Fortune, civil servant.'

'Ms Fortune.' Dr Pottinger peered at her over his spectacles. 'Forgive me if I don't....' He waved his white-gloved hands. 'In what capacity are you here?'

'She discovered the first body,' Rowlands said before Cassie could respond. 'And identified the *kotwica* tattoo.'

'Clever civil servant,' Pottinger said as he peeled off his gloves and crossed to a sink. 'You're very honoured, Andrew doesn't usually bring anyone else on to his cases.' He wiped his hands on a towel.

Honoured wouldn't be the word I'd use.

'So what can you tell us, Bill?'

The pathologist led them over to the steel trolley beneath the window and turned the white sheet back, revealing the body of the young man from the burial chamber.

'The first victim is a Caucasian male, mid-twenties, I would say from the dentition. No identifying marks except the tattoo on the bicep. His throat has been cut.' Pottinger indicated the brown line around the throat. 'Expertly, with a very sharp blade, trachea, carotid and jugular all severed. Major bruising and grazes to the arms, torso and abdomen suggest that he was in a fracas and someone restrained him forcibly. There are signs of anal penetration, again, probably forced.'

'He was raped?'

'I can't say for sure, but it looks like it. Either that or some very heavy S&M, but, taken with the bruising, I think that unlikely.'

'Semen?'

'Not that I can find. Condoms were used, I'd guess. We'll check for any DNA. I would say he's been dead for about fifty-six hours now.'

Saturday night. Poor boy.

She still thought of him as a boy. The discovery that he was in his mid twenties was something of a surprise. He looked younger.

'His system contained traces of chemically manufactured methylenedioxy-methamphetamine, so-called E, a common party drug.'

'That makes sense.' The inspector took a deep breath. 'A rave took place on Saturday in a deep basement near where the body was found.'

So, he's decided to trust me.

The pathologist moved on to a second trolley. This would be the man found at the depot.

'Our second victim is also Caucasian, but his darker hair and skin tone suggest some southern European heritage.'

Like a magician revealing the rabbit under the hat, Pottinger turned the sheet back with a flourish.

Cassie gasped.

'What? Do you recognise him?'

'Yes. He was at the Palace of Westminster yesterday evening, a workman replacing the floor tiles in Central Lobby. That's why CSL was familiar, it was the logo on his overalls.'

I had my pass when I saw him, I'm sure.

'Another young man,' the pathologist continued, his echoing voice strangely disembodied. 'Also mid twenties. No signs of a struggle with this one and no evidence of anal penetration, though cause of death is the same.' He pointed to the tell-tale circle of blood encrusted around the throat. 'Again, expertly done.'

'By the same person?' the inspector asked.

'Both cuts are clean and rise to the left,' the pathologist shook his head. 'Whoever the killer is, he knows how to wield a blade and is probably right-handed. I'm not a gambler but I'd bet on this being the work of the same man.'

'Was it a man?' Cassie asked.

'Unknown,' Pottinger corrected himself. 'It could have been a woman. The first victim was restrained; the second could have been surprised. Whoever did it, he or she was very skilled.'

'Time of death? Approximately?' the inspector asked.

'I estimate the early hours of this morning, probably between two and four o'clock. When was the body discovered?'

'About five thirty this morning.'

'Hmm, that would be consistent.'

'OK, thanks Bill. Unless you've got any questions?' The inspector glanced in Cassie's direction.

'I assume he hadn't taken drugs?'

'Not that I can trace, though there was a low level of alcohol in his system. He had no tattoos either,' the pathologist grinned.

'Thanks, Bill.'

The inspector led her from the mortuary.

The warmth of the sunlight on her skin felt reassuringly normal and Cassie exhaled in relief. Both she and the inspector checked their phones. She had an urgent email from Siobhan.

'So, two young men, both from continental Europe, killed in the same way, probably by the same hand, but there the commonality ends,' the inspector said as they began to walk back to Cassie's office.

'There is one other link, aside from me,' Cassie replied. 'This morning I asked my PA to do some research on old London plague pits, in case the Press Office asked for more background. Aside from finding plenty of nutcases online getting hysterical about the plague, she found a map. Look.'

She handed the phone to the inspector.

'So, the depot was a plague pit site too.' He stopped walking. 'Is that just a coincidence? Or is there a deeper significance? Do we have a serial killer with a predilection for plague pits?'

'Intriguing, isn't it. Why plague pits? But at least we now know when the dead Spaniard might have got my access pass, though we don't know whether I lost it and he found it, or if he stole it.'

'If he was a thief, it won't be the only item missing,' the inspector said, resuming their course. 'Something for DS Patel to follow up.'

'Tell her to contact the Serjeant at Arms office and the Parliamentary Security Department. The set up in the Palace of Westminster is unusual. It has its own internal police. They'll be able to help.'

They had drawn level with Cassie's office building.

'Thanks, I will.'

So that's that. Goodbye sleuthing and goodbye Andrew Rowlands.

'Well, best of luck with the case.'

'Thanks, bye.' With a small nod, Rowlands strode off.

Cassie caught herself staring after him as he left. He didn't look back.

◊ NINE

As Cassie approached her desk, Siobhan rose from her seat.

'You're wanted on the sixth floor,' the secretary said, handing over Cassie's notebook. 'Sir Terence's office, right away. Duncan's already there. They're waiting for you.'

What does the head of the whole department want with me?

As she walked from the lift on to the sixth floor, Sir Terence's secretary was waiting for her.

'Siobhan told me you were on your way,' she said as they hurried along.

'What's up?'

'Search me,' the secretary replied. They had reached Sir Terence's office. 'But it was after a phone call with the Deputy Prime Minister that he asked me to get you, if that helps.'

'Thanks.' Cassie stood up straighter as the secretary knocked on the door to announce her.

'Cassandra, come in.' Sir Terence sat at the head of the long glass meeting table with Duncan seated on one side of him. 'Join us, please.'

Through the floor length windows Cassie could glimpse the towers of St John's church in nearby Smith Square. She sat.

'The Deputy Prime Minister has been told about your quick thinking yesterday. Well done.' Sir Terence gave her a mirthless smile. 'He has also been informed about your macabre find, as well as this morning's discovery. I understand there is reason to believe that these two occurrences are linked; two bodies in two days. I suppose you're familiar with this sort of thing.'

Not really.

Her former job had had its moments, but, by and large, it hadn't been so gory. She said nothing.

'The DPM is concerned by the Palace of Westminster connection,' Sir Terence said. He walked over to the window where he closed a blind, seeming reluctant to continue.

She waited.

'You must not, under any circumstances, mention what I am about to tell you outside of this room,' he said, looking from Cassie to Duncan. 'The DPM and senior party officials expect the Prime Minister to announce at the Party Conference that he will be stepping down in the near future.'

Bloody hell!

'The DPM is aware of the current Home Secretary's...um... desire to take the PM's place.' He gave a small cough. 'David Hurst has made no secret of his ambitions and the party would accept him. But it would be disastrous to have a new Prime Minister who might then be implicated in any scandal, especially including murder, if only through connection with his previous department's mistakes. The reputational damage to the government could be incalculable.'

And perhaps Charles Morecombe has ambitions of his own? Any such implications of scandal would scupper the leadership chances of his rival.

'There have been investigations into historic abuse allegations in Parliament, as well as an independent enquiry into the role of the Metropolitan Police in investigating, or failing to investigate, such cases.'

Where's this leading? And what does it have to do with me?

'So the DPM wants to ensure that the Met and the Home Office are doing everything by the book this time. This won't be an official investigation, but he wants to know enough to allow him to take a view before any announcement is made and, if necessary, persuade the Prime Minister to defer it.' He paused. 'It's unlikely that there is any connection between these deaths and Parliament. The murders of a Polish apprentice and a Spanish workman are not exactly corridors of power stuff, but in the current climate the murder of EU nationals might draw attention to any other failings. This is a question of reputation management.'

How does Sir Terence know about the victims? Rowlands didn't know earlier. This is new.

Sir Terence focused his gaze on Cassie.

'You have investigated highly sensitive cases in the past and are already personally involved, so you seem ideally placed to take on this task. I need hardly add that this is an opportunity for you to demonstrate your continued usefulness. Such an opportunity to retrieve your old reputation is unlikely to come along again. It is, of course, up to you whether you accept or decline.'

Her heart leapt.

For real? A chance to get my old life back?

She calculated the timescale. Parliament rose for autumn recess and the party conferences next week, meaning seven days at most to learn whatever could be learned, from people who would not want to share it, then to reach her conclusions and report back.

'The DPM wants to know if there is anything in these deaths, and their investigation, which could compromise the police, the Home Office or the Home Secretary,' Sir Terence said and sat once more.

To ask anyone to do that in a week is absurd.

It was a poisoned chalice. It could be suicide to take it. And yet, it would be worth the risk to get back what she had lost – a career that really counted.

'If I may ask, Sir Terence?' Duncan said.

'Yes.'

'Given the little time available and the, er, unofficial nature of any enquiries, exactly what does the DPM want by way of assurance?'

Thank you, Duncan, narrow it down. Bless your Scottish Presbyterian heart.

'To know that this isn't another scandal in the making; the fact that the Spaniard worked in Parliament is incidental; that there is no link with previous cases and, finally, that the police are investigating this correctly.'

Duncan shot a glance in Cassie's direction.

She knew that look. You can turn this down, he was saying. Decide what you want to do and I'll back you.

But I can't turn it down. It's what I've prayed for and dreamt of: another chance.

A chance to get out of the backwater into which she had been allowed to crawl, to lick her wounds and keep out of trouble. To return to doing something she was good at, which she had a natural aptitude for, something she loved; a chance for her to get back to the centre of things. To get back to where she ought to be, to where she belonged.

If I fail..?

Her career would be finished forever. She wouldn't get another shot. She might not even be allowed to wallow in obscurity, but would lose what she currently had: a salary, a decent boss, a pension. Then what would she do? The stakes were high and this was a high-risk commission.

'I'll do it,' she said.

'Good,' the Permanent Secretary pursed his lips. 'You will work with the existing police team, though your role is different from theirs, don't forget that. An Inspector Rowlands is in charge, I understand, I'm sure he will welcome someone with your inside knowledge of Whitehall.'

Like a hole in the head.

'Begin immediately. You will be given full security clearance, including for the Palace of Westminster. Your previous vetting is sufficient. My secretary will organise your pass. Just as well you're getting a new one....'

He turned to Duncan.

'Given the short timescale involved, Cassandra will not be replaced. Defer activity or hand it off to other members of your team.'

So no help for Duncan, payback because he supported me.

It was the end of the meeting but she had two more questions.

'Is there anything I should know about David Hurst? Any skeletons already identified?'

'Outside your remit,' the Permanent Secretary said.

So there is something. That's why I'm being asked to do this.

'So how will I know if anything I discover is new?'

'You won't.' He snapped his mouth shut.

Move on.

'To whom do I report? And when?'

'I'll speak with the DPM,' Sir Terence said. 'For the moment, let's schedule in a meeting before the end of the week.' He stepped out of his office. Cassie and Duncan followed. The secretary was already holding Cassie's new pass.

'You didn't have to accept,' Duncan said in a low voice as they walked over to the lifts.

'I know, and it's probably the wrong thing to do, but...'

'You couldn't resist the mystery and it's better than overseeing procurement projects.'

'It's not that I dislike my job here.'

That was a lie, but a necessary one. Duncan was a good boss and had stuck his neck out to support her. In so far as she was fond of anyone these days, she was fond of him.

'It's only... I can't resist a conundrum. Pride comes before a fall - isn't that the saying?'

'"Pride goeth before destruction and a haughty spirit before a fall",' Duncan quoted as they walked towards his office, passing Cassie's desk on the way. 'Be careful Cassie, especially when it comes to reporting, verbal or not. You've only got seven days. You won't have time to do more than the most cursory investigation and, if this thing blows up, they'll be looking for someone to blame.'

Been there. Done that.

'I'll come along to the meeting tomorrow morning but duck out of everything else,' she said.

With a rueful grin Duncan continued on towards his office.

She had been asked to do the almost impossible and she'd accepted. She was about to step back into the murky world of crime and murder, and yet her heart felt lighter.

Seven days isn't long. Best to tackle this head on and hope the inspector has been informed.

'Siobhan, would you get me Inspector Rowlands of Scotland Yard on the phone, please.'

◊ TEN

Rowlands had been instructed to cooperate with her, but it was clear that he wasn't happy. She would have to tread carefully if she wanted his help, as he most definitely didn't want hers.

The investigation team included three other detectives and a couple of uniformed officers. They sat beside a large whiteboard at one end of what had been designated the incident room at New Scotland Yard, an open-plan office on the fifth floor overlooking the Thames. Rowlands' glass box of an office was next door. The inspector was bringing them up to date with his trip to the mortuary.

'So, we have two victims. One raped and murdered, one just murdered. The only thing linking them at the moment is method of killing, but, as Bill made clear earlier, he wouldn't swear to it being the same killer in court. We need to see if we can find a link between them. Find the link and maybe we can understand why we've got one killer and two very different crime scenes.'

'Or they might not be linked at all,' Cassie added, punctiliously, as she approached.

'Ms Fortune,' Rowlands snapped. 'Everyone, this is Cassandra Fortune, she'll be joining the investigation in an advisory capacity. Please make her feel at home.' The last sentence hung in the air.

'Hello,' Cassie said, looking around the group. 'Sorry I'm coming to this late. What have I missed? Did you manage to find out anything more about either victim?'

Rowlands gave DS Patel a meaningful look and she took up the narrative. 'The first victim is Tadeusz Jablonski from Gdansk in Poland. He lived in Croydon and was an apprentice, an electrician working for a company called Union Building.'

'Did he have a record or prior arrests?' Cassie asked.

'One,' Serjeant Patel replied. 'He'd been found carrying drugs during a stop and search. We wouldn't have arrested him, except that he was aggressive. The report says he fancied himself a kickboxer.'

'That aligns with the pathologist's view of a fracas. He would have fought. Sexual orientation?'

'The electrician he was apprenticed to, another Pole, says Tadeusz

had a girlfriend back in Gdansk,' Rowlands said. 'He carried a photo of her in his wallet.'

'Hm, it doesn't mean...'

'I know what it does and doesn't mean.'

Cassie shifted the focus of her questions. 'And the rave he attended? Is there a link there?'

'DS Patel is meeting with the events company in Shoreditch this afternoon.'

Hmm. What about me? I'd better not be sidelined, kept away from the evidence.

'And José?'

'From Madrid. No prior arrests or known criminal connections.'

'That doesn't fit with him being a professional thief.'

'It doesn't mean he isn't one either.'

'José's girlfriend is pregnant,' Serjeant Patel stated.

'A child would mean a lot of extra expense,' Cassie said. 'But stealing an access pass isn't going to bring him any cash. Was anything else missing?'

'I spoke to police at the Palace. They confirmed that other items have been reported missing. I asked for a list,' the serjeant said.

'Did you speak with Parliamentary Security?'

'No, why speak with them as well?'

'Ah,' Cassie hesitated. 'Perhaps you should. Forgive me if you already know what I'm about to explain... but policing and security in Parliament is rather unusual.'

'This is a double murder enquiry.' The inspector was terse, his grey eyes cold. He clearly didn't envisage the possibility of anybody not being entirely compliant, not to say helpful, in such a case.

'I'm sure we'll get full cooperation but the Palace of Westminster isn't subject to laws in the same way as elsewhere. Our investigation will go more smoothly if we take account of that.'

'The law of the land is the law of the land,' the serjeant said.

'Parliament makes the laws; it isn't subject to them. It sits at the very top of the tree, above the executive and the judiciary, including the police service.'

The inspector gave her a long, cold stare. There was an embarrassed shuffling among the other officers on the team.

There's no time for any misunderstandings. The timetable's too tight. Make it clear.

'That's not to say the law doesn't apply in the Palace of Westminster, it does,' she continued. 'The Met provides security and policing but it does so because the Speaker allows it to. Parliamentary privilege means MPs in the Chamber cannot automatically be bound by law, so, for example, they cannot be sued if they name individuals as suspected wrongdoers.'

'So the legal framework we work within...the powers which we have...' a uniformed officer began, an incredulous look on his face.

'Will still apply,' the inspector said. 'The rule of law is fundamental, without it there is chaos. We assume that the law operates there, that murder is a crime to be investigated and that we have the powers to investigate it.'

'I'm not saying to do otherwise,' Cassie said. 'But you should be aware that some police powers, like surveillance, aren't automatic in the Palace of Westminster. MPs are concerned about being overwatched, by the security services, for example.'

'Bizarre.' Patel rolled her eyes.

'And, if I might make a suggestion....?'

Everyone looked at her expectantly.

'We should get information from In-House Services. They handle the contract staff. Most people who work there are on the Palace payroll but sometimes outside contractors are used, especially when specialist skills are required. José was a contractor, he worked for CSL.'

'Perhaps you could arrange that?' the inspector said.

'I'll get my office to ask some questions.'

'Have we talked with the girlfriend, Daljit?'

'No. I thought you would want to do that yourself.'

'I do. Get me her address please. Ms Fortune and I will pay her a visit.'

The serjeant nodded but didn't look particularly happy about it. The team began to disperse.

So, I've usurped her place. He's not shutting me out after all. Good.

As she and the inspector made ready to leave, she remembered her old pass.

'Did you get anything from my pass? Fingerprints, DNA?'

'Nothing, nothing at all,' the inspector replied. 'I can't give it back, I'm afraid.'

'Don't worry, I've got a better one.'

◊ ELEVEN

Iñes Vaquera lived on the twelfth floor and her living room had a spectacular view. Northwards sunlight sparkled on the Shard and the towers of the City and, to the east, the chunky skyscrapers of Canary Wharf jostled for space on the Isle of Dogs. To the south east Cassie could see Crystal Palace Hill rising, bedecked by strings of terraced streets, to the high transmitter mast at its summit.

The flat was in a large 1970s municipal tower block, one of several standing on both sides of a busy triple carriageway. The lobby and lift well were litter-strewn and smelled of urine. This was a very different south London to Clapham's gentrified Victoriana or that visible on Crystal Palace Hill.

The living room was off a tiny hallway, half-filled by a large baby buggy. A white-haired woman, who introduced herself as Rosa, ushered them through. The smell of paint almost eclipsed the underlying whiff of damp and Cassie noticed the ill-fitting metal window frames.

Short and brown-haired, Iñes Vaquera was already showing her pregnancy. There were dark rings under her eyes and a pallor which told of a sleepless night waiting for her partner to come home. She had been informed of his death only that morning. Now she was folded into an armchair, opposite the sofa where Cassie and Rowlands sat. Rosa brought in mugs of coffee and placed them on to little crocheted coasters on the coffee table.

'As you know, we're investigating the death of your fiancé, José,' Cassie began. They had agreed that, as a Spanish speaker, she would lead the interview. 'We think that he took some items from the Palace of Westminster where he was working last night--'

Iñes interrupted. 'I do not believe it. Why do you think this?'

'Because one of those items was in his possession when he was found,' Cassie said. 'A Palace of Westminster pass. It belonged to me. I was at the Palace on Monday night, I saw José working there, though it didn't seem important at the time.'

'You saw him. You saw him alive!' Iñes stared, her eyes wide and pleading, as if Cassie could conjure José into their presence. Rosa reached across and took her friend's hand.

'Yes, I did.'

Take care with the description, she'll visualise him from my words.

'He was working on the tiled floor in Central Lobby with a group of colleagues. He kept sweeping his fringe out of his eyes. He was smiling and joking. He had a broad smile. He was enjoying his work.'

'Yes, yes, he was happy. He was waiting for the birth of our son.' Iñes wiped her cheeks and scrunched the tissue into a tiny ball.

'When is the child due?'

'The end of January,' Iñes replied. 'We already prepare.'

'Yes, I saw the buggy,' Cassie indicated the door to the hallway. 'And you've been decorating.'

'*Si.* José did it himself, he insisted. We make a nursery too. He worked hard, even after double shifts.' Her mouth twisted into a sad smile. 'Now he will not see his son.'

'Children are expensive,' the inspector said.

'It must have been a struggle to afford everything,' Cassie added.

Iñes Vaquera sat still and said nothing but Rosa looked sidelong at her friend.

'Where did he find the extra money, Ms Vaquera?' the inspector asked.

'We have it,' Iñes insisted, her chin tilting upwards.

Cassie looked around the small room. It was spotless and well-kept, but its furniture was scuffed and looked secondhand. Rag rugs were strategically placed, probably to cover threadbare parts of the carpet. Iñes and José had been trying hard to make a good home but there was no spare money here. Her eyes met those of Rosa. Cassie gave a little shake of her head.

The older woman looked away.

'You can tell them,' she said to her friend in Spanish. 'It might help find José's killers.'

Iñes' face crumpled but she pressed her lips together.

'He did not steal, he borrowed it,' she said.

'Who from?'

'I don't know their names,' she said. 'But they are not *buena gente*, not good people.'

Loan sharks.

'I told him not to. We manage, but he wanted to buy things, to decorate,' she paused. 'I was afraid that they would find out where we lived and come here.'

Cassie suspected they already knew, but she asked.

'How was he going to pay them back, Ms Vaquera?'

'No lo se. I don't know.' Tears rolled down her cheeks.

'What about work? You said he had already been working double shifts?'

'Yes...but he asked for more.'

'And...?'

'I don't know. A woman named Karen Woods gave out the jobs,' Iñes frowned. 'Everyone has to be nice to her. I do not like her. And her husband, he's not good news.'

Rowlands wrote down the name.

'José was anxious? Worried?' Cassie said.

'Yes... pero...'

'But what?'

'He was worried for many weeks. Then he changed. Like he had found the answer.'

'When was this, Señora?' Rowlands asked, quietly.

'The end of last week,' Iñes replied. 'I thought perhaps it was because he got his assignment for this week. Sometimes the company doesn't say if there's work until the last minute, it's how they keep control, but this time José knew in advance so he didn't have to worry.'

So José was a contract worker, not even a CSL employee.

'Did he know he'd be working at Westminster?' Cassie asked.

'Oh yes. He liked it there. He hoped he would continue, though they never really let you settle in one place in case they get into trouble with the tax people.'

'But this wouldn't have solved your money worries? It wasn't enough for José to pay back the loans?'

'No, but it meant he was sure of being able to give them... something.

And... he said there would be more this time.'

'Did he say why?' The policeman asked.

Iñes shook her head. Her lips were pressed closed and she had a determined look on her face. She wouldn't say anything more. Cassie exchanged looks with Rowlands.

'Thank you, Ms Vaquera,' Rowlands said. 'Only one more thing...'

'Yes.'

'How did José usually travel home and at what time would he normally arrive?'

'It depended. He was often late, especially when he was at Westminster. That place is falling down, they do urgent work after hours. He used the night bus, the 148. It was an easy journey, another reason why he liked working there.'

'Thank you,' the policeman reiterated.

'Yes, thank you and thank you for the coffee,' Cassie added, as they stood. 'I hope all goes well with the birth of your child.'

'So do I,' Iñes replied. 'I am going home, back to España, soon. I'm going to my family. I cannot stay here without José. Please find out who killed my baby's father.'

◊ TWELVE

'So, José owed money to loan sharks; that would explain why he stole,' Cassie said, as they walked along the Embankment towards the Houses of Parliament. In an attempt to prove her usefulness she had offered to show DI Rowlands around the Palace of Westminster.

'It appears so, though there may be more to it than that,' Rowlands said. 'We'll follow up on the company and the Woods woman and her husband.'

The crowds grew denser. Ahead, camera-clicking tourists surrounded the black railings, even though Big Ben was silent and its tower shrouded in scaffolding. Piles of newspapers stacked on the pavement screamed 'Return of the Black Death' in thick black letters.

At the gate the security guard inspected her pass and his warrant card and waved them through. They crossed New Palace Yard to enter Westminster Hall, one of the oldest parts of the Palace. The inspector gazed around the enormous space while Cassie punched in the code at a controlled access side door. Once through the door they climbed a small staircase to a long corridor.

'This is the back way to the Commons Lobby,' she said.

At the end of the corridor they passed through an arch into a lofty rectangular space. 'Only MPs, security and lobby journalists are allowed here when the House is sitting. We count as security. We can get to Central Lobby this way. That's where I saw José.'

As they crossed the pale stone floor they attracted the attention of more than one of the men who stood at its periphery. These men wore an antique uniform of a black tailcoat, breeches and stockings. One stepped forward to intercept them and Cassie raised her pass.

'Security,' she said as the man took a long look at the pass. 'This is Detective Inspector Rowlands.'

The inspector produced his warrant card.

After scrutinizing it, the man stepped back and waved them on their way.

'Doorkeepers,' she explained as they walked on. 'They eject those who aren't supposed to be here.'

'How do they know who is and who isn't?'

'They memorise the faces of all the Members,' she said. 'No, it's true. Honestly. They carry a pocketbook of photographs. They're a sort of human CCTV only better, as they can take action immediately. You'll see them all over but especially near the Chambers.'

'Novel,' the inspector said.

'There is CCTV, but only in certain parts of the building – Central Lobby, for example, or outside the Strangers' Bar. There are no cameras in the non-public side of the palace. Much of the business conducted here is privileged; the Speaker won't allow blanket coverage.'

'So there's no chance of tracking the plumber's movements on CCTV while he was working?'

'None,' Cassie said as her phone buzzed. 'Here we are, Central Lobby.'

'Yes, I recognise it from TV,' Rowlands said, looking up at the arched ceiling. 'It's impressive.'

'Tourists and visitors see only part of the Palace,' Cassie explained.

'The rest isn't open to the general public. It's really like a small town, with shops, places to eat and drink, even a barber's and hairdressers and a Post Office too. Business is focused on the Houses of Commons and Lords but the Palace has a life all of its own, twenty-four seven.'

She checked her phone for the message.

'Last night José was working here,' she said. 'My secretary tells me that CSL is a regular specialist contractor, so he was probably with members of the Craft Team.' Cassie strode across the chamber. 'They were re-laying this floor.' She stamped lightly on the patterned tiles. 'I didn't take much notice because I was watching for my boss.'

'And when he arrived you went straight to the Terrace?'

'Yes, I'll take you there now.'

Cassie took the same route as the day before, but, she reflected, today she was feeling rather different. For the first time in a long while she felt content and comfortable in her work. She was doing what she loved once again.

So don't screw it up this time. Give them what they want.

'Cassie, you're the only sane person I've ever met who seems to enjoy being a murder suspect.'

Cassie grinned at him. 'I am enjoying it, I have to admit. Does that sound awful? Two people have died.'

'I understand,' Rowlands said, a smile lifting the corners of his mouth. 'It's the job. Tell me, how long did you do investigation work for?'

'A while.'

He waited, then asked, 'Why did you stop?'

He's been checking again. Perhaps he called in a favour and got lucky.

'What does my file say?'

'I haven't seen it, if that's what you're thinking.'

Cassie said nothing.

'Who did you cross, Cassandra?'

'It was in a different life,' she said. 'I rarely think about it these days.'

I used to think about it all the time.

He said nothing, but neither did she. He was, she noticed, good at using silence.

'OK, you don't have to tell me,' he said, raising both hands and laughing. 'I want to ensure it doesn't hinder the case, that's all. By the way, it would be helpful if you would accompany me when I speak with various officials here. You know the ropes, I don't.'

'May I suggest you leave the Palace of Westminster people to me. It'll save time and be so much easier.'

Rowlands stopped and looked down at her. He was half a head taller and was using that for the first time since they'd met, she realised.

'Cassandra, this is my case and I intend to run it. If you think you stand a better chance of getting somewhere because you're on your own, in specific instances, I'll consider stepping aside. But I'm not giving you *carte blanche.*'

Cassie raised an eyebrow. This was a reasonable compromise, she supposed, if he kept to it. She decided to assume he meant it, but she would test him.

'I have a personal contact in the Parliamentary Security Department, an old friend. I want to talk to him alone.'

Rowlands frowned.

'I promise to report everything back,' she said quickly. 'And bring you in as soon as I can.'

He said nothing. She assumed consent.

'And I promise not to lecture you about the law again,' she said, smiling. 'I wouldn't like it in your place, but it was important that the team understood how things worked here.'

He looked at her sidelong as they resumed walking.

'You needed to establish your credentials, I understand,' he said, then paused. 'Though apology accepted.'

'I wasn't...'

He was laughing at her again. The corners of her mouth began to curve upwards and she pressed her lips together, stifling the involuntary smile.

'We're here,' she said and led him out on to the terrace.

As always in the evening it was in shadow. A young female MP was escorting a group of constituents and a clutch of sharp-suited young men sat drinking with two more Members.

'Lobbyists,' she said, leading him over to the river balustrade. 'This place was full last night: ministers, MPs, people from business, civil servants, lobbyists and catering staff. Duncan and I stood here for a while, watching. I was here at the Minister's invitation because of the cave-in underground. I wouldn't normally be asked to something like this. He wanted to thank me.' Cassie's lips twisted.

'What was the reception for?'

'The Thames Estates Programme, though it's not formally launched until Thursday. It's a multibillion pound programme to refurbish a high-profile part of the government estate. Every major corporation wants a part of it. Before he was killed, Tadeusz was working in one of the buildings that will be refurbished.'

'The original New Scotland Yard.'

She nodded.

'So, lots of important, powerful and wealthy people in town then? Here on the Terrace last night?'

She nodded. Where was this leading? But he said nothing more. He turned to rest his forearms on the parapet and look at the river. She followed his gaze.

On the opposite bank the buildings were still in sunshine, red-orange light reflecting from the windows of St Thomas's Hospital and the County Hall Hotel.

'Those hospital wards must have one of the finest views in London,' he said.

'They do... and the hotel too.'

A tourist boat chugged past, its commentary heard over the water. 'On the left the Houses of Parliament and Westminster, the site of royal buildings since Anglo Saxon times....'

'I find it fascinating,' she said, looking back at the Palace. 'So much power being concentrated within this small area. All because, centuries ago, the ground of old Thorney Island, as it was then known, was a bit higher than the Thames Marshes around it. Now, everything's here: Parliament, Downing Street, the Supreme Court, Whitehall and the Abbey.'

The inspector relinquished the balustrade.

'And the building itself? You're not interested in that?'

'No. If you discount the older bits which survived the fire, it's really a fake, a Victorian idea of what they thought the past looked like. The history lies beneath it: the old Whitehall Palace, the Abbey. There are relics of the medieval buildings, you know, traces of almost everything.'

The inspector had a slow, lazy smile. The grey of his eyes grew smokier when he was relaxed.

'Everything leaves fingerprints,' he said.

Cassie's own smile faded.

'But not on my pass, not even my own. Doesn't that strike you as odd? Who wiped them off?'

◊ THIRTEEN

He stood at the full length windows, hands in the trouser pockets of his suit, watching the sun set. On the opposite bank stood the Palace of Westminster, the finial on its central tower catching the sunlight, the riverside and terrace in shadow. Seven storeys below, traffic crawled over Westminster Bridge and the clippers and cruisers skimmed over the waves of the slow-moving Thames. A tourist cruiser chugged by. Had the window been open he was sure he would have heard its commentary.

The police were already nosing around there. It was dangerous.

He folded his arms. Up until now he'd been careful to minimise the risk of detection, which was why he'd succeeded for so long. The Spaniard had demanded more money. The stupid man didn't know who or what he was dealing with. But something had gone awry, his body had been discovered and somehow the link with Westminster had been made and made quickly.

From his vantage point he could see a forest of towers. The Victoria and Elizabeth Towers of the Palace, the Gothic towers of the Abbey and, beyond, the slim, Byzantine column of Westminster Cathedral. To the north lay the domes of the Treasury, the square towers of the Foreign Office, the chunky blocks of the Ministry of Defence, and to the south Millbank Tower dwarfed the Tate Gallery.

'Won't be long!'

A call came from the bedroom of the suite, in a southern US drawl. The Texan. So tiresome.

The visitor was important in pharmaceuticals, so important that he had judged it better to deal with him himself. Something he was regretting now. The man was a bore and a boor. His own involvement was tedious in the extreme and these days he didn't really need, or want, to appear in the enterprise at all. He had no intention of taking part later. The entertainments were useful, but he found them distasteful. At least the dining rooms in St James's were private and the wine would flow, smoothing the social infelicities.

Who else was attending tonight's dinner? Who would be a suitable companion for the visitor at that evening's event, in its suitably orgiastic setting? Someone who would be an enthusiastic participant and wasn't crucial to the immediate project. Yes, he had just the man.

There were people on the Terrace opposite, tiny figures watching the boats travelling up and down the Thames. Yesterday's reception there had been a good opportunity to see some of the main players together. She'd been there too, though she'd left early.

The woman intrigued him. Why was she, with her background and talent, buried away doing tiny procurement contracts? He'd used all his contacts to find out more about her but they had yielded little, other than that she had once worked at GCHQ. She seemed to have no friends. Her mother and sister knew nothing about her professional life and even her ex-husband had proved uncommunicative.

Former colleagues were reluctant to talk about her but they made it clear she was not to be underestimated. Only one, well into his cups, had confided that she had been the single most ambitious person he had ever met, but when questioned again had been more careful, which was interesting.

Now she worked for Morecombe, the Deputy Prime Minister, yet she hadn't been near him yesterday: which was odd in itself. Senior civil servants never missed a chance to bring themselves to the notice of their Minister, but not her. There were other ways, he supposed, in which she could command the DPM's attention, private meetings and back channels.

Something else was going on, there had to be, there was someone else she was working for. The procurement post had to be a cover, nothing else made sense, but a cover for what? Had the security services placed her there? What was her real role? There were rumours swirling around Westminster about the Prime Minister. Was she involved?

He would charm her and find out everything he wanted to know. The Thames Estates Programme would be a useful point of contact.

His arms dropped to his sides.

Yet there was something else this woman provoked in him, an unfamiliar sensation. He examined himself with the same ruthless forensic logic he applied to any situation and found what surprised him, though it shouldn't have done. She might answer a need. The one thing he lacked was a companion, someone to share his success with.

His sort of status and wealth attracted women, the beautiful and the talented. Yet none of them had his hunger for power – that overwhelming urge to reshape the world. His associates were, by and large, unimpressive or uninterested, his international rivals dangerous and untrustworthy. There was no one who had the inside track, no one with his mix of ambition, drive and vision. Did she have it? Would she appreciate what he had achieved and what he still wanted to do?

Yet she might also destroy him – he was aware that this was part of her appeal.

The Texan came to stand at the windows, whisky tumbler already in hand.

'Wonderful view, but I guess it should be, the amount this suite costs. Can I tempt you?' He shook the glass so that the ice clinked.

The Texan would be useful, once he could be put to work.

'Oh no, I don't think so. Shall we go?'

WEDNESDAY

◊ FOURTEEN

Telephones rang as Cassie walked between rows of empty desks towards the lifts. She had to collect papers for the meeting she had promised to attend and had come into the office early to avoid colleagues curious about her new commission; colleagues who still thought of her as an outsider even after two years. Now she wanted this morning's meeting over with, so she could contact Parliamentary Security and get on with the case.

People were arriving as she left the building and headed for Whitehall. By the Abbey she slipped through the stationary traffic in Parliament Square. Out of habit she glanced up at the clock but it was shrouded by netting.

Her watch told her she had fifteen minutes to walk along Whitehall. That was cutting it fine.

'Cassandra!'

Andrew.

She looked round to see the inspector striding across Parliament Street towards her. She slowed.

'I've been trying to contact you,' he said. 'You're not answering any of your phones.'

'Walk with me, I have a meeting –'

'No.' He stopped. 'It's important. We have a new lead.'

Cassie came to an abrupt halt.

'Very early this morning a police constable found a young French-Algerian woman wandering the streets of Mayfair,' Rowlands said. 'She was half naked and distraught. The constable couldn't understand what she was saying but it was clear that she was greatly distressed.'

'She'd been assaulted?'

'It seems so. As far as he could make out she claimed that she'd been held underground against her will, where she was raped repeatedly.'

'Like Tadeusz.'

'Exactly. I think this may be our lucky break. She could be the one that got away. They've taken her to St Mary's Hospital in Paddington. I'm on my way there now. Are you coming?'

'Of course. I'll text my boss to say I can't attend the meeting. Andrew, was the girl found near a plague pit, like the others? How do we...?'

But the inspector was already hailing a cab.

◊ FIFTEEN

She was there, only yards away. It was as if an electric charge had scrambled his insides.

He checked his watch. She shouldn't be there. She had a nine o'clock meeting.

He veered across the pavement out of her sightline and drew his phone from his inside pocket as if he were taking a call. Don't behave suspiciously, it was the most elementary of mistakes. If she sees you, she sees you. It doesn't matter. You've every right to be here.

He could feel his anger very near the surface. It was the shock of seeing her unexpectedly, where she ought not to have been, so close after the debacle of last night.

How could they have allowed the French girl to escape? The American couldn't be blamed but Harris was slipping, he should have secured all the exits before they began. He was usually efficient. It wasn't his fault that the Polish boy's corpse had been found, under normal circumstances the body would never have been discovered, but this...

Of course he had not been there himself. The girl couldn't identify him personally. But she had seen too much. Now they had to find her and kill her.

Someone was calling Cassandra's name.

He glanced across quickly, then looked back down at his phone. Detective Inspector Rowlands.

He knew the names of all the senior police, who was ambitious, who would cut corners. Rowlands was clever but he did things by the book. He was still a DI because he'd screwed up a case a few years ago when his wife left him, but he wasn't corruptible. Was this the policeman who his people had sensed on their trail before? Was Rowlands the reason why operations had had to be closed down to let the trail run cold?

If so, he would have to settle the score with the inspector.

Rowlands and Cassandra together – he watched them out of the corner of his eye.

The man and woman were standing close to each other. He was taller and she was looking up at him, intent on what he was saying. The inspector was telling her something, from his demeanour something important.

Did they know about the French escapee? Had she gone to the police? Or had they found her?

He stepped towards them, listening, as a black cab braked in response to the policeman's hail. Rowlands opened the cab door to let the woman in.

'St Mary's Hospital,' the inspector said to the driver and climbed in behind Cassandra.

He turned away, tapping a speed dial key.

'Hello. The girl you managed to lose has been found by the police and taken to St Mary's. Do we have any contacts there?'

He paused.

'Then get someone there immediately. We have to prevent her from talking.'

The taxi carved a U-turn to go back into Parliament Square.

'And Harris, if necessary you will take care of this yourself, do you understand? No more mistakes. Report back to me when it's done.'

◊ SIXTEEN

Cassie lengthened her stride to keep up with the inspector as he paced along the busy corridors of the trauma unit at St Mary's Hospital.

'Have you interviewed rape victims before?' he asked, not waiting for a reply. 'It's important not to be aggressive. There's an interpreter already there.'

Rowlands pushed through a set of double doors and spoke to a uniformed constable standing at one side of the corridor.

'Second door on the right, sir,' the man said. 'Doctor's just over there.'

A white-coated young woman standing at the nurse's station introduced herself as Doctor Naipaul. She took them aside.

'Ms Tabriki has been severely traumatised,' she said. 'Endured rape, beating and other abuse. There are no life-threatening physical injuries, but psychologically, she's very fragile indeed. The interpreter's already in with her, as well as a policeman.'

'Samples and DNA?'

'You'll get them but unfortunately we're understaffed at the moment. Many of our lab scientists are elsewhere dealing with various outbreaks,' she said. 'And we're inundated in A&E. It's the plague pit - people believe the nonsense they read online and every ache or pain is a symptom of the Black Death. As if we didn't have enough to cope with. Ten minutes, no more,' she added.

'We'll keep it short,' Rowlands said. 'Thank you, doctor.'

A constable stood inside the room, well away from the beds. Only the bed by the window was occupied and a woman sat by the side of it. She rose and came towards them.

'Patrice Legrange.' She held out a well-manicured hand.

'Detective Inspector Rowlands and Ms Fortune.' The inspector kept his voice low. 'Is she talking?'

'Yes, though she's very unstable. Sometimes says nothing, sometimes you can't stop her. Mainly French and Arabic but she can speak English.'

Cassie looked over at the figure in the bed. The young woman was tiny, lost in the striped hospital gown, with huge eyes in a thin face. Her arms, smudged with black and purple bruises, lay atop the white sheets, right wrist in a pink plaster cast. She looked like a child.

'She's twenty-two years old.' Patrice anticipated Cassie's question. 'It's hard to believe, I know. Her name is Silana.'

The inspector brought two more chairs over to the bedside, seating Cassie closest to the girl.

'Ask her to tell us what happened,' he said.

The interpreter's question elicited a flood of words, jumbled and almost incoherent.

'Let's start with something easy,' Rowlands said. 'Does she know where she is?'

'*Londres*,' Silana replied.

So she could understand English.

'Do you live here?' Cassie asked. 'Or are you visiting?'

Slowly the girl's story emerged.

'She is from Paris, but she works on the Eurostar train service, that's how she learned English. When her shift finishes at St Pancras, she stays in London with another young Frenchwoman.'

'We'll need a name and address, please,' Rowlands said and wrote down the information given. 'Now, tell us what happened.'

'She was going to her friend's yesterday evening as usual, but she was accosted and bundled into a van. She says she was drugged. At some point, she's not sure exactly when, she awoke, lying naked on the ground, her hands and feet tied. It was pitch black and smelled dank and earthy.'

'Underground?' the inspector asked.

'Yes... it seemed... very old.'

There was a torrent of words from Silana.

'She lay there, not knowing what was going to happen, afraid that she'd be left there to die in the dark. Then she heard someone approach. A man brought a light and he lit a flambeau, an old-fashioned flaming torch. She was released and made to walk about. He gave her clothes.'

'Did they fit?' Cassie asked.

Silana nodded a yes.

So this was completely premeditated.

'What happened then?' Rowlands continued.

'She was taken into another room and two other men came in.'

Cassie controlled her urge to lean forward. She sensed Rowlands' anticipation too.

'The room was larger, a chamber with a shallow pool in its centre. It was ancient, Roman. It had furniture of an old style, couches and low tables, flaming torches on the walls, deep shadows. She was taken to a stone table or altar and made to drink from a goblet.'

The young woman became very distressed. It took the interpreter some time to calm her.

'They made her do things. She was raped, several times. They were disgusting.'

'More than one man raped her?' the inspector asked.

'Yes.'

'How many? Were all the abusers male?'

'Two. Yes.'

'Did any of them refer to each other by name?'

'No.'

'Can you describe them?' Cassie asked Silana. 'First the man who abducted you.'

The young woman shuddered and closed her eyes before speaking. Mme Legrange translated.

'Middle-aged, not tall, forty to fifty years old, but hard-bodied and strong, with short hair, like a soldier, she says. He wore gloves, medical gloves, all the time. He didn't take part but was more like a servant. There were two others. One was American, she thinks. Also middle-aged, but paunchy. The other was a tall, straight-backed man who the American called *monseigneur*.'

'My lord?' Rowlands queried.

The interpreter checked.

'Yes.'

'Could you tell if the two men knew each other? What was their relationship?'

Silana answered, but the interpreter asked her more questions.

'She says they had both been drinking. The American seemed to be the guest of the other man. She was for the American's pleasure, to do with as he wished. She was a plaything, a slave. She was whipped and beaten, as well as raped. She wasn't treated like a human being at all. What was important to the other man and the servant was that the American enjoyed himself.'

Vile.

'How did she escape?'

'She pretended to pass out and they left her alone, starting drinking again. She saw there was a passageway behind one of the columns in the chamber and she followed it, going upwards in the dark. They must have realised she was gone because she heard shouting so she ran. She knew if they caught her she would be killed.' The interpreter took a deep breath. 'It must have been terrifying, running in the blackness, knowing there was death behind but not knowing what lay ahead.'

'Eventually she ran into a wall, where the passage ended, but there was light coming in through a hole. She was able to crawl through it into the cellar of a shop. The shopkeeper was just opening up. Then she ran out into the street and shortly afterwards the police found her.'

The young woman began to weep, the words interspersed with sobs.

'She says she wants to rest now,' Patrice said.

'Very well.' The inspector reluctantly agreed. 'Though we'll have to come back later.'

'Tomorrow,' said the doctor. She stood holding the door open. 'She needs to rest.'

◊ SEVENTEEN

The artificial light in the corridor was white and harsh. An orderly wheeled a patient along on a hospital trolley. Nurses in white and medics in blue scrubs talked and joked as they passed, untouched by the horror of what Cassie had just heard.

How could this have happened in central London in the twenty-first century?

She felt a hand gently take her elbow.

'This way,' the inspector said and led her along a different corridor.

Soon she heard chatter and the clink of cutlery and crockery. They rounded a corner and she saw that they were in a staff canteen. The inspector steered her to an empty table.

'Coffee?' Rowlands didn't wait for her reply.

Cassie watched him as he walked to the serving counter, took a tray and joined the queue. He spoke on the phone while he waited, looking slightly out of place in a business suit.

'Here,' the policeman said, returning with coffees and croissants. 'Get your sugar levels back up.'

'Thanks.' Cassie ripped into a croissant.

'This wasn't random,' she said. 'She's tiny and they had clothes to fit her.'

'Silana or someone like her.' He took a sip of coffee. 'Someone small, childlike.'

Or a child.

'What about the setting?'

'I've asked Daljit to have someone check. It might be a real Roman site.'

'There are plenty around,' Cassie said, mouth full of pastry. 'Mostly near the City, though there are baths near the old Aldwych tube station.'

'Too far south. She was found near Grosvenor Square.'

'There must be others.'

'Yep.' The inspector was eating too. 'We should also check if there's been a missing person report filed by Silana's friend, or keep a look out for one.'

'Could we cross-check Roman sites with plague pits? And–it occurred to me this morning–have there been any earlier instances of young people found dead at similar sites?'

'You mean, has this happened before?' the inspector looked over his coffee cup at her. His expression was serious and guarded. He put the cup down. 'There've been others. I have quite a file, going back five years.'

'How many?'

'I can't be sure, but I think at least seven and probably more. Young people sexually abused and killed. I attended a funeral only the other day of a Danish boy, not unlike Tadeusz. His body was found tangled in an anchor chain of a Thames cruiser. I think we're getting close to something I've been tracking for some time.'

'A serial killer?'

The inspector took a sip of coffee.

'The previous victims were all foreign nationals, their bodies dumped in central London. I couldn't convince my superiors that the cases were linked and should be pursued as such, until now.'

'Because of the Westminster angle?'

He nodded. 'That got their attention.'

'Method of killing?'

'Where we can tell, the victims had their throats cut.'

'Is it a serial killer?'

'I thought so but now I'm not so sure. Serial killers are loners but Silana's story suggests that this isn't the work of one person.'

'It could be something new? A gang of psychopaths, perhaps?'

'It could be, though profiling suggests that psychopaths work alone. Silana wasn't a victim chosen at random, she was targeted, abducted and taken to a predetermined location where she was made to play a role in someone else's sexual fantasy.'

'The American's.'

'I've spoken with colleagues in Organised Crime and the gangs they pursue don't provide services like this. Girls, yes, and young boys, trafficked mostly. They operate in brothels or safe houses in the suburbs and the kids earn, they're too valuable to kill. The flavour of this operation is different. '

'Something Organised Crime hasn't seen before?'

'It seems so. At least now we have the Bond Street site to work with and the depot. We've never had a crime scene before, to check for physical evidence. Now we have two. Not that we've found anything so far.'

Which suggests they clean up after themselves.

'Andrew, I know it's unusual for psychopaths to work together but it's not entirely unheard of. Fred and Rosemary West, for example, or Ian Brady and Myra Hindley.'

'Bonnie and Clyde,' Rowlands added with a sceptical raise of the eyebrow.

'It's rare but it does happen. What we know is that this is well organised and involves at least three people who enjoy exotic or outré locations – a plague pit, a Roman baths – women or girls and boys or young men. What if they help each other out to satisfy their needs? Then clean up afterwards.'

'You make them sound like boy scouts: they cooperate, they take turns, they clean up after themselves.' His lips twisted.

She understood his reaction. Yet it made sense, it was logical. This wasn't a lone psychopath but a small group, hunting in a pack. Infinitely more dangerous than a loner, but find one and the others would be scooped up too.

'Andrew, when you came to my office yesterday, you didn't really suspect me at all!'

'I never discount anyone or anything,' he said. 'That's how clues and evidence get missed. Having seen you the day before, however, it seemed unlikely.'

'Thanks a million.'

She smiled at his sheepish expression.

'It has been going on for five years?'

'As far as I know; it could have been going on for longer. Often I begin an investigation but then everything goes silent. It's as if they sense I'm on their trail and disappear. Then something turns up, months, years later.'

'Or you haven't found the other victims yet.'

'Unfortunately, yes, that's possible.' The inspector frowned. 'And the body count is rising. Our sick trio, if that's what's at work here, haven't sated their appetites yet.'

'But that's typical of serial killers too. The more they kill, the more they need to kill. They may be encouraging each other.' Cassie paused, overcome with the horror of what she was describing. 'This is frightening, Andrew. It's a hell of a lot to absorb and rather more than I bargained for.'

'I know.' His smile was sad. 'I'll send you my file. See what you think.'

'What will happen to Silana now? If her abusers are scared that she'll lead us to them, they'll want to silence her and quickly. We must protect her.'

'She'll stay here, with her police guard, until the doctors say she can go. We'll question her again, see if she can remember anything more. Then we'll take her to a safe house.'

His phone rang.

'Yes,' he answered. 'Excellent. Where?' He paused. 'On our way.'

He pocketed his phone as he stood.

'That was Daljit. She thinks she's found the location of the Roman baths.'

'Where?'

'North Audley Street, just off Oxford Street. Not far from your plague pit. Come on.'

◊ EIGHTEEN

Cassie climbed from the cab outside the *Huang Chen Golden Emporium*, a newsagents and general store. A short, neatly dressed man, Mr Chen, she assumed, stood next to DS Patel. From the shop a forensic officer, clad in his white plastic oversuit, was emerging.

'We've found small footprints in the passageway, Sarge,' he said. 'Someone ran up it barefoot and through a door into the cellar.'

'Yes, yes,' the shopkeeper stammered excitedly. 'She frightened the life out of me, appearing from down there like that.'

'Looks like this is how the woman got out, boss,' the DS said to Rowlands. 'There's a big sewer running nearby beneath Oxford Street, with regular access points which could provide another way in. A man from Thames Water is on his way.'

'What's down there?' the inspector asked the forensics man.

'A couple of old rooms, one with a sunken bath. It looks Roman, like we were told.'

So this is where it happened.

'The passage is clear to go down now.'

Cassie was given an electric torch and she followed the others through the shop and down a set of steps to a brick-lined passageway. The rough stone floor went down at a steep angle as the walls became earth and stone. Airless and oppressive, this was completely unlike the smoothly engineered tunnels of the tube. It felt more like the earthfall, constricting and suffocating. As light from her torch bounced off the walls Cassie became conscious of her own breathing.

She could hear voices up ahead, other members of the forensic team at work.

The passageway opened out into a long and narrow chamber, stretching away from them. The roof was supported by stone arches branching from columns and portable lights threw dramatic shadows from the pillars on to the walls. Broken pieces of mosaic tile glinted from the pools of water in the shallow stone bath at its centre. A stone plinth, once the base for a statue, stood in front of them. It was exactly as Silana had described.

One of the lights spluttered and dimmed for a moment, causing the forensic officers to halt in their work. Full luminescence returned and they carried on.

In flickering torchlight it must have been terrifying. Silana would have felt totally powerless, Cassie shivered in sympathy. And not dissimilar to the terror Tadeusz must have felt when he saw the skeletons.

Was terrorising the victim part of the plan?

'Found anything?' the inspector asked one of the forensic team.

'No.' He shook his head in bafflement. 'It's as if the place has been swept clean, sir. Whoever cleaned up did a thorough job.'

'Our victim was raped. There must be something.' Cassie heard the frustration in Rowlands' voice. His crime scenes weren't yielding the clues he'd hoped for.

'There's nothing sir. That's what's odd about this place,' the forensic officer hesitated, but Rowlands nodded that he should continue. 'You would expect some footprints, because of the water and mud, but there's nothing. It's as if the whole place has been industrially cleaned.'

'Thank you, Constable. Don't give up yet. The people who were down here didn't enter the way we did, so there will be another entrance. If we can find it you'll get a second chance to search.'

'There's another room, sir, through the archway. One of the team's already – here she is.'

With a rustle of her plastic suit, an officer entered. She carried a plastic mould.

'There's nothing in the room next door,' she said. 'But there is another passageway which leads from it. And look...' She showed them the mould which contained a reverse imprint of the toe and the side of a shoe. 'I found this at the mouth of the passage. The shoe was wet when it sank into the earth there. They were careful, but not careful enough. '

At last, something tangible to follow up!

With a sharp crack a light failed as heavy footsteps sounded. Cassie spun around to see a distorted shadow stretching across the arches. The black water in the pool glittered. Someone was in the passageway behind them and approaching the baths.

'The Roman baths! Somebody else come across them, 'ave they?' A voice with a flat, cockney twang rang out and a man entered the chamber.

He was of middling height and build but seemed larger because of the thick rubberised overalls and coat he wore. The hard hat on his head had a raised crest, like a cockerel, so his shadow resembled a strange form of bird or reptile.

'George Bindel, Thames Water, at your service,' he boomed.

'Inspector Andrew Rowlands.' The inspector dealt with the introductions quickly. 'You speak as if you knew these were here?'

'Bless me, yes. They were discovered back when the work was done enlarging the old Great Conduit in Oxford Street to turn it into one of Sir Joseph Bazalgette's Victorian interconnecting sewers. It ran all the way to the City. Brilliant man, Bazalgette.'

'Can we get to the sewers from here?'

'Oh yes. There's a link to the sewers.'

'Where does this other passageway go then?' The serjeant led the way through to the next room.

George pursed his lips. 'Hmm, that'll go up to the surface.'

'Have you finished in there?' Rowlands asked the forensics woman.

'Yes, we've got all we're likely to get.'

'Right. Come on, Mr Bindel, let's see where this tunnel goes.'

Ten minutes later they emerged from a door on to North Audley Street. The pavements were busy with commuters heading homeward via the tube stations at Bond Street and Marble Arch.

'Daljit, get the team to start asking around and check for any CCTV footage,' the inspector pointed at the rows of shops and sandwich bars and a large pub. 'The crimes took place on Tuesday night. See if anyone can remember anyone coming and going from this doorway. And make sure forensics have covered the door too.'

'Boss.'

'Would you mind coming to the Yard with us, Mr Bindel? It would be useful if we could talk about the sewers,' Rowlands said.

'No problem. I'll get my van.'

◊ NINETEEN

It was almost an hour later when George Bindel was shown into the incident room at New Scotland Yard. In the low evening sunlight, Cassie could see that he was in late middle age.

'Mr Bindel, do you have a map of the old sewers?' the serjeant asked.

'It's George,' he said. 'I thought a map might be useful, so I brought some along.' He tipped the contents of a plastic bag out on to a desk. 'These are old maps I've collected over the years.'

'Do you work for Thames Water?' Cassie asked.

'I'm retired but they offer me freelance work when they need someone who knows the sewerage system. I've an interest in the history. Here, this is probably the best one, it shows the modern and the Victorian sewers as well as the earlier ones.'

A constable took the map and stuck it to a whiteboard. Everyone clustered around it.

'Here's where we were today and there's the big interconnecting sewer under Oxford Street,' George pointed to a heavy line running from east to west. 'This used to be the Great Conduit, installed back in the 1200s.'

'What's that?' Cassie pointed to a line intersecting the conduit near Bond Street and running southwards.

'That's the old Tyburn. It's one of London's 'lost' rivers. Water from the Tyburn would originally have fed those Roman baths we've been walking around in. Years later the Great Conduit was supposed to deliver it to the City. Look, see the way Marylebone Lane bends, though all the other streets north of Oxford Street are in a grid pattern?' He traced a line on the map. 'That's because the lane follows the course of the Tyburn. There are several lost rivers under London, the Westbourne, the Fleet, the Wandle –'

'So.... the River Tyburn,' Cassie interjected before the history lesson could begin in earnest. With her finger she followed the line of the river to the south on the map. It ran beneath Mayfair, across Green Park to Buckingham Palace.

'Yes, well, it's essentially a sewer today. It was incorporated into Bazalgette's system in Victorian times,' George went on. 'After Buckingham Palace it splits in two. The southern arm reaches the Thames west of Vauxhall Bridge. The outlet's marked here.'

He pointed to a symbol on the map.

'And the northern arm?' Cassie asked.

'Goes into St James's Park, where its water was once used to feed the lakes. It follows the line of Tothill Street towards Westminster, then it splits again. One spur goes north under the government buildings in Whitehall. South of Downing Street it turns towards the Thames and exits at what used to be called Whitehall Stairs, yonder.'

He gestured towards the river out of the window.

'The other spur goes south down Great College Street and exits to the Thames on Mill Bank. The Abbey monks used it to drive a mill wheel back in the day; you can see it marked on really old documents when the river was above ground. The Tyburn surrounds what used to be known as Thorney Island – not the one in Chichester Harbour but our very own, original island on the edge of the Thames.'

Cassie followed the line on the map again.

Centuries ago the delta of the River Tyburn entered the Thames and the river's arms created Thorney Island. Thorney Island was now called Westminster, the centre of government in the United Kingdom. The Crown, the Supreme Court, Downing Street, Parliament itself, Scotland Yard and even the MI5 building on Mill Bank all lay in Westminster.

And the Tyburn...?

The hidden river was a dark mirror, running beneath the streets and avenues linking all the institutions of government.

The inspector's voice broke into her reverie.

'Is this river network usable by people walking or with a boat?'

'Bits of it are,' George replied. 'More when it's dry. The rain still floods the old river courses and water backs up from the Thames when the tidal river's very high. The sewers are dangerous and some of them are only three feet high. It's not advisable to travel them, unless you know what you're doing. '

So it's possible.

Everyone looked at the map.

'Hmm. Thank you, George. You've certainly given us something to think about,' the inspector said. 'Can you give your details to Serjeant Patel please. I think we might need your expertise again.'

◊ TWENTY

The French girl couldn't have told them anything of importance and she would be dealt with before she could tell them more.

They might find the Roman baths. Let them, the site was clean. That one of the men had been an American, well, London was full of Americans. What's done couldn't be undone. The future could still be determined. That was what he must concentrate on.

Yet it galled.

More than that, the police were too close for comfort.

Rowlands. He would have to deal with that annoying inspector.

Outside the window the trees quivered in the breeze. He took a sip of the finest *amontillado* imported direct from Jerez. Turning his back on the view he contemplated his study, the leather-bound volumes, the oak desk and antique militaria. Behind the panelling, state of the art technology provided access to information, information which gave him power and control.

Under normal circumstances the entertainments would cease, before starting again later. That had sufficed to throw any investigation off the scent in the past. At this precise time, however, London was especially full of wealthy individuals and corporate investors, or their representatives, so the events were particularly useful. He was reluctant to abandon them. It was best to strike while the iron was hot.

It was time to make life more difficult for the forces of the law, the plodding inspector and the beguiling Cassandra. To hamstring them. To see what they were made of, what *she* was made of.

The French girl's death might serve a dual purpose. The police hadn't released details of the other two recent killings, yet this was bound to happen soon. Why not pre-empt them and frame the narrative for the public, putting more pressure on the police? It was a calculated risk. They might devote more resources to the case but they would also be more likely to make mistakes.

What had he overheard Cassandra say when he'd seen her on Whitehall that morning? She asked if the girl had been found at a plague pit *like the others*.

There was already a growing panic about the possible return of the Black Death, an entirely spurious idea and contrary to all the science. Yet in the era of fake news, reason was abandoned. The public would believe what they wanted to believe, especially given encouragement in a certain direction. He would set people to work online and the story would be picked up by the TV and print media. A plague panic was good for business too - particularly if you had money in pharmaceuticals.

Add in a serial killer narrative, a modern Ripper who killed his victims on sites where plague-ridden corpses lay, and the story would run and run. It was suitably *grand guignol* for the TV and clickbait for the online news outlets and the conspiracy theorists, who were already having a field day. If the establishment wasn't telling them about the murders, what else wasn't it telling them about? Yes, that would do very well.

It was time to unleash his attack dogs. At least two editors of national newspapers would do his bidding. There were others in the media who owed favours and yet more would be grateful for the tip-off. They would be primed, waiting to pounce.

The French girl's body would have to be found in a more public place, not somewhere that could be closed off. Then one of the villains of the piece would be the police, who had kept the facts of the other murders from the public and failed to protect their latest witness.

Let DI Rowlands deal with the media pressure and the inevitable demands from his superiors.

And the lady? Why not set a hare running to bring her out of the shadows and see how she dealt with being in the limelight? It would confirm whether or not she was really worthy of his attention.

Something else too. To let her know that she was in his sights and to see how she reacted. And possibly provide him with some useful information.

He took another sip of sherry and picked up the phone.

◊ TWENTY ONE

Once George Bindel left the members of the team in the incident room drew up chairs to sit in a semicircle around the whiteboards.

'To summarise,' Rowlands began. 'We have two recent murders, possibly three, taking into account the Danish boy found in the river, and two rape cases. There are similarities between them which could mean a serial killer, or a group of serial killers who come together to commit multiple crimes. There are also significant differences between them.'

'The two most recent murder victims, Tadeusz and José, were killed in the same way, almost certainly by the same person. In the cases of rape, of Tadeusz and Silana, we are awaiting results regarding DNA. There are no known links between any of them or with the Dane who was found in the Thames. But whoever did this was careful and very well organised.'

Rowlands eyes flicked around the team.

'First, Tadeusz; last seen by a neighbour in Croydon on Saturday afternoon. This is the location of the chamber where he was found.' He placed a red marker on George's map. 'It's close to a deep basement where a rave took place on Saturday night.' Another marker. 'Forensics have found nothing at these locations.'

'Did anyone see him leave the rave?' Cassie asked.

'Unknown. We've got someone talking to the bouncers?'

'Yeah, but don't hold your breath,' said the serjeant.

'We'll issue an appeal for witnesses when we go public,' Rowlands continued. 'But I doubt how much verifiable information it will bring in. We don't know why he left the rave but we can be reasonably sure that his abusers got into the chamber through the entrance next to a pub in nearby Woodstock Street. We can't be certain how they persuaded him to join them, maybe the promise of drugs.'

'Forensics are on it and we're making enquiries about anyone seen going in or out at Woodstock Street,' the serjeant added. 'Though, so far, no one has seen anything and there are no CCTV cameras which cover the entrance. There were none at the North Audley Street site either.'

'Something of a coincidence, in one of the most surveilled cities in the world,' Cassie noted, her tone arid. 'But these are busy parts of town anyway. Wouldn't someone have noticed a group of people?'

'During office hours or the evening, yes, but in the early hours these streets are empty,' DS Patel countered. 'They aren't residential areas.'

'Final point we should make about Tadeusz,' Rowlands added. 'He was young, fit and muscular, an amateur fighter. Since it seems that he was lured into the underground chamber, I would suggest that at least one of our rapists has a particular sexual interest in that kind of physique, and given how bruised he was and the fact that he was chained to the wall, that interest was also a violent one. That's a very specific requirement.'

There was silence around the room. Rowlands continued.

'So, José, victim two.' The inspector pinned another marker near the bottom of George's map. 'Last seen on the 148 night bus and found at the disused Underground depot, on his way home from work. He went there willingly, he was neither restrained nor raped. So, this is very different to the circumstances of Tadeusz' death.'

'And his body wasn't hidden either,' the serjeant said.

'It was hidden in as much as it was left in what looked like a disused train yard,' Cassie said. 'His killer might have thought it was hidden.'

The serjeant frowned and looked about to respond but Rowlands continued. 'We suspect that José stole items from the Palace of Westminster. We know he needed money, but, aside from the one access pass we know about, any other items have disappeared.'

'We've received a list of missing items from the Palace of Westminster.' The serjeant hesitated. 'It's largely what you would expect but also includes ten access passes, so nine are still missing. With the obvious exception of Cassie's, the list isn't specific about who owned any of the missing items.'

'What?' Rowlands glowered at her. 'Didn't you make yourself clear?' When she didn't reply he turned his glare on Cassie. 'What's going on?'

Oh dear.

Maybe an overzealous junior administrator was withholding information, or was it at the behest of the Speaker? She hoped it wasn't the latter, otherwise it would complicate matters. It would certainly impact on her report to the Deputy Prime Minister.

'I don't know, Andrew,' Cassie replied. 'It could be a mistake by a junior, or there could be politics involved. I'll try and find out.'

'Do that,' he snapped. 'In the meantime, Daljit, go back to the Palace and ask them for the full information and, in addition, get a list of all the attendees at Monday night's reception on the Terrace. I want to know who was there. Please handle this carefully but make plain the difficulty of solving a murder case if evidence is withheld. I will take this to the Commissioner if necessary.'

The serjeant nodded, saying nothing.

'The passes will be useless now anyway,' Cassie said. 'They'll have been removed from the system as soon as they were reported lost or stolen. Anyone trying to use a cancelled pass is identified immediately.'

'So why were they stolen?' an officer asked. 'Unless they were used straight away?'

'The security system will show if they were,' Cassie said.

'Can you take that?'

She agreed.

'Assuming José stole them, did he know that they would be useless?' the serjeant asked.

'If he'd been working at the Palace for a while, I think so,' Cassie said. 'But if he was selling them on, maybe his potential purchaser didn't know.'

'Unfortunately, this brings a further complication; potential terrorist involvement,' Rowlands said.

So the security services will be muscling into the investigation.

A meeting with them would be unavoidable. Something she could do without. Cassie consciously unclenched her jaw.

'Did you inform MI5?' she asked.

'Of course.' He gave her that blankly professional, arms-length stare.

The rivalry between the Metropolitan Police Force and MI5 was legendary, but Rowlands had followed the correct procedure.

'What have the stolen passes to do with the other crimes?' a uniformed officer asked, pointing at the whiteboard. 'Parliament is a long way from Bond Street and from North Audley Street.'

'We found one of the stolen passes on José, who was killed in the same way, by the same person, who killed Tadeusz,' the inspector said. 'That's the link.'

'How did you find my pass? Where was it?' Cassie asked.

'It wasn't immediately obvious, we found it in an inside pocket in Jose's jacket,' Rowlands replied.

'So the killer may not have known it was there?'

'We only found it because we examined his clothing minutely, as we always do with murder victims. It was very carefully hidden.' He paused, frowning. 'But why would José keep one pass, if he had sold the others?'

'Insurance? Extortion?'

'Against what, or from whom? Let's stick to the facts. On to victim three, at North Audley Street.'

People shuffled in their seats as the inspector picked up another marker.

'Silana Tabriki was working on the Eurostar from Paris yesterday. She was abducted and taken to the Roman baths where the rapes took place last night. She escaped and is our best chance of tracking down the criminals. She described the man who abducted her.' He flicked open his notebook. 'Between forty and fifty, not tall, but hard-bodied and strong, with short hair, like a soldier.'

'Could apply to a lot of people,' said the serjeant.

'Silana also described the rapists,' Rowlands went on. 'One is a middle-aged American and the other is a lord, or someone called Lord. He is tall and straight-backed. We're still awaiting samples for DNA testing, as the hospital lab is short staffed at the moment.'

All contemplated the whiteboard in silence.

'Tomorrow we'll speak with her again, find out if she knows the other victims,' Rowlands said. 'A point to note is that they had a costume for her to wear – she's physically tiny. To have deliberately chosen someone with a childlike physique implies, again, that they have specific sexual requirements.'

'Rape to order?' the serjeant asked.

'I fear so.'

'More than that, in my view,' Cassie said. 'Not just rape. The victims are terrorised too: held underground in frightening places, places which are dressed or prepared beforehand – there were candles at the plague pit site and flaming torches and a costume at the Roman baths.'

'So the rapists get off on not just the rape, but also the terror they inspire and then the murder,' said DS Patel.

'Exactly.' Cassie paused. 'The staged nature of these crimes suggests to me that the abusers want to enjoy the power they have over their victims. We know from scientific research that the wielding of power generates testosterone and increases levels of dopamine, the brain's chemical reward system. Power acts like a drug and, as with any drug, the individual needs more of it as time goes on to get the same effect. The power of life and death is the ultimate and I think that's what they are after.'

'We know there is organisation behind these crimes,' Rowlands continued. 'This is no lone serial killer. It's possible that this is a group of psychopaths. Some studies have up to twenty percent of serial killers as part of a team.'

'So how are the victims found? Are they linked in any way?' the serjeant asked.

'We'll ask Silana about this tomorrow,' Rowlands replied.

'What about locations? Is there a link there? North Audley Street isn't an old plague pit?' A uniformed constable asked.

'No,' Rowlands replied.

'So maybe plague pits aren't the link,' the serjeant said. 'Or we're missing something. And the depot is south of the river, which is on a separate sewage system. So the crime scenes aren't linked underground by sewers or rivers.'

So much for the Tyburn then.

Frowning, Rowlands stared at the map on the whiteboard. 'I'm convinced that the locations tell us something. They like to operate underground and there are plenty of places in a city like London for them to do so - sewers, rivers, conduits, plague pits.'

'And Second World War shelters, even here,' added Cassie, pointing to her feet. 'Churchill's bunkers. But really, we're speculating. Without more evidence we'll go round in circles.'

'To state the obvious...' the serjeant's tone was dry.

'We have to follow up on what we have and hope that we can turn up something new,' Rowlands said, quickly. 'Otherwise there are likely to be more killings. The shoeprint from the Roman baths might give us a lead. And, crucially, we will speak with Silana again tomorrow.'

He threw the marker pen back on to the table. There was nothing else to be done.

It was already Wednesday night and Parliament dissolved on the following Tuesday. The clock on the wall was silent but Cassie knew that, for her, time was running out.

◊ TWENTY TWO

Cassie could hear Spiggott's mewling before she turned her key in the lock.

'Hello, lovely.' She picked up the cat, fondling her silky ears while turning off the alarm. 'Waiting for your dinner?'

She switched on the lights, tossed her keys into the dish on the hall table and walked through into the kitchen. 'Here you go,' she said as she opened a tin of cat food and scooped it into one dish of Spiggott's double bowl.

Cassie checked her phone. There were messages from Duncan inviting her to the launch of the Thames Estates Programme the following evening. He had been assigned to join the Programme but could not attend, so she was to attend in his place.

She shrugged off her clothes and walked into the shower.

Washing off filth of another kind tonight.

She towelled her hair dry and pulled on some old jeans and a grey T-shirt, while Spiggott wound about her legs, purring and rubbing against her as she sat.

'My, you are affectionate today,' Cassie said as she picked up the cat. Spiggott immediately began to knead her T-shirt. 'Anyone would think I'd been away for days.'

She had papers to read. Siobhan had sent her the fruits of further research into plague pits and the draft minutes of that morning's meeting and she had received a file from the inspector on the previous murders. She would print out everything to read over a late supper.

She also needed to get her thoughts in order about the case, to decide what to say to Charles Morecombe, the Deputy Prime Minister. She didn't have to report yet but time was moving on. Better to deal with Morecombe direct; Sir Terence would put his own gloss on things, which might have little to do with the facts. She knew all too well what might happen if information wasn't delivered in person.

She had to gain Morecombe's confidence, especially if she was to persuade him to support her return to the world of intelligence and investigation.

Interesting that Andrew's still curious about my past.

Andrew Rowlands was a professional but he had the investigator's itch to know and, if he didn't know, to find out. She understood that. She had it herself. It was one of the reasons why she was enjoying this commission. She was enjoying Andrew's company too, she admitted. She found him attractive and he had been thoughtful and kind at the hospital. His physique – the height, the broad shoulders, the masculinity – was never used to intimidate, at least not to intimidate those who worked with him. He would be formidable, she suspected, in any physical confrontation.

She pulled back her hair and contemplated herself in the mirror; a professional woman, nothing special to look at, but pleasant enough, with a high forehead and a pointed chin. Her skin was OK and she still had a good figure and a certain amount of style.

Stop it.

She was judging herself as a woman because she had been thinking about Andrew Rowlands as a man. Romantic or sexual involvement with a fellow worker was professional suicide. Anyway, he probably already had someone, even if he didn't wear a ring.

Never get involved with a colleague.

'Off you go, Spig,' she said as she stood, reaching for her mobile. Walking along the flat's corridor to the kitchen, she ducked into the little room that served as her study and switched on the lights and the printer. With a few deft taps on her phone she sent the files and the printer began to whirr.

Spiggott wound around her ankles, still demanding attention.

'What's up with you, lovely?' She scooped the cat up against her chest.

The printer chunked.

'Ow!'

Spiggott had dug her claws into Cassie's shoulder.

Why so agitated and nervous?

'Hush, it's alright, it's alright.' Cassie calmed the cat, stroking her repeatedly. Spiggott subsided into a rolling purr as little flowers of red appeared on the grey cotton.

With one eye on the printer she casually checked the security app on her phone, just in case. She scrolled through the security checks and... froze. According to the log, the alarm had been turned off at eight o'clock that evening and reactivated ten minutes later. Half an hour ago.

Someone's been here. Inside the flat.

Cassie studied the room. Everything was in its place. Putting the cat down on the floor, she walked into the kitchen, checking the locks on the windows and the door into the garden. Her temperature plummeted, the passionless frigidity and logic which sustained her under pressure kicking in. Becoming glacial when threatened had served her well in the past.

The door to the spare bedroom was closed. She hesitated. Was the intruder still here? Could someone be behind it? Unlikely, but why risk it?

Because I need to know.

She opened the door.

All looked untouched. The window was locked. She retreated through the kitchen and checked that the bedroom doors to the garden were locked and bolted. In the jewellery box on the dressing table her one or two good pieces of jewellery were still there. If someone had been inside then they'd left everything exactly as they had found it.

Could it be a problem with the alarm system? No, that wouldn't explain Spiggott's nervousness.

She re-entered the study. That window was closed and locked too. Her eyes ranged over the reading lamp to the broadband router, the telephone and the closed laptop. The technology would have to be interrogated, in case of infiltration and the flat checked for covert surveillance devices.

The printer's whirr ceased and she drew the papers from the tray and took them into the living room, Spiggott weaving around her ankles.

The front windows were locked and the road outside was dark and quiet. She drew the curtains closed and switched on the large Chinese lamp, then stood at the centre of the room, slowly turning to scrutinise everything. It was all as it had been, except... on the mantelpiece, where she placed her cards and invitations, there was an addition. A bright red 'Sorry You Were Out' card, the sort the Royal Mail pushed through the letter box if they had been unable to deliver something, couldn't be missed. The hairs on her arms lifted.

She grabbed for the card. There was nothing written on it. There had been no trace left except the one they wanted her to find. She hurried to the front door to pull the chain across and draw the bolt.

Someone has been here and they want me to know it.

On the floor at the side of the hall lay a tell-tale piece of plastic, the cover on the topmost sensor attached to the door frame. She'd missed this when she came in. Somehow it had been removed from the sensor, preventing an alarm from sounding until the door had been opened and the alarm switched off. It was a professional job.

She had to tell Andrew.

But first she needed to speak with the security firm and get one of their technicians around immediately to ensure that the alarm signal could not be interrupted or deactivated again, by anyone but herself.

THURSDAY

◊ TWENTY THREE

The ringing was insistent.

Cassie groaned. It had been very late when she had finally got to bed last night.

Once she'd telephoned Andrew Rowlands, things had started to happen. He was the first to arrive and had sat, questioning her, in a police car while forensics did their work. Was she sure there wasn't anything missing? What did her alarm record show?

The job was professional and, almost certainly, connected to the case. She insisted that they sweep the flat for listening devices but none were found.

It was frightening. It was meant to be.

When they returned to her flat the others had gone, except for Serjeant Patel, who had made a friend of Spiggott. The alarm company technician, deployed after she had exchanged heated words with one of the managers, had been there for over an hour installing new sensors. It had been past eleven when they all left, a PC remaining, at Rowlands' insistence, in a patrol car out front.

The phone was still ringing.

Silver-grey light filtered through a gap in the curtains. It must be very early, the sun wasn't up yet. She dragged herself out of bed and reached for her mobile. It was Andrew.

'Yes.'

'Switch on your television.'

'It's not even six o'clock.'

'BBC News 24.'

She pulled her robe around her shoulders, padded through to the living room and picked up the remote.

A reporter was doing a piece to camera in a leafy square.

'The body was discovered in Golden Square during the early hours of this morning. Eyewitnesses say that the young woman's throat had been cut. This is the third such killing in as many days, with other bodies discovered near Bond Street and south of the river at London Road transport depot.'

The screen showed a map of central London, the locations ringed, then returned to the reporter.

'Are these murders the work of a serial killer? Sources confirm that there are strong similarities between them. If there is a serial killer in central London, why hasn't the public been informed? And what are the police doing to catch the criminal? These are questions for the Metropolitan Police to answer. Now we go over to St Thomas's hospital for more on the plague panic and a statement from the Chief Medical Officer for England and the UK.'

Cassie pressed the mute button.

'Who?' she asked.

'Silana.'

Damn! Damn, damn, damn.

Cassie felt tears forming at the back of her eyes. Poor Silana. To be tracked down and killed, just when she'd believed herself to be safe.

'How did they get to her? She was under guard.'

'I don't yet know,' Rowlands' voice sounded weary. 'We'll need to find out. I've announced a press conference at the Yard at midday. There's a media feeding frenzy. The body was found at around four this morning, so it won't have made most of the morning editions. But the Standard will have it, and later editions of other papers. It's all over the internet. The location couldn't be worse, given the number of media companies based here.'

He must be in Golden Square. She could hear sirens in the background.

'I've sent a car for you.'

'Uh, OK, I'll have to get ready,' Cassie said, dragging fingers through her hair. 'And I'll have to go into the office. There'll be questions for me to answer.'

'Come here first. Don't worry, Daljit's the driver. 'Bye.'

'I – oh...'

He had rung off.

Cassie released Spiggott from the kitchen and fed her, then washed and dressed. She heard a car horn toot outside the flat. Opening her living room curtains, Cassie saw a silver-grey Corsa parked opposite, Daljit Patel behind the wheel. She waved.

She still hadn't read the documents from last night: the inspector's file on the previous murders, the draft minutes and Siobhan's research on plague pits. She would have to take them with her.

Was Golden Square another plague pit site?

She flicked through her papers until she found Siobhan's list and map; it had more detail than the one she had shared on Tuesday. Golden Square was on it. It too had been a plague pit.

A lone serial killer, as the TV reporter had claimed and the print media would doubtless pick up on, was Andrew's first thought, but she knew that it wasn't what he believed now. It didn't fit. These crimes were too organised, too many people were involved.

Yet there were obvious links too. Three recent deaths, the method of killing the same, all found in locations where the diseased dead of long ago had been buried in mass graves, shunned places of putrefaction and corruption. But what was that supposed to signify?

Thus far, she had trusted Andrew's analysis and, despite the press reports, this most recent tragedy had confirmed her view. There were significant differences between what had happened to Tadeuz and José. What had happened to Silana was different again. The theory of a single serial killer was too convenient. It was much more likely to be a group.

That wouldn't stop the media running with it.

'Come on, lovely,' she called to Spiggott. 'I'll give you some biscuits before I go.'

In the kitchen, she filled one dish of the cat's bowl with kibble, put plenty of soft food in the other side and refilled the water bowl.

The papers she put into her satchel and, stooping to fondle Spiggott's ears one more time, she set the alarm by the front door. This time, the alarm company had assured her, no one would be able to break-in without the sensor connections being tripped. She closed and locked the door.

'What time were you dragged from your bed?' She asked as she slipped into the passenger seat of the Corsa.

'About five,' the DS replied as she pulled away from the kerb. 'All hell's broken loose at the Yard.'

'I'm not surprised.'

'The boss is under a lot of pressure. He needs all the help he can get.'

'I know. You'll get no argument from me about that.'

'Yeah, but you've got your own fish to fry.'

What does she mean by that?

'Daljit, it was my flat which got broken into, remember?' Cassie responded. 'Besides, I only want to help as much as I can.'

The DS gave her a speculative look, pursing her lips, but she said nothing more.

The dual carriageway at the top of the road was busy and the pavements became crowded as they neared Clapham Common Station. Streams of people were disappearing into the maw of the station beneath the glass cupola, going down, as they did every day, to the hidden transport network beneath the streets. Stationary at the traffic lights, Cassie noticed the rotunda above the entrance to one of the deep shelters built during the Second World War as havens from air raids. London was riddled with tunnels, shafts and passageways beneath the earth.

The traffic lights changed and they headed off into the centre.

◊ TWENTY FOUR

Golden Square was besieged. Crowds of media people, with a few tourists and commuters mixed in, spilled into the road. Cassie saw three TV crews filming. The car inched forward along Air Street, the serjeant tooting the horn to make people move out of the way.

'Surely it isn't usually like this at a murder scene?' Cassie asked.

'It's never like this,' the serjeant replied. 'Someone's been stirring the pot.'

A uniformed constable came forward to direct them away from the square. When DS Patel waved her warrant card he began trying to clear a way for them through the crowd, but this only created more interest in the occupants of the car. Cassie faced front, ignoring the shouts of photographers. They parked on the square's south side.

Golden Square was a place Cassie had walked through many times on her way to somewhere else. It was leafy and pleasant, lined with benches which were always full at lunchtimes. A stone statue stood at its centre surrounded by small bushes. Now a large tent was set up to the right of the statue.

Inside it, Rowlands was speaking with Bill Pottinger, while at the scene of the crime, officers were still at work. There was no sign of the body.

'The victim wasn't killed here,' the pathologist was saying. 'Too little blood. I'd guess she was placed here so as to be found.'

'My thoughts exactly,' Rowlands said. 'Got a time of death?'

'Best guess, sometime between twelve and three.'

Dr Pottinger nodded a greeting to Cassie as he passed her, making his way out of the tent.

'Placed where?' Cassie asked.

'Lying at the foot of the bronze,' Rowlands indicated a metal sculpture.

'So why here?' Cassie felt slightly nauseous and was glad that she hadn't eaten breakfast. 'And how the hell did they get to her, Andrew?'

'I don't know.'

'When we saw her yesterday she was traumatised and terrified. Was she frightened into leaving? Or was she taken?'

'I don't know! There appears to have been some sort of incident at St Mary's late yesterday,' he said and she realised she sounded accusatory. 'We'll go over there later.'

She took a deep breath. 'So is there anything else to learn here?'

'Time of death sometime in the early hours, killed elsewhere then brought here for half the press corps to find.' Andrew's mouth was a thin line.

'But how come there's so much media attention? Daljit says this is unusual.'

'Somehow they've got wind of the other two killings, and they think we're hiding something.'

'Have they made the plague pit link yet? You know that –'

'Golden Square was a plague pit. I don't know if that link has been made. I hope not. There's already talk of a serial killer.'

'The more this case progresses, the more that doesn't fit.'

She'd read his report on the earlier murders while travelling in. The parallels between the earlier crimes and Tadeusz' murder, as well as what Silana had described, were striking. The degree of organisation required suggested a highly efficient operation.

'I know!'

'Anyway, I must report to my bosses, they're probably already trying to get hold of me.'

I'll need to think about what to tell them.

'I'll be back for the press conference,' she said, eventually. 'Is it at New–'

'New Scotland Yard. In the largest of the briefing rooms I'd say.'

His lips were pressed closed, tension in his jawline. He was angry, she realised. Angry at himself for letting this happen, probably angry that he'd spent yesterday evening looking after her instead of protecting someone far more vulnerable.

'OK, I'll see you later.'

There was nothing she could do here but annoy him further. He barely acknowledged her departing wave.

Cassie ducked beneath the tent flap and started northward. She wanted to walk, so, with head down and a closed expression, she braved the crowd at the police barrier. No one would notice her. Caffeine was what she needed and somewhere to gather her thoughts and check her emails on the way back to Whitehall. There was a little place she knew in Ham Yard that would do very well.

'*Ciao*, Signora Cassie.' The round-faced, black-haired matriarch behind the counter greeted her.

'*Ciao*, Signora Fattori. The usual please.'

Cassie sat in a little booth and took out her phone. She smiled gratefully as the signora placed an aromatic black coffee in front of her, with a small Madeleine in its transparent packet beside it.

She'd received a flurry of new emails and messages. The earliest was from Duncan at seven thirty. He'd seen that morning's discovery on the news and immediately understood it was linked to the case she was working on. He asked if she was alright.

Quickly she dashed off an email to the Scot, then tweaked it and sent it to Siobhan, reassuring her little work family that she was fine, despite the latest gruesome discovery. There was no one else to tell. She sipped the thick coffee, its caffeine boosting her into greater wakefulness. Her phone pinged. It was Duncan responding. She was to go to the Permanent Secretary's office on Whitehall to meet him and Sir Terence at nine o'clock.

Cassie tossed back the rest of the coffee and slipped the Madeleine into her bag. She fished out some coins and left them on the counter, shouting '*Addio*' to the signora, who had disappeared into the kitchen to make a breakfast. Hefting her satchel on to her shoulder she opened the café door.

In the narrow street outside, people strode past going to their work. For a moment Cassie stood, watching them in the sunshine. How pleasant, she thought, to be free of the knowledge of rape, terror and murder; to not know what she knew; to be concentrating on getting to work on time or thinking about that evening's date.

That life wasn't for her. Those commuters were blissfully ignorant of so much: the extent to which they were surveilled, the lengths to which the state would go to keep them safe, the things done in their name. No. She needed to know, to be on the inside. Only by knowing could she begin to have some power and control.

And that was only possible if she got her job back, or something like it. She would do it, she would succeed. No one said it would be easy or safe. But still... a thought chilled her to the bone. Could Silana's killer have been the same person who had broken into her flat yesterday and left a calling card?

It could have been me.

A shiver went down her spine.

All the more reason to get back on the inside.

Cassie straightened her shoulders, tilted her face to the sun and stepped out into the flow.

◊ TWENTY FIVE

At the gateway to the Old Admiralty building Cassie presented her pass to security. The Deputy Prime Minister had offices there but it was also a Whitehall base for Sir Terence, the Permanent Secretary. Sir Terence's rooms were at the rear on the third floor, looking out on to Horse Guards Parade and to the greenery of St James's Park beyond. It was almost nine when she arrived at his office.

All the Admiralty buildings had been refurbished and Sir Terence's office was no exception. Ornate plaster cornicing sat above the silk-lined walls and a huge Adam-style fireplace dominated the room. An elaborate baroque clock hung above it, ticking loudly. Sunshine shone through the windows opening on to the parade ground.

Both men rose as she entered, Duncan striding forward to grasp her hands.

'Cassie, I was concerned when I heard the news this morning. It's very distressing.'

'I'm fine, Duncan, really. Thank you.'

Just as well that he doesn't know about the break-in. He'd insist I come off the case.

'Cassandra,' Sir Terence greeted her. He indicated the boxy modern sofas. 'Please sit. So, where are you in terms of your report?'

'There are a lot of unanswered questions,' she answered. 'But as yet, I have found nothing to suggest that there's any reputational damage to the Home Secretary or his department. If there is, it's likely to be peripheral only.'

'Hurst's got his hands full with plague panic at the moment, causing all sorts of public order problems,' the Permanent Secretary said. 'There will be a COBRA meeting on it shortly. Number 10 needs to get its communications strategy in order. Things seem to be escalating. What about the death of the Spaniard who worked in the Palace of Westminster?'

'He had no criminal record yet it seems he stole a number of items, including access passes. Why, we don't yet know. The passes would have been removed from the access system as soon as they were reported missing.'

'Any terrorist links?'

'None that we know of, but the security services have been alerted and a meeting is arranged,' Cassie continued. 'I doubt very much that there are terrorist implications. Nonetheless, you asked me to find out whether or not the Spaniard's working at Westminster might be linked to his death and I think that it is. I cannot yet say how but we're pursuing several leads.'

'Hmm... but go on, you've more to tell us?'

'The police investigation is likely to be criticised. The first two murders were not immediately made public and the press are now claiming that the Met has been deliberately keeping people in the dark about a potential serial killer in central London.'

'Pff,' the Permanent Secretary was disdainful. Duncan winced.

'There were good policing reasons not to go public for forty-eight hours,' Cassie added. 'Inspector Rowlands will defend the decision. He has called a press conference for midday. It may also be that the media are being manipulated by someone involved with the case, there's more interest than usual and more facts are known than have been released.'

'And –?' Sir Terence was relentless. 'What else?'

'Silana Tabriki, the woman whose body was found this morning, was important to the case. She was a key witness.'

'Wasn't she given police protection?'

'Yes. She was a patient at St Mary's, with an armed police guard. I saw them, Sir Terence, when we went to interview her yesterday.'

'So how did she end up dead?'

'I don't know,' Cassie said. 'Neither does Inspector Rowlands. We'll try to find out after the press conference.'

'Incompetence rather than conspiracy? Again?'

Don't speculate without evidence.

'I can't say.'

Sir Terence raised an eyebrow.

'Who do you think is behind this, Cassie?' Duncan asked.

'Inspector Rowlands has a theory that these are organised events. There were earlier killings, which he believes are linked to these cases and, having read the files, I agree. Before she was killed, Silana told us how she had been abducted and raped. We think she was chosen specifically to meet someone's sexual requirements, a task which must have taken a fair degree of organisation. Physically, she was very childlike. Her abusers seem to be wealthy and high ranking.' She took a breath. 'One of them could be a lord.'

'From the House of Lords?' Sir Terence gave her a sharp look.

'Unknown. Silana's story echoes what we know about the death of the young Pole.'

'Is it paedophilia?'

'No evidence of it as yet.'

'Blackmail then?' Sir Terence said.

'Again possible, but unlikely. Organised Crime doesn't recognise it.'

'I see.' Sir Terence drew in a deep breath, stood and walked over to the windows.

Cassie heard the tick of the clock and outside, a shouted order. The guard was changing. She risked a look at Duncan but he was watching the Permanent Secretary closely. Sir Terence turned to address her.

'If the Upper House is involved in any way this could result in a major scandal and we don't know how far it might reach,' he said. He seemed to make a decision. 'Not a chance we can take. You have until next Tuesday to find out more, though the DPM may want a report on your findings so far.'

'I'll wait for a call from his office?'

'Do that, and Cassandra...'

'Sir Terence?'

'If we could apprehend those behind this we would be able to manage matters much better.'

So now he wants me to help catch the culprits. So much for just managing the reputation of David Hurst.

'Yes, Sir Terence.'

The Permanent Secretary walked over to stand behind his desk, his signal that the meeting was over.

Cassie and Duncan rose and, nodding goodbye, left.

Neither said anything until they were descending the stairs.

'And can you see if you can find a way to stop global warming while you're at it,' Duncan's voice echoed in the stairwell. 'As a sideline to solving a major crime.'

She started to laugh and found that, once she started, she couldn't stop. The chuckle turned into a guffaw and she leant against the wall, her shoulders shaking as she laughed silently.

'Hey,' Duncan bent forward to look into her face. 'You alright? You mustn't let this get to you, you know. Maybe you should stand back from it, let the police do their job and merely observe.'

Too late. She was too deep in to withdraw now, the intruder in her flat had made that plain. She doubted that there was any going back even if she wanted to – which she didn't. The laughter eased and she took a deep, calming breath and wiped the tears from her eyes. She gave Duncan a small embarrassed smile. It was just as well that little spasm of... not laughter exactly... hadn't happened in front of anyone else.

'You going back to the office?' she asked as they emerged on to Whitehall.

'Yes. You?'

'No. I've promised to go to the press conference. Tell me, how did the procurement meeting go yesterday? And I understand you're on the Thames Estates Programme now too.'

'For my sins. The briefing papers are piled high on my desk and the bid documents – from the usual big conglomerates, like Diagio and Group 4, but also from smaller, local firms too, London & City, CSL. Can you do the launch tonight, by the way?'

So CSL is bidding for Thames Estates contracts.

Distracted, Cassie nodded agreement.

'Come on, I'll buy you a coffee and tell you about it.' He waved in the direction of Carlo's cafe on the other side of Whitehall. 'It's on your way.'

◊ TWENTY SIX

The briefing room at New Scotland Yard was already full when she arrived.

She squeezed into the back of the large room. On a raised dais at its front was a long table fitted with microphones integrated into a modern sound system. Normally there was an echo, but not today. It was packed full with people.

Cassie scanned the room for familiar faces. She knew the lobby journalists from most of the media outlets and some of the business correspondents, even one or two security specialists, but this crowd wasn't of that sort. There was a well-known reporter from the BBC and she recognised one or two who appeared regularly on TV news, but no one else.

'Here, love,' a red-faced man, cameras about his neck, moved his equipment case so that she could sit. 'Who are you with?'

'Nobody,' she said as she took the seat offered. 'I'm a civil servant.'

The man frowned and seemed about to ask her more questions when a door at the front of the room opened and a group of people entered, led by the Metropolitan Police Deputy Commissioner, Malcolm Edgerley. He was a long-serving policeman who had climbed the career ladder until almost the very top. At the moment, he looked supremely annoyed. Andrew Rowlands and two women wearing press officer badges followed in his wake. The man sitting next to Cassie rose, as did many others and there was a cacophony of clicking and whirring as photographs were taken. Cassie stood in order to see.

The Deputy Commissioner took the centre right seat, with Rowlands seated on his right. He allowed the audience to settle and then rose.

'Good morning,' Edgerley said, pausing only a second to allow a muted response. 'This morning a body was discovered in central London. This is linked to an ongoing investigation led by Detective Inspector Andrew Rowlands who will brief you on the case. There will be time for questions at the end.'

He sat and the inspector stood. Rowlands looked professional and in control.

'Good morning. At two o'clock this morning the body of a young woman was found in Golden Square, W1. Her death is being treated as suspicious and her family is being informed. We believe that this is connected with two other killings.'

The audience shifted and murmured. This was what they were really interested in, the potential vulnerability of the police, the opportunity for righteous anger in the next day's editions.

She understood why so many of her fellow senior civil servants referred to the press as 'reptiles'. En masse and hungry, they weren't a pleasant sight. Around her some of the journalists were already growing restless, wanting to ask questions.

'The first body was discovered three days ago, on Monday, following an earthfall close to the works on the new Crossrail link. Details were not released because of the need to determine point of access, and to preserve the highly unusual crime scene until it had been fully investigated. A second body was discovered two days ago, on Tuesday, in Lambeth. The families of both victims have been informed. We believe that the cases are connected; there are similarities. Further details will be released when the investigation is concluded. Thank you. I'll take questions now.'

'Were they all killed by the same person?' a woman near the front asked.

'We believe the same people may be involved but it's too early to say conclusively.'

'Is this a serial killer, Inspector?' she followed up.

'Is it true that all the victims were EU citizens residing in London?' another journalist asked.

'Polish, Spanish and French?' someone else added.

How can they know that?

'I am not able to confirm the nationalities of the victims at this time.'

There was little else he could do but stonewall. The journalists knew it too and questions were shouted thick and fast.

'If a serial killer is at work in central London why hasn't the public been informed?' The first journalist asked.

'As I explained–'

'Is this linked with the possible plague outbreak?'

'And if you're not telling us about the killings, what else aren't you telling us about?'

'Was the first body found in the plague pit? Did they die of the plague?'

What? Not the plague again?

At her side the photographer looked at Cassie again. He nudged the man standing next to him and said something. Both turned to look at her.

They've recognised me, maybe from the TV news. Time to go.

She moved away, slipping out into the corridor.

There she listened to the quickfire, shouted questions, sensing the angry mood.

Why had the police endangered the public by keeping them in the dark? Was this another case of Met Police incompetence or was there more to it? She heard Operation Yewtree mentioned and then the Police Complaints enquiry. She no longer needed to make the link between the current investigation and previous scandals, the press was doing it for her. They were also making a link with the plague.

That could be dangerous. Fear of the plague had a way of short-circuiting people's brains. It might make it more difficult for the police to do their job and solve the murders before there were more victims.

The meeting was coming to an end so she made her way to the corridor behind the briefing room. She heard the Deputy Commissioner's staccato delivery before she saw him and stood to one side of the corridor, trying to make herself as invisible as possible.

'Just as things were beginning to die down,' he was saying. 'We can ill-afford a rerun of the scandals of recent years. This is unacceptable.'

Oh dear.

'And this plague business has got out of hand. We've already had incidents at pharmacies and doctors surgeries, it's turning into full-scale hysteria.'

As bad as that? Already?

'You failed to protect the one witness you had, Detective Inspector. Why?'

'You know I can't answer that now.' Rowlands was barely controlling himself.

'Make sure that by the next time we speak, you can. I want a full briefing by this evening. My office, six thirty. Alone. You can leave your civil service minder elsewhere, though preferably not skulking in corridors.'

'Sir.'

The Deputy Commissioner swept on with his entourage as Rowlands stopped and looked back to where Cassie was standing.

'Were you there?' he asked as she walked forwards.

'Right at the back, in the scrum. They were out for blood. There was nothing you could do.'

'Wait 'til we see tomorrow's headlines,' he said, a rueful look on his face.

They had reached the incident room. It was empty. Cassie assumed that his colleagues were giving Andrew space after the press grilling. At least it meant they could talk unheard.

'How did they know about the nationalities of the victims?' Cassie asked. 'Very few people knew all three of them.'

'That was interesting,' Andrew agreed, with a deep sigh. 'Daljit's convinced that someone is stirring up trouble for us with the press.'

'Maybe it's whoever's behind the crimes?'

'Or a junior or a temp, someone in a clerical position, giving information to a journalist in return for a favour. You'd be surprised how often it happens. But it's nonsense we could do without, it's taking me away from the investigation and we have few enough resources as it is!'

Cassie didn't know what to think.

'Now we have to find out how Silana went missing,' he continued. 'I'll have to interview the two police constables who were supposed to be guarding her.'

'Yes,' Cassie said. She hesitated – this wasn't going to be easy. 'I'd like to accompany you when you question them.'

The inspector stood very still. Cassie avoided eye contact.

'It will be more efficient if I do this alone.' His voice was tight.

I've got to do this properly if I'm to succeed. The conduct of the police is crucial to my enquiries.

'That's as may be,' she said. She liked Andrew Rowlands, maybe more than she should. He was a good man doing a difficult job and doing it with integrity and commitment. Cassie hated herself for continuing. 'But my brief, as you know, is to satisfy myself that there is no possible scandal attached to the circumstances of this case... including the investigation.'

Rowlands glared down at her, his mouth clamped tightly shut, a twitching muscle in the side of his face his only movement.

He had offered to step back from interviewing the staff at the Palace of Westminster if she thought it better, but she could not afford to be so accommodating. She wanted to tell him that she wasn't calling his integrity into question, that in her eyes he was beyond reproach. Yet she couldn't, because, in one sense, calling his integrity into question was exactly what she was doing. Besides, any policeman felt loyalty to his organisation, to the force. If she cast suspicion on the Met she cast suspicion on him. There was no getting round that.

He forced out a reply.

'Very well. We'll go now.'

◊ TWENTY SEVEN

'Constable Goodwin, you were assigned to St Mary's Hospital to ensure the safety of the witness, Ms Silana Tabriki yesterday evening. Correct?'

The inspector sat behind a plain, modern desk with the young police constable opposite him. The room at Paddington Green Police Station was small but airy and light, windows stretching the width of one wall on the sixth floor. Outside the sun glinted off the planes processing in an orderly queue above the London skyline. Cassie sat in the corner, pen and notebook in hand, trying to look like a secretary.

The constable looked nervous and uneasy, he shot glances her way as if she might help him.

'Yes, sir.'

'Where were you standing?'

'Outside the door of the witness's room, sir.'

'And,' Rowlands consulted the file on the desk in front of him, something Cassie knew he didn't need to do. He was easing the constable into the interview, giving him questions he could answer. 'Your colleague, Constable Khan, was stationed inside the room?'

'Yes sir.' The young policeman stared straight ahead.

'When did the witness leave her room, Constable Goodwin? When did she leave the hospital, as we know she did? How could she have done so without your seeing her?'

'Don't know, sir.' The young officer swallowed, his Adam's apple bobbing up and down.

'Did you, at any time, leave your post?'

'I...'

'What?'

'I went to the nurses' station to find out what the fuss was about, sir.'

'Fuss?' Rowlands' eyebrows were raised, his voice scathing.

'There was a commotion, sir, noise, staff rushing around, patients being moved.'

'How long were you away from your post?'

'Five minutes, sir. Ten minutes max.'

'So there was no one outside the witness's room for ten minutes?'

'No sir, Constable Khan came to stand outside while I went. Be a visible presence, sir, in case anyone was nosing around.'

Clever. Constable Goodwin might survive this, after all.

'The witness was left alone?'

'Not at that time, sir, but...'

'But what, constable?'

'The commotion was because of a fire, sir, on the floor below at about seven thirty, eight o'clock. Medical staff were taking stretchers and equipment down to help get patients out. There was a bit of a panic.'

'You said the witness was not left alone at that time. When was she left alone, Constable?'

Goodwin hesitated.

'Out with it.'

The young policeman's face had turned bright red.

'One of the staff asked Constable Khan and myself to help move some valuable medical equipment...'

'And you left the witness unprotected.'

'Yes sir,' the young policeman hung his head. 'She was gone when we came back but we thought she'd been evacuated with all the others. So we went to find her but couldn't in all the chaos. She was only left alone for a moment, sir.'

'A moment was all that was needed, Constable.' Rowlands sighed. 'You know that the young woman was killed?'

'Yes, sir. It was...'

'What?'

'My fault, sir.'

'You didn't kill her, Constable Goodwin. But you failed in your duty to protect her.'

'I'm – I'm sorry, sir.'

'You may go.'

'Yes sir. Thank you sir.'

The young man rose and left. Rowlands slumped back in his chair.

'Do we get Constable Khan in next?' she asked.

'He'll corroborate Goodwin's story,' the inspector said. 'They were duped. I've no doubt that Silana was taken while they were distracted. It wouldn't have been difficult to sedate her and put her on a stretcher, then simply wheel her out, like so many others. This was well planned. The fire was a big risk. It could have turned into a major disaster, caused loss of other lives, especially with the overcrowding in A&E because of the plague scare.'

'It's ruthless. These people are willing to cover their tracks, whatever the cost,' Cassie frowned. 'Does this mean that the break-in at my flat wasn't to do with the investigation?'

'What makes you say that?'

'Well, Silana's abduction seems to have happened at about the same time as my flat was broken into. It seems unlikely that three men could have done both at the same time. Taking Silana must've required enormous amounts of reconnaissance and organisation.'

The inspector looked thoughtful.

'I can't think of a single reason why your flat would have been broken into, if not because of the case. Nothing was stolen, no damage was caused, intimidation was the sole purpose. It's unlikely that two people could have pulled off the abduction while another broke into your flat. The obvious explanation is that more than the three men Silana encountered in the Roman baths are involved,' Rowlands paused. 'In fact I think it's now clear what we are dealing with. This is an organisation, a crime ring. These people aren't amateurs. They're selling their victims for rape and murder to the highest bidder.'

They both sat in stunned silence for a moment.

'That's vile. And terrifying.'

'Yes. And they are incredibly good at what they do, that's why we've never been able to catch them. The only mistake they've made since I began tracking them is letting Silana escape.'

'They tricked the constables. You can't really blame Goodwin and Khan.'

'I can.' Rowlands stated, flatly. 'They should have stayed at their posts, regardless, and denied access to anyone who wasn't medical staff, the authorised interpreter or police. They were her guards!'

Someone would feel Andrew's wrath. She hoped the constables wouldn't find their careers destroyed.

He was speaking to her again.

'What?'

'I said, are you ready for Khan now?'

'Yes, yes, Constable Khan it is. Then I'll have to head for the launch of Thames Estates,' Cassie replied. Time was moving on. 'It could be useful to see who is, or isn't, there.'

'OK, we'll meet up afterwards at the Yard.'

'Maybe, it depends what time it finishes.' She also wanted some time to gather her thoughts about her report. 'It might go on until quite late.'

'Oh,' the inspector said, after a pause. 'Right.'

'Constable Khan?'

'Right.'

◊ TWENTY EIGHT

Cassie raised her hand to shade her eyes. The windows of the Queen Elizabeth II Conference Centre were ablaze with reflected light from the setting sun as she approached. The ziggurat of concrete and glass squatted on Broad Sanctuary opposite the soaring gothic glories of the Abbey and beside the majestic Victorian rotunda of Methodist Central Hall. The flags in front of the entrance lay listless against their flagpoles.

The Thames Estate launch was taking place on the third floor. Before she went up, she checked her phone alarm app again. The flat was secure.

An animated buzz of talk, shot through with laughter, met Cassie as the lift doors opened on to the event anteroom. It was the sound of artificial bonhomie, of commercial dealings well-lubricated by alcohol and the promise of serious money to be made.

No sign of plague panic here.

Cassie took a glass of water from a waiter's tray and wandered further into the building. A massive diagram filled one wall, showing some of the priciest real estate in Europe, integral to the functioning of government. The budget was in excess of four billion pounds and that figure would rise. Every large corporation wanted a piece of that pie.

Commercial pitches advertised the intrinsic merits of the large or expensive. Those belonging to the big audit and accountancy firms extolled a strict virtue little seen, in Cassie's experience, in the world of big business. Smartly dressed young men with sharp haircuts competed with tanned and polished young women to press glossy brochures on to conference goers.

The great and good were in attendance, checking out the possibilities of non-executive positions in which they could barter their knowledge and influence for tangible rewards. Discrete groups of elegantly suited finance types were glad-handing as they watched events unfold.

Cassie stepped up on to a slightly raised area to watch the currents and eddies of motion in the room; the distinct flows as people circulated around those who had money and power.

There were few politicians, many MPs having already left London for their constituencies. Cassie saw Charles Morecombe, the Deputy Prime Minister, a head taller than all those around him, at the centre of a vortex. She could hear Simon Joliffe's guffaw and located the Transport

Minister at the centre of another. The leonine white head of Sir Percy Dugdale, the Chair of the Parliamentary Oversight Committee, was surrounded by a small scrum and the recently appointed Programme Director held court in the corner. Senior executives from big business stood within their own whirling galaxies. Many of those who had been at Monday night's reception were here too, including all the Committee members.

Is this linked to the case, the headlong rush for the spoils of such a major public project?

She had only experienced small projects, though even they had examples of greed and avarice.

'Cassandra!'

Cassie turned at the sound of her name. A short young woman was wending her way towards Cassie. She recognised Beverley Allott, Charles Morecombe's personal assistant. They had met before.

'Hello, Bev. Looks like almost everyone's here tonight.'

'Not the PM,' Bev said. The PM liked to remain above such commercial events, which any hostile press could paint as money-grubbing and tawdry. He left such things to his Deputy. 'Home Secretary isn't here either,' Bev added, with an arch look. So she knew about the PM's imminent departure and what it might mean for David Hurst. 'Charles would like a word if you've got a moment.'

Dutifully, Cassie plunged into the crowd to follow the young PA.

'Sir Terence is with him,' Bev said, wrinkling up her nose in distaste.

'Ah, Cassandra,' Sir Terence greeted her, as she and Bev joined the small group around the DPM. 'Charles, this is the civil service investigator--'

'Yes, I'm aware,' Charles Morecombe interrupted him. 'Your name has been drawn to my attention in the past. You handled a number of sensitive GCHQ cases, handled them well.'

'Thank you, Deputy Prime Minister.'

'I trust you'll do the same with this. Use your skills to good effect now and you might even get your career back. I'm expecting results.'

I get it: failure is not an option.

'Bev will schedule a meeting for us tomorrow at Westminster. You don't need to attend Terence.' Sir Terence looked as if he was about to object. 'I'm going back to my office now,' the DPM said. 'Bev.'

'Coming.'

'I'll come too,' the flustered Sir Terence said, depositing his half full glass on a passing waiter's tray. The group exited, the crowd parting before them.

Cassie was left standing alone. It wasn't long before others joined her, looking curious: about who she was, why she was speaking with the DPM and, of course, how she might be of use to them.

'Hello, I'm Frank Cairns,' a tall, slim man with large blue eyes and hair cut close to his scalp introduced himself. Of indeterminate age, his stance was assured, athletic; he was someone who looked after himself. 'How do you know Charles? I used to work with him before I got elevated.' He grinned and pointed his finger upwards.

'To heaven?' she suggested, smiling. She recognised the former junior minister who had been given a peerage. Now he was a government whip in the Lords. 'Cassandra Fortune.' She offered him her hand.

'Oh, not heaven,' he answered as he shook it. 'Somehow I don't think I'd fit in there.' He had a mischievous lopsided grin. 'Much too boring. A bit like this event.'

Hmmm, very attractive and trying to charm, too.

'Are you involved with Thames Estates?'

'I represent the Lords on the Oversight Committee, me and William Priess. He's around here somewhere. Hey,' he beckoned to a waiter. 'Do you only have this stuff? Nothing stronger? Whisky, sherry?'

'Only wine, sir.'

'Ah well.' Cairns waved the man away as they were joined by a short man in a turban.

'Amit Kumar of Deloitte,' he said. 'Are you on the programme team?'

'No, I'm not, I'm afraid. I'm Deputy Prime Minister's Office.' She couldn't help smiling at the disappointed look on Amit Kumar's face.

'And yet you're here?' Cairns said, one eyebrow arched. 'Why is that?' He sipped his wine.

'My boss has been assigned to the programme. Duncan Macfarlane, you'll meet him.'

'Cassandra, what a pleasure to meet you again.' It was William, Lord Priess exuding old-world charm. In a well-tailored silver-grey suit he looked rather more as if he belonged to the twenty-first century than the last time Cassie had seen him. And younger. He was definitely only in his early forties. She had forgotten how pale his eyes were against his sun-weathered skin.

'You two know each other,' Cairns raised his eyebrows. 'I shouldn't be surprised. William seems to know everyone, or everyone who is anyone, especially if they're female and attractive.'

Cassie was saved from having to respond by the arrival of a dark-haired man, who looked vaguely familiar.

'Hello again' he said to the startled-looking accountant from Deloitte. 'It seems like we've all reconvened on the other side of Parliament Square.'

'Oh, yes, Monday,' Amit Kumar replied. 'Er...' The accountant hesitated.

'Lawrence Delahaye,' the man offered his hand to each of the men, then to Cassie.

'Cassandra Fortune, Deputy Prime Minister's Office.'

His handshake was firm and he surveyed the company with studied disinterest but his wide mouth carried a faint smile. A businessman, she guessed, no, a financier.

'What's your interest here?' she asked.

'I like to keep an eye on major capital projects, especially when they may involve companies in which we have holdings. I run a hedge fund.'

Frank Cairns gave a silent snort. He raised a hand in salute, dropped an overtly salacious wink to Cassie and disappeared into the crowd.

'You're not the only fund manager here,' the accountant said. 'Which is yours?'

'Barton Management. I live in Barton Street, hence the name,' he explained. 'Do you live in London, or commute?' He focused on Cassie, ignoring the accountant.

With an address like that you must be very wealthy. Now, where've I seen you before?

'South London, not quite as grand as Barton Street,' she half-smiled up at the dark eyes.

'It's so grand I sometimes don't believe I really live there.'

Cassie was amused. Priess looked unimpressed, but then, she supposed, he lived somewhere equally as expensive, which had been in his family for generations. To the manor born. Kumar had drifted away.

'So who is this mysterious *femme* who has been conspiring with

Charles Morecombe?' Sir Percy Dugdale said as he sidled up, far too close, to Cassie.

'Cassandra Fortune, DPM's office,' she said, standing back and offering her hand.

'Lovely lady.' Sir Percy held her hand between both of his own, not letting go immediately.

Tut, tut.

She twisted her wrist and extracted her hand.

'I'm so sorry, my dear,' Percy gushed, his eyes full of mischief. 'It's a social minefield these days, one can't compliment a woman. Shows I'm growing old.'

A bell sounded, indicating that the presentation was about to begin.

I'll take my leave.

The group moved towards the conference room but Delahaye showed no sign of joining them.

'I'll be on my way,' he said.

'I'm going too,' she said and turned to walk by his side.

'I don't suppose you have time for a drink?' he asked, as they entered the lift.

I ought to go home.

'Just one, maybe,' she said, tilting her head to one side.

'There's a place I know nearby,' he said, with a grin. 'It's a private club and will be quiet. If that's OK?'

'Sure.'

◊ TWENTY NINE

The bells of St Margaret's began tolling eight o'clock as Cassie accompanied Lawrence Delahaye out of the conference centre.

This is silly. I need to head home and get some quiet time to absorb what's happened over the last four days.

She sneaked a look sideways. Tall, loose-limbed and rangy, her companion cut a dashing figure. Very dark, almost black, eyes gleamed above sharp cheekbones. He looked down at her and smiled as the breeze ruffled unruly curls. She remembered where she'd seen him before – at the reception on the Terrace on Monday night, speaking with Duncan.

She returned his smile.

His interest in her, and he *was* decidedly interested, made her feel attractive and desirable. So there was a spring in her step as they walked through the narrow Georgian lanes south of St James's Park.

'Here we are,' he said, pointing to a wide black door beneath a fanlight and ushered her into a broad entrance hall hung with paintings.

'Mr Delahaye,' a doorman greeted him.

'And guest,' he replied. 'We'll be in the garden room. This way.'

Cassie noted the Turkish rugs, the shiny brass lights and door fittings, the airy stairwell. Off to the left, a hum of conversation came from a well-appointed room with a bar. All understated, it shouted money. She saw him watching her appreciate the surroundings.

They entered a large rectangular room beyond the staircase. Its elaborate cornices and grand marble fireplace reminded her of Sir Terence's office. One wall was all French windows, some of which were open to allow the air to circulate. Beyond was a terrace and shallow lawn, ending in a border of shrubs and high iron railings.

A waiter appeared at Delahaye's side as they sat on a plush sofa next to the windows.

'Champagne, I think,' the financier said. 'Unless you'd prefer something else?'

'Prefer? No, no, it's your choice.'

This is a different world.

'I enjoy the finer things in life,' he said. 'Who wouldn't if they had the money?'

She smiled. She liked fine things, though she couldn't afford them.

'I especially enjoy them because I wasn't born into wealth,' Lawrence explained, meeting her eyes with an intense gaze. 'My father was a school groundsman, my mother a teaching assistant.'

You didn't attend an ordinary school, though. You have that confidence, the hallmark of a private education, even if by grace and favour, or a bursary for the very bright.

The waiter returned with an ice bucket and stand and went off again.

'Believe me, I'm well aware of my own good fortune, though I've worked hard for it too. I will take some of the credit for my success.' He grinned. 'It's one of the reasons I support numerous charitable foundations. The wealthy should use their money for the benefit of the less fortunate: the Americans have got that right. Governments are not the sole vehicle for social engineering. When governments and charities pull together, that's when things can really change.'

A hedge fund manager with a conscience? How original.

Cassie gave a noncommittal smile.

'I was scouting for talent at the conference, looking for someone to manage my European portfolio of charities. A linguist. Do you know anyone suitable?'

'No one springs immediately to mind.'

What would it be like to work for him? Might be fun.

The waiter returned with glasses and the champagne.

'Leave that please. I'll deal with it,' Delahaye said and sat forward to open the bottle. 'By the way, I thought you were very restrained in dealing with some of those people this evening.'

The odious Sir Percy.

'It goes with the territory,' Cassie said.

'Even in the twenty-first century?'

'I fear so.'

'Hm, it shouldn't. Here.' He handed her a glass of fizzing liquid and grinned. 'To better times.'

'Better times.'

The champagne was delicious.

'So why were you at the Thames Estates launch?'

'My boss has just joined the Programme Board, I was deputising.'

'And I'm guessing that you don't particularly enjoy such events? I know I find them tedious.'

Delahaye placed his glass on the low table in front of them and sat back into the sofa, legs crossed at the ankles, one arm stretched along its back, the other along the sofa arm. He studied her, openly, appraising and admiring.

Two can play at that game.

She lifted her chin and gave him look for look. He was a fine specimen: the black hair and eyes, a wide, flat torso, slender wrists and large, long-fingered hands. His lips quivered into a half smile, his eyes glittered with amusement.

Pure desire, he had made sure she saw it.

She felt a flush rising from her chest and glanced away.

'I'm sorry,' he said, eyes cast down. His eyelashes were long and dark, many a girl would envy him them. 'I went too far. I didn't mean to make you feel uncomfortable.'

Uncomfortable!

'I'm unused to being looked at,' she said. 'In that way,' she could have added.

'I find that hard to believe. But it's not the thing to do.' He took a sip of champagne. 'I seem to be doing nothing but putting my foot in it tonight, constantly apologising.'

'Please don't, I feel very spoilt.'

'Then let me spoil you some more,' he perched on the edge of the sofa, eager as a schoolboy. 'We could have dinner. The chef is very good here. Do say yes.'

This is madness.

'Yes.'

'Right.' He stood. 'I won't be a moment. I'm sure they'll be able to accommodate us.'

As he strode off, she heard the ring of her phone and reached inside her satchel. It was Andrew Rowlands.

Damn.

'Hello, Andrew.'

'Hello. Where are you?'

'Why?' she answered, her tone dry.

'Your shindig finished has it? Had enough champagne?'

Where's that mood come from?

Of course. He'd been summoned before the Deputy Commissioner earlier that evening. It couldn't have gone well. If the last few days had been difficult for her, they must have been worse for him.

'My shindig, as you call it, wasn't a party. There wasn't champagne and actually many of the people there figure in our case.'

She kept her voice mild and hoped the 'our' might show solidarity, as well as being relatively accurate. As she had told the serjeant it was how she now thought of their enquiries, despite her original brief.

'That's timely then. I've received the full list of attendees and the list of the missing items from Monday evening's Westminster reception. Your input would be useful.'

'What? Now?'

'Yes. I'm at the Yard.'

'Andrew, can't it wait until tomorrow?'

'If Parliament is involved in this we have only a limited amount of time left to investigate before it closes on Tuesday. The chances of the criminals simply dispersing again are too great. We must use all the time we have.' The phone went dead.

Damn, damn, damn.

Lawrence was returning.

'They can fit us in,' he said.

'I'm sorry,' she brandished her phone. 'Work. I have to go.'

'Oh,' he looked crestfallen. 'Well, perhaps another time?'

'I'd like that.' She stood, gathering her bag.

'How about Saturday night?'

Saturday? Work on the case, then sit in front of the TV with Spig. Dinner sounds better.

'I think I'm free.'

'Shall we say eight o'clock. Here?'

'That would be lovely.'

'I'll reserve a table. I hesitate to do this after Percy's grabbing, but...' he took her hand and stepped closer to her, 'til Saturday.'

'Saturday,' she murmured. His proximity disconcerted her. She resisted the urge to tilt her face upwards.

'The doorman will call you a cab.' He stood back and relinquished her hand.

'Don't worry. I'll manage.'

◊ THIRTY

Her heart was hammering as she scurried down the steps on to Queen Anne's Gate. Determined not to look back she strode across the narrow road into another pool of light as she headed for New Scotland Yard.

Lawrence Delahaye, handsome, fascinating and wealthy was interested, very interested, in her.

Why?

That was a good question.

She was no expert in relationships but she trusted her analytical judgement. Delahaye was a member of that exclusive club of the internationally wealthy and he was unattached. So why was he so interested in a civil servant who had seen better days?

Power? He obviously enjoyed proximity to power, that much was clear from earlier in the evening, but she wasn't close to power these days, however it might have looked earlier. Knowledge of Whitehall? No, he could buy better. What advantage could she possibly bring him? Other than pleasure; there was definitely a frisson between them.

Maybe Lawrence Delahaye was one of those men who pursue one woman at a time, enjoying the thrill of the chase, the seduction and conquest? Then lose interest and move on. She'd seen men do this before and, in fairness, she'd seen women do it too. If it left scarred lovers, that was all part of the game – it was supposed to.

She considered the event where they'd met. Everyone seemed to be seeking advantage, from parliamentarians and civil servants looking out for lucrative posts or promotion, to companies and consultants seeking government contracts. The opportunities for corruption were huge.

Whoever had elected the slimy Sir Percy Dugdale to Chair of the Oversight Committee needed their head looking at. The academic researchers she'd quoted yesterday to Andrew and the team would have had a field day with Sir Percy. Though nothing had, to her knowledge, ever been proved, rumours of corruption were constantly circulating about him. He was a perfect example of how power, like the plague, was a contagion. Those of equally dubious ethics surrounded him.

Even those sharks among capitalists, the hedge fund managers, had been there.

Like Lawrence Delahaye.

Sexy and rich he might be, but he had probably made his millions on the back of misfortunes and disasters.

Though those misfortunes and disasters couldn't be laid at his door.

She would check out Barton Investments though she didn't hold out much hope of learning anything. It was almost certainly registered in a tax haven somewhere. As an attendee at the reception on the Terrace and at tonight's launch event, Lawrence Delahaye was, at least peripherally, involved in the case. He would feature on Andrew's lists.

She had reached the lights of Parliament Square. As she crossed towards Whitehall, a phalanx of police cars, lights flashing and sirens wailing, screeched into the square and a pair of ambulances followed them up Whitehall.

What's going on? A large accident somewhere?

Focus on the case, she told herself, sternly. Be careful. This is your one chance, remember, the one chance to get your career back, your own access to power. Something no boyfriend can replace, however attractive, however powerful. That's what you must concentrate on.

Maybe it was just as well that Andrew phoned.

Reflections of the Embankment lights were shimmering in the river as she walked along to New Scotland Yard. Glancing up she saw the incident room and Andrew's office were well lit though much of the building was dark.

He would never give up, not until he found some justice for those young people so far from home.

Concentrate on that. Try and help him as much as you can.

◊ THIRTY ONE

There were still a number of people in the incident room despite the hour. Two uniformed officers broke off their conversation as she entered and, from the looks she was given, Cassie had the distinct impression that she'd been the subject of their discussion. Rowlands was sitting at a desk in his glass fronted office, papers strewn before him.

'Cassie.' He rose when she entered. 'Look, I'm sorry for being sharp with you.'

He looked worn; the skin beneath his eyes was grey. He'd been working while she had been enjoying herself, flirting with all and sundry. She felt an unaccountable tenderness, an urge to offer physical comfort, to hold and stroke, to make things better.

'How did it go with the Deputy Commissioner?' she asked, wanting to console.

'Not well.' His expression hardened. 'I'd rather not talk about it now. Too much else to do. Here...'

He handed her the list of attendees at Monday's reception. It included the ministers, Sir Percy Dugdale and many of the same people who had been in the Conference Centre that evening, like William Priess, Frank Cairns and Lawrence Delahaye. Only some of the attendees had reported items stolen, which were marked against their names.

'I think the only odd thefts here are the passes,' he said. 'Is there anything about any of the other items which you think suspicious?'

The list of missing items included ten Palace of Westminster passes, eight of which had been taken from offices and two, including her own, from the Terrace reception. Sir Percy Dugdale was the other missing pass owner. The other items stolen were personal, such as purses and wallets.

'No,' Cassie answered. 'But if anything incriminating or embarrassing was stolen from an MP, its owner probably wouldn't report it missing anyway.'

'Incriminating?'

'Something the owner wouldn't want the whips to get hold of.'

'So, it's true. The whips get to know everything?'

'Not everything but they know a lot. Who's sleeping with whom, whose child almost got arrested for drug offences, who keeps a lover in a house in Kennington. Ordinary morality often goes out the window during the Westminster week. There are plenty of MPs who are decent, dutiful partners and parents at home in their constituencies who change character once they arrive at the Palace. It's a world unto itself, a self-contained town full of gossip and plots. The information the whips have is very useful arm-twisting ammunition when it comes to forcing a vote.'

'Blackmail,' his mouth twisted up at one corner into a grimace. 'Maybe you should speak with the whips then.'

'Actually, that's not such a bad idea, though they won't want to share sensitive information.'

She could at least speak with the Deputy Prime Minister about talking to the government whips. Perhaps she could co-opt Frank Cairns to help in the House of Lords? He would probably enjoy that.

'Should we be doing background checks on the people at the reception?'

'There's no reason to suspect the attendees,' the inspector replied. 'Why would José have stolen a pass and left the Palace, if he could have just handed over the goods then and there?'

'What if he wanted a private audience? He didn't want to be overheard so he drew them away?'

'What I've learned over the years is the simplest answer is usually the right one. If José left the Palace to meet someone, it was probably because that person wasn't at the reception. Anyway, we can't ride roughshod over people's right to privacy without a reason.'

'So why did you ask for the list in the first place?'

'Information is power,' said Rowlands with a wry smile. 'Besides, if the Palace of Westminster people think they can refuse to send over information crucial to a murder enquiry, I'm not going to make their lives easy.'

'Most of the owners of missing passes can be discounted,' Cassie said. 'The ministers and the civil servants are vetted and cleared. I suspect the only real person of interest, aside from myself, that is...' she gave the inspector an arch look, 'is Sir Percy Dugdale.'

Rowlands smiled. 'I'll get Daljit to do some digging on him then.'

'Yes. Where is Daljit by the way? Somehow I expected her to be here.'

'She would've been if I hadn't insisted she go home. She's got a family you know, two kids.'

Oh.

That was a surprise. Somehow Cassie had assumed that the serjeant was married to the job, just as she herself had been, husband or no husband.

'So what's next?' she asked.

'Security services want a meeting. Tomorrow at the Home Office, nine o'clock.'

Marsham Street. Home ground.

'It's likely to be MI5,' Cassie said. 'Do we need to involve SO15?' She hoped not. MI5 and the Met's Counter Terrorism Command Unit were permanently at loggerheads.

'I don't think so.' Rowlands shook his head. Their eyes met. That would make the meeting easier.

'Deputy Commissioner Edgerley?'

'Let's leave Malcolm Edgerley out of it too.'

Was Andrew sticking his neck out? She would do her damnedest to try to ensure that he didn't get his head chopped off.

'One more thing. I've arranged for George Bindel to give us a tour of the lost River Tyburn tomorrow,' Rowlands said. 'I don't think we should rule it out as a link. It runs close to two of our crime scenes.'

'That'll be interesting,' Cassie replied. She slung her satchel over her shoulder. 'If that's it for today, I will brave the flashing lights of Whitehall and go home. What was all the fuss about, by the way?'

'A riot outside Barts Hospital, people demanding treatment for plague symptoms and some so-called 'Plague Truthers' smashing up the vehicles.'

'But there is no plague. And smashing ambulances isn't going to help anyone, just the opposite.'

'I know, but logic has taken a holiday. Anti-vaxxers, plague truthers, centuries of scientific advance wilfully abandoned. It's getting out of hand. I'm worried that it might slow us down, distract people from the real crime. Anyway, there's a car waiting downstairs to take you home and a detective constable to see you're safely inside an empty flat.'

So that was the real reason he insisted I come into the Yard. To make sure I was safe...

'Be gentle with him, he's only doing his job.' Rowlands came to stand by her side and looked down at her, a sardonic gleam in his eyes.

'I don't need a bodyguard.'

'He isn't one but he'll see that you're safe tonight. And Cassie, be prepared tomorrow morning. The headlines will not be good ones. The press will have a field day in tomorrow's editions.'

Of course, the press conference was only the beginning. Reassure him, make him feel better.

'We have to trace whoever is behind all of this. And we will.'

'Oh yes,' the policeman sounded unconvinced as he looked out into the darkness. 'We will.'

FRIDAY

◊ THIRTY TWO

Cassie nodded to the man with the *Racing Post* who sat on the left at the back of the bus every weekday morning. She took a seat in the other corner and drew the newspapers from her satchel. That morning's TV coverage had been bad enough but the print headlines were worse.

'The plague murders' screamed the *Daily Mail*, something picked up by the *Express*. 'Secret plague cult' made the front of the *Sun*. The broadsheets were little better. 'Met Police questioned about cover-up' was on *The Guardian*'s front page and 'A serial killer in central London?' in *The Times*. There were stories about the Black Death too, linked with the murders. She would read them later.

A search on her phone yielded over a hundred stories online, everything from HuffPost to Guido Fawkes. She emailed Siobhan asking her to print out hard copies. Siobhan responded immediately.

'Check out attached,' her message said.

Cassie clicked on the link.

'Plague Spy' was the title of the article. 'Who is the shadowy civil servant at the centre of the investigation into the macabre murders in central London?'

What?

The article was by Victoria Ngoni, a lobby correspondent. It mentioned GCHQ and suggested that Cassie was an espionage expert, which she most definitely was not. She winced. The people who mattered, Duncan and her close colleagues, would know her well enough, she hoped, to know that she hadn't approved this. Others would assume that the piece had come from her, which wasn't going to make her popular.

The article described her as single and living in south London. It included photographs, one of which must've been taken recently, because it showed the travelling circus ferris wheel currently pitched on Clapham Common. So a photographer had been sniffing around.

The piece wasn't offensive. It was the fact that it had been written at all that disturbed her. After the break-in this felt like another intrusion. Why was she even on the media's radar? She wasn't important or central to the case. And why was a political journalist writing this sort of article?

As they crossed Vauxhall Bridge she almost forgot to look for the outlet of the Kings Scholar's Pond sewer, one outflow of the Tyburn. A quick glance at the glittering waters of the Thames below told her that the tide was high and she wouldn't see anything.

Today's starting out well.

'Morning,' Siobhan called as Cassie approached her desk. 'Andrew's already gone up to the sixth floor.' She stressed his name with a sly smile and raised eyebrows, tilting her head at a flirtatious angle. 'I've been making him comfortable.'

Not this nonsense on top of everything else.

'I'm sure you have.' Cassie dumped her satchel and picked up a document holder. Yet she hadn't been able to meet her secretary's eyes. She chose not to think about it as she headed for the lift.

The meeting was in the Permanent Secretary's office, not Sir Terence this time, but Sir John Sparrow of the Home Office, who dealt with the security services. Both had offices on the sixth floor because, it was said, neither was willing to concede the higher ground to the other.

Cassie took a seat next to the inspector on the low sofa in the waiting area.

'How are you this morning?' Rowlands asked her, a genuine question in his eyes.

'OK' she said. 'Or at least I was until I saw this.'

She handed him her phone with the article open on it.

He swore softly as he read it. 'Do you know who Victoria Ngoni is?'

'She's a lobby correspondent. What she's doing writing a piece like this is beyond me.'

The door to the office opened and Sir John emerged. 'Both here. Good.' He spoke to his secretary. 'Hold all calls except the Minister, please. This way.' He led them back into his office.

A lean man with a high forehead rose from his seat at the meeting table as they entered. Ex-military, Cassie thought, noting the straightness of his posture and his stillness.

'Detective Inspector Rowlands, Ms Fortune, this is Peter Bradley of MI5.' The Permanent Secretary didn't waste time. 'He's here to discuss the theft of the Palace of Westminster access passes and possible links to terrorist activity. Mr Bradley.'

'I understand that ten passes were stolen, belonging to a variety of individuals, two of them during a reception on the Terrace on Monday evening,' Bradley began. He'd obviously got the same information they had. 'And that one of them, yours, Ms Fortune, was found the following day in the possession of a dead man, a plumber who had been working the previous evening at Westminster.'

Cassie assented.

'The plumber, named Ortega, was Spanish, I understand, resident in Elephant and Castle and a regular contract-worker at the Houses of Parliament.'

'That's correct.' It was Rowlands who answered. 'He was the second victim discovered within twenty four hours, both killed in the same manner. Subsequently there's been a third. Ortega didn't have previous convictions for theft, or any criminal record. So we're still investigating why he had the pass at all.'

'You didn't know him?' Bradley asked Cassie.

'No. I recognised him when I saw his body in the mortuary. He was at Parliament when I was there the previous evening.' Cassie redirected the conversation. 'I'm not convinced that these thefts are linked to terrorism. The passes were cancelled as soon as they were reported missing. They'd have become useless very quickly and we'd know if they had been used during the interim.'

'I agree. But there is still a risk and we need to be as certain as we can be that the risk is minimal. I think there's more here than meets the eye.'

'That we can all agree on,' Rowlands said, in a dry tone.

The door burst open. A large, muscular man charged, bull-like, into the room. David Hurst, current Home Secretary and Prime Minister-in-waiting, had begun his adult life working in the docks before a union sponsored scholarship took him to Oxford. He had a reputation of being a bruiser and someone of unlimited ambition.

Be careful. Make a good impression.

'Sir John,' he said, nodding curtly at the Permanent Secretary. 'Thought I'd come along. See what Charles' tame spook had to say for herself when faced with the real security services.'

Insulting and inaccurate.

Cassie looked down at the table.

'Home Secretary,' Sir John was on his feet and everyone else rose. 'Please join us. We're just summarising the position so far.'

Peter Bradley repeated his summary. The politician was the outsider here, Cassie recognised, even if they were all his servants. He was in command.

But we aren't entirely powerless.

'So what are you going to do next?' Hurst asked her.

'The police investigation continues,' Cassie said. 'I'm sure Detective Inspector Rowlands will set that out for you. I, meanwhile, will be speaking with the Parliamentary Security Department and the Serjeant at Arms in the Palace of Westminster and, potentially, the Whips' offices.'

See what he makes of that.

The Home Secretary's head swivelled towards her.

'They may know something about the individuals who had items stolen that we do not.'

David Hurst and Sir John exchanged looks. There was the faint suggestion of a smile on Bradley's lips.

'And your investigation, Inspector?' Hurst turned his gaze on Rowlands.

'We have found the location where the third victim was raped and abused before she escaped,' he began. 'It's unlikely to yield DNA evidence, though we still await the forensic report. We have a description of events and of her attackers. We are also tracing a footprint found at the scene.'

'Good. I want a full report on what you find,' the Home Secretary said. 'And immediate briefing on anything brought to light by your enquiries at Westminster.' He looked pointedly at Cassie.

Her report was to the Deputy Prime Minister and he knew it. Was this a test?

Cassie glanced across at Bradley. His eyes were on her, he was waiting to see how she handled David Hurst.

'I will be reporting to the Deputy Prime Minister, Home Secretary,' she said.

Hurst bent forward across the table, his jowly face flushed, his eyes cold. Cassie prepared for an onslaught. Instead he laughed. She sensed the inspector relax beside her and even the Permanent Secretary sounded relieved as he drew the meeting to a close.

'Unless you have anything further, Home Secretary? No, well, that seems to be all.'

'I want to speak with you on another matter,' Hurst said to Sir John as everyone stood and Cassie, Rowlands and Bradley moved towards the door.

'Charles Morecombe won't be around forever you know, Ms Fortune,' Hurst called after her. 'I suggest that you give some thought to your future when he's gone.'

Oh no, I've offended him. So much for making a good impression.

As the door closed behind them, Cassie heaved a sigh of relief.

'Bollocksy old bugger isn't he?' said Peter Bradley cheerfully. The MI5 man had a wry grin on his face. 'Hadn't you met him before?'

'I hadn't.'

'After your time, probably. Good meeting you, Inspector.' Bradley shook hands with Rowlands. 'If you can copy your report to me, please. I'm pretty sure you're right, though one can't rule out a terrorist connection completely.'

He took Cassie's hand. 'Goodbye. I know better than to ask for your report.'

'I've no doubt you'll get it,' she said. 'Just not first, I hope.'

'You never know.' He smiled and headed for the lift. Cassie and Rowlands watched him go.

'Er, Ms Fortune, Cassie?' It was the secretary. 'Beverley Allott's been trying to contact you.'

Rowlands raised an eyebrow.

'Bev is the Deputy Prime Minister's PA,' she explained as she led him away. 'I wouldn't be surprised if David Hurst had told the DPM that he was meeting me this morning with MI5.'

'This is above my pay grade,' Rowlands said.

'It's above mine! The DPM probably wants me to go over to Parliament.'

'See you back at the Yard? Then we can check out our lost river.'

Cassie agreed. At that moment, clambering around a rat-infested sewer seemed infinitely preferable to another grilling by a politician.

◊ THIRTY THREE

Central Lobby wasn't crowded. Only private members bills were debated on Fridays, when most MPs returned to their constituencies. She spotted Bev Allot coming from the Commons Lobby.

'He's only got a few minutes,' the young woman said. 'David Hurst phoned him.'

'I thought he might.'

Before their earlier meeting or immediately after?

'Come on, I've arranged for one of the messenger boxes.'

The PA led the way to a cubbyhole-like room tucked away behind a wooden panel off Central Lobby. Charles Morecombe, the DPM, sat reading papers, his knees reaching to the underside of the small table.

'Cassandra,' he nodded by way of greeting. 'I don't have long – too much going on. Let me have a brief summary of where we are.'

Cassie reported as she and Rowlands had done earlier that day, adding her conclusions to date.

'I have no evidence of any link with previous allegations about illegal activity in Westminster. Nor is there any issue with the Home Secretary as far as I can tell. But there is a connection with the Palace of Westminster and there is organisation behind these crimes. We think it's a criminal gang.'

'With links to the media,' he said. 'I saw the piece about you. Not Vicki Ngoni's usual beat at all.'

'Quite. And my flat was broken into on Wednesday.'

'Cassie!' Bev looked shocked.

'Are you certain it was linked with the case?' the DPM thrust his head forward, looking at Cassie intently.

'They left a calling card.'

Morecombe slapped his hand down, making the table shake. 'Then make sure Rowlands organises full protection for you. I'll speak with Hurst about it. What – didn't you tell him?'

A protection officer would only get in the way.

'Er, no. It wouldn't help. I had to persuade the inspector not to fill my road with plain clothes police!'

'So the police are carrying out their function? There's nothing to substantiate any allegations of corruption?'

'No, sir.' Cassie pressed on. 'But I'd like to probe further into people at Westminster, talk to the whips. Can that be arranged?'

'David told me that you mentioned that,' the DPM said with an amused air. 'How did you think the meeting with him went?'

Why's he asking?

'OK.'

'Hmm.' The DPM raised an eyebrow making him look even more like a bird of prey. 'David can be... somewhat forceful. At the moment he's on the back foot, having mislaid the only witness in the case.'

'Silana died, sir.'

'Yes, tragic, quite indefensible.'

'Right now, I can't tell you more,' Cassie said. 'But I want to start digging.'

'Very well, I'll speak with Robert Partington in the Chief Whip's Office. Keep at it. The more we know before the House rises for conference, the happier I will be.'

'Whatever I find?'

'Whatever you find. Report back on Tuesday at the latest. Bev'll carve some time in my diary.'

Morecombe unfolded himself from his seat, filling the small space as he stood. He left, a rueful looking Bev trailing in his wake clutching his papers.

As she returned to Central Lobby Cassie spotted Victoria Ngoni in the Commons Corridor, in conversation with a shadow junior minister. She signalled to the journalist that she wanted to speak with her.

'Cassie, can you give me five minutes to finish here? Meet you in New Palace Yard?'

'OK, but I have to do something first. See you in half an hour, say?'

Victoria agreed and returned to the MP.

Now for Parliamentary Security.

Cassie entered the Peers side of the Palace. She was looking for Jack Martineau, with whom she had worked in the past and who currently held a post in the Security Department at Westminster. Jack would know everything there was to know about what went on here.

Yet who should she see strolling towards her but Frank Cairns and William Priess.

'Well, I am doubly fortunate,' Cairns said with his lopsided grin, blue eyes twinkling. 'Meeting you twice in two days, Ms Cassandra Fortune of the Deputy Prime Minister's Office.'

Priess smiled and held her gaze. 'Cassandra,' he said, inclining his head. Today his pale eyes were slightly bloodshot but he still stood ramrod straight.

'We're off to the Woolpack for a hair of the dog,' Cairns referred to the Houses of Parliament Sports & Social. 'Last night went on too long, I'm afraid. You left early, I was looking for you.'

You certainly don't look the worse for wear. Rather the opposite.

'Yes, I left early.'

I don't owe you any explanations.

Cairns' smile widened, he seemed to be able to read her thoughts. She suspected he would relish any sparring. William Priess, meanwhile, was watching the exchange very closely, his smile frozen.

I don't have time for this.

'If you will excuse me,' she said and slipped by them. 'I'm late.'

'Until we meet again,' Priess murmured as she passed.

◊ THIRTY FOUR

The Parliamentary Security Department was at the river end of the oak-lined East Corridor. Before she reached it, Cassie tapped at an unmarked door on the same side of the passageway and stepped into the Westminster Security Control Room.

The modern office was squashed into a space too small to accommodate it. It contained four desks, two against each sidewall, with windows looking out on to a courtyard lawn. One wall held a series of antique looking screens showing the output from the few CCTV cameras inside Westminster. The desk in front of them was occupied by a young man.

'I'm looking for Jack,' she explained at the same time as Jack Martineau entered behind her. His shock of grey hair above a ruddy face was unmistakable; he was beaming.

'Cassandra! I thought it was you.'

'Hello, Jack.' She bent to kiss his cheek.

'Let's go and talk somewhere.'

He patted her hand and led her out of the office into one of the small waiting rooms.

'You're working on something here?' he questioned. 'Can I help?'

'I hope so.' Cassie took a seat by the window. 'I have a little list. First, the access passes stolen during the reception on Monday.'

'Including yours.'

'Mine was found in the possession of a dead man, one José Galan Ortega, a Palace plumber.'

'I knew he was dead, but I didn't know he had your pass,' Jack said. 'What do you want to know?'

'Anything about him. I'd like to talk with his workmates if possible and bring in the DI who's on the case. We want to speak with CSL too.'

'I'll set up a chat with the Craft Team. Tomorrow morning? There are major works happening once Parliament rises next week and the Palace closes, so best to talk with them before then.'

'That would be great, Jack. Thanks.'

'The CSL directors are usually here on Fridays. Karen Woods likes the connection with the Palace so she still comes to give the work out herself. I'll give you a bell later when they arrive.'

'You're a star. Also, were the stolen passes used later that night, or in the early hours? Have any attempts been made to use them since?'

'It's easy enough to interrogate the system; I can do that right away. What else?'

'We think a titled man features in our case, could be an aristocrat, a life peer, a baronet or knight. We believe he took part in at least one rape, on Tuesday night. Is there anyone you know of with a title and a reputation for violence and sex? From either House.'

'I'll ask around,' Jack said. 'Though this is very dark. And?'

'When the Met asked for a list of missing items and their owners, all we got at first was a list of things stolen,' Cassie began. 'I know the Speaker can be touchy about such matters but this seemed excessive. Could you find out if it was an official block, or something else?'

'Of course. Did you get what you needed?'

'Yes, eventually.'

'Good. Is that all?'

'Isn't that enough?' Cassie handed him her card as she stood. On it she had scribbled the number of the secure fax in the incident room. 'You can reach me at New Scotland Yard.'

'About time they brought you back into the fold. It wasn't right what happened to you.'

'Thanks, Jack.'

'I'll be in touch.'

New Palace Yard was at the other end of the building so Cassie hurried through the ornate corridors and halls. She was breathing quickly when she emerged into the small garden next to Westminster Bridge. It wasn't long before she was joined by the journalist.

'Sorry I took so long,' Victoria said. 'Coffee?'

'I'm afraid I don't have time. But I'll walk towards Carlo's with you.'

The two women set out, manoeuvring round a scrum of banner-waving demonstrators demanding that the government take action against the plague. The demo had taken up permanent residence on Bridge Street and Abingdon Green.

'This is ridiculous. There is no plague,' Cassie said to her companion. 'Why does your lot go along with it? You're making it worse. I've seen so many scare stories but the bacillus can't survive for hundreds of years and, anyway, bubonic plague is treatable now.'

'The scare stories would be there anyway,' the journalist replied, 'on the internet, in chat rooms. We've had ebola, SARS, Zika and Covid-19, so now it's *yersinia pestis*. Some news outlets would pick up on this, however irresponsibly, and the TV needs to fill the 24-hour news cycle, so we all do it.'

'But it's dishonest and dangerous.'

'That's one way of looking at it.'

No, it's not a way of looking at it. It is dishonest and dangerous!

They crossed Bridge Street and walked through the crowd of tourists emerging from Westminster station.

'I was surprised by your piece this morning,' Cassie said. 'Isn't it usual practice to let the subject of an article know about it and ask for comment before publication?'

'It is and I'm sorry that wasn't done. That's partly what I wanted to talk with you about.' Victoria cast a guilty glance at Cassie. 'I was expressly forbidden to warn you. And Cassie - I was instructed to write that piece. My boss gave me no choice. I think the order came from above and whoever ordered it has a lot of clout further up the food chain. Someone's out to get you but neither my boss nor I know who, or why.'

That sounded right. Vicki was a political correspondent; that morning's piece was of a different type. Cassie appreciated her honesty.

'What's going on, Cassie?'

Cassie shook her head. 'I don't know. I wish I did.' The two women came to a stop on the corner. 'Tell me, have you heard any rumours about Thames Estates? Anything odd?'

'Funny you should ask. There's a smell attaching to it. Lots of money involved. I sniff a story.'

'What kind of story?'

'Corruption. Lots of backstairs manoeuvring,' Vicki said. 'Strings are being pulled. '

Cassie frowned. Investors in contract winning firms stood to make a small fortune and stock prices would rise or fall as the frontrunners for the contracts emerged. Last night she had marvelled at the amount of interest but thought it was simply about a lucrative government contract. Maybe it was more than that? An MP like Percy Dugdale or lords like Cairns or Priess could be raking in the kickbacks. And Duncan was with the Programme now too.

'Do you have anything concrete? About anything out of the ordinary?'

'Not as yet, but my sources say that though the standard process is being followed, the contracts aren't being awarded in the usual way. This is make or break for many companies, you know all about procurement... Have you heard of a company called CSL? They're one of the bidders.'

'Palace contractors aren't they,' she said, keeping her voice noncommittal. 'If your suspicions firm up, will you let me know? Confidentially, of course. I'm sorry but I need to go now.'

'Wait, Cassie,' the journalist hesitated. 'There's something big coming – we can all sense it – do you know?'

'I've been concentrating on this case–'

'OK. Look, I'm sorry about this morning's piece, I really wasn't given a choice. I know that's not much of an excuse.'

'Apology accepted,' Cassie said and meant it. 'See you around. In the Lobby maybe.'

Vicki smiled and turned back towards Parliament. Cassie headed for the Embankment.

So Daljit was right, the media was being used against them. Someone had prompted that profile of her. Who had that kind of power? And why use it against her? She was small fry.

And CSL – that company's name kept coming up.

The people doing this were clever and could command others to do whatever was required, even within the media. She set her jaw and squared her shoulders. However formidable their adversaries, she and Andrew would find them and expose them; that was what they did, what she did, what she was good at. A small frown drew her brows together as she strode into New Scotland Yard.

◊ THIRTY FIVE

There was only one more entertainment. On Monday, something special for his Russian business partner. The arrangements were all in hand. He stopped exercising and mopped his neck with a towel. Why then did he feel uncertain? All his instincts told him to withdraw, to close everything down. But Oleg was important and he wasn't the type of man to understand the difficulty; he would see any change as a sign of weakness. Being seen as weak would be yet another problem he'd have to solve.

Irritated, he went to change out of his gym gear; he was expecting a visitor. When he entered the sitting room ten minutes later, Sir Percy Dugdale already awaited him. The MP had helped himself to a whisky.

For an instant, he regretted not filling the decanters with something less pleasant, cyanide perhaps. But no, for now Percy was too useful to eliminate.

'Hello, old boy. Hope you don't mind.' He waved the tumbler.

'Sir Percy. Is everything arranged for our Russian friend? It is, as you know, particularly important to impress upon him just how far we can reach and what power we wield. Oleg is not an ally I wish to lose. He could be a dangerous enemy.'

'Yes, everything's hunky dory, don't worry. We've found a suitable woman, a redhead, as requested. Oleg will be impressed. Is it just the Russian? No Chinese interest?'

'No.' He gave a tight smile in response. Percy was becoming too familiar. Annoying and possibly dangerous.

'Will you be attending?'

'Probably not.'

Percy laughed. 'You never do.'

'I have other business.' He kept his voice calm and walked over to the window.

'I'm sure. By the way, I spotted Cassandra Fortune in the Commons Lobby earlier. Ah, that got your attention! She was speaking with the black bint from *The Indie*. I assume that this morning's story about her originated here? Something to stir things up.'

He nodded, not trusting himself to speak.

'The Met has a list of the people who lost their passes. My attempt to deflect their enquiries didn't work, even if I did slow them down a bit. My name is on that list, thanks to that Spanish thief.'

'You shouldn't have got drunk and left your pass lying around, Percy. Besides, as far as the police are concerned, you're just the victim of a petty theft.'

'Well, the lovely Cassandra went to the Security Department today, so she'll get all the dirt. I don't like things being raked over.' Sir Percy's tone grew more demanding. 'It's too close to home. When are you going to do something about her?'

'Do something?' His voice was completely flat, devoid of inflection.

'Isn't it time Harris paid her a visit?'

'That is my decision, Percy. I suggest that you concentrate on the tasks you have at hand.'

'Can't help speculating, old boy, she must be a sizzler between the sheets.' Percy slurped his whisky, a salacious smirk crossing his face. 'Too crude for you am I?' There was a feral cunning in Percy's eyes. 'Well, I checked her out and I think you've got competition. My sources tell me that someone else shares your taste in intelligent women. If you want her, you'd better move quickly or you'll lose your fun.'

'What's that to you?'

'Oh, nothing. You take your pleasure where you find it. I certainly do. Though when it comes to a GCHQ spook, it's dangerous. But then, maybe that's what you find so exciting, eh?'

'I shall do as I please, Percy, and I suggest you remember that. Otherwise, you might find Harris visiting you.' Again, he made his voice empty of any emotion.

Percy's face lost its colour and his mouth twisted.

'Steady on, old boy,' the MP's jollity rang hollow. 'Mutual benefit, you know, mutual benefit. I'm useful to you too.'

'There are over six hundred MPs, Percy.'

'But only one chairs the Oversight Committee.'

'Then you'd better remember who put you there,' he said. This time, he allowed a faint sting of contempt to colour his voice. 'Go and prepare. Let me know when plans are in place. Cassandra Fortune won't be the only one snooping round the Palace on Monday evening. The trusty Inspector has had yet another tranche of overtime approved. Your diversion had better be good. We cannot afford for this to go wrong.'

'We'll be ready.' Percy drained his glass and slammed it down on the sideboard with rather more force than was customary, before leaving.

Percy was becoming tiresome. Once this phase of activity was over, it would be time to replace him. Yet the man had a sixth sense for survival, which might make things tricky. He would already be planning his next move, which would have to be countered. But later. After Monday. For the moment, let him concentrate on the task at hand. There were other purposes that the Palace of Westminster passes could be put to, but it wasn't necessary for Percy to know that. This event would be a useful test.

But on one thing Percy was right. Cassandra Fortune was dangerous and so was his interest in her. The police investigation was getting too close, he needed to take steps. He would have liked to reel her in slowly, but he needed to press on. She would soon have to decide which side she was on.

◊ THIRTY SIX

The blackened brickwork seemed to sweat. Vast distorted shadows moved on the walls and the lights they carried reflected in the water.

It was hot, though the stream running along the foot of the egg-shaped passageway was cold. She stooped beneath the curved roof and took a deep breath.

Bad move.

She tasted the humid tang of detergent as well as less pleasant odours. Her breathing mask hung low on her chest, ready if needed. George had explained that each mask contained a sensor to identify the dangerous mixture of gases - the explosive carburetted hydrogen, sulphurated hydrogen or carbonic acid – which miners called chokedamp. As soon as it sensed the gases a beeping alarm would sound and she'd have to put on the mask. It had its own small pressurised oxygen supply, slung on a strap over her shoulder.

They waded along the tunnel in single file. Rowlands was immediately ahead of her following George the sewerman at the front. Two other sewermen were behind her, carrying collapsible boats, ready for when the water deepened as the sewers approached the Thames. They all wore heavy-duty bib and brace oilskins, waterproof coats and thigh-high waders, with reinforced soles and toecaps. Cold sludgy liquid pushed at the back of her waders, forcing her onwards. Her feet sank into whatever was hidden by the murky water.

She and the inspector had met George at Green Park and had followed him down an iron ladder fixed into the wall of a small shaft beneath a manhole cover. When they reached a concrete terrace they checked that their hardhat lights and mini-radios were working.

'The flushers didn't have none of this technology in the old days,' said George. 'When I started they used to carry chemical strips which would change colour in the presence of certain gases. And they'd have to keep an eye on them, as the shit often holds pockets of gas. Least it kills the rats and eels though.'

He ushered them down a further shaft for another twenty feet to a small chamber which sloped gently down to the sewer. After that Cassie lost track of time, the never-ending tunnel became as monotonous as it was disgusting. She wasn't about to remove her gauntlets to check her watch.

Suddenly, without warning, it opened out into a cavernous arched chamber, twenty feet high, supported by pillars and concrete buttresses.

Like a cathedral. It echoes like one, too.

The water trickled over a weir into a lower chamber. What it would be like in a flood, the cavern would be a mass of roiling water? A sluice gate, hung about with detritus, was suspended from the ceiling.

'We've crossed the park and are south of Buck House now,' George said, pointing upwards. 'This sluice was installed to block the smelly stuff which used to back up the sewer from the river when the Thames flooded. Too strong for the royals' delicate olfactory organs.' He chuckled. 'There are ventilator gratings for a while from now on.'

He pointed to a grey shaft of light up ahead, coming down into the cavern from above.

'And there are access doors.'

Interesting.

Cassie exchanged looks with Rowlands.

'Do you know where they go?' she asked.

'Mostly,' George replied. 'They often have numbers on them.'

He shone his torch towards a wide metal door set deep into the brickwork. There was a raised coat of arms in the metal.

'Though not that one, obviously,' he chortled.

He started off again along the tunnel and they followed. There were occasional small side passages from the main sewer leading to steps.

'Storm sewers,' George said. 'And some old private ones. The brickwork's not so good on those.'

They sloshed along from one light shaft to another. Gradually the tunnel ceiling grew lower again.

Then George stopped. They had reached a division where the tunnel branched into two.

'Down there is Victoria and Pimlico,' he waved his torch at the right-hand passageway. 'The sewer follows the line of Tachbrook Street to the Thames. If we go that way we'll probably need the boats. Do you want to try it?'

He looked at Rowlands.

'No. Take the other passage, the one that goes to Westminster.'

The tunnel narrowed as they walked, its contours forcing them into its centre. The brickwork seemed to be closing in around them. She concentrated hard on trying to remember any distinctive features of the tunnel, but it all looked the same.

Then, up ahead, there was another division and again George turned to consult.

'This is the Thorney Island split. We can go either north or south around Westminster Abbey.'

'South first,' Cassie said. 'The right-hand tunnel. Then back here to go down the other one?'

'Right-hand it is,' George said. 'Be careful here, the level changes, it gets much shallower and there's a dog-leg turn to the left. This tunnel is very old. It has brick buttresses, at least until the Abbey. Then there's the stone. Not like a Bazalgette tunnel at all. You'll see soon. '

Cassie was glad that he had warned them as the floor rose suddenly and she would have tripped and fallen into the effluent. To either side brick piers spread into the tunnel, slowing their progress. They weren't far along when the brickwork gave way to stone.

'We're underneath where the old Abbey walls stood,' George said. 'You can see the entrance to the lower crypt coming up on the left.'

There was a corbelled arch and a stone-roofed passage leading away from the main tunnel.

'We'll be under Westminster School soon. Then the tunnel runs along beneath Great College Street.'

There were more doorways, some up short flights of steps. Cassie pointed her flashlight at each one.

'What are you looking for?' Rowlands asked.

'I don't know, exactly,' she said, sotto voce. 'George, where do these go?'

'School buildings mainly, though there are private houses too. Did you know Sir John Gielgud, the actor, used to live round here?'

'Do you know which door belongs to which house?'

'That's the School on that side.' George had halted and was shining his torch along the left-hand wall of the tunnel. Then he swung it around. 'That's the corner of College Street with Barton Street. Shows you how quickly the slime takes over, that door's new, though it don't look it.'

Cassie shone her torch on to a black metal door, set back up some shallow steps.

Barton Street. Isn't that where Lawrence Delahaye lives?

'How far to the river now?' Rowlands asked.

'About a hundred yards or so,' George said. 'But the tunnel doesn't go straight there, it cuts back. The Tyburn would have been part of the moat of the old Abbey and Palace of Westminster. Now it runs beneath Abingdon Gardens.'

Cassie wished she had spent more time looking at George's map. She'd have to consult it later.

'Do you want to go on further, or retrace our steps and take the northerly spur?' George asked.

'Retrace our steps,' Cassie answered.

As they did so, Andrew dropped back to talk to her.

'What are you up to?' he demanded, a smile in his voice.

'Don't worry, I'll explain everything when we get out of here.'

After the dog-leg turn the other branch of the tunnel had blackened Victorian brickwork again and the periodic gratings resumed. Every twenty yards or so columns of grey light reached down to reflect from the moving water. A series of small tunnels branched off to the right.

'What about those, George?' Cassie asked.

'Second World War bunkers,' he said. 'Disused, shut up decades ago. I'd always meant to explore them but never got the chance. We're under Broad Sanctuary now. Soon we'll swing left under the Treasury building. You'll see the change.'

He was right. There was a modern concrete roof, with regular concrete pillars in the walls, though the gratings had stopped and they were in complete darkness again, save for the lights they carried.

'They reinforced the brickwork when they refurbished the building,' George said.

Cassie imagined the rooms above them. The cycle store and cloakroom in the damp lower basement. When they came to a door she shone the beam of her torch on to the HMRC insignia.

Directly ahead the tunnel hit a concrete wall but branched off to left and right.

'Dead end that way,' said George, indicating the left-hand passage. 'This one goes to your neck of the woods.' He nodded to Andrew. 'Old New Scotland Yard.'

'The first New Scotland Yard, in fact,' Andrew said. 'If you mean the Norman Shaw buildings. One of our victims was working there. Can you take us there and out where the sewer meets the river?'

'Not quite. This runs into one of the big intersections, like the one you saw near Buck House and that diverts the flow. The tunnel beyond is very small, about three feet high, so I suggest that we come out at the crossing point.'

'Fine with me,' said Andrew, glancing at Cassie.

'And me,' she said.

It would be good to get back to daylight again.

◊ THIRTY SEVEN

Without his oilskins and hard hat, George Bindel looked frail, standing in the incident room clutching a mug of coffee. He'd dismissed the other sewermen once they'd got to the surface.

'Look, there's the big east-west intersectional which the Tyburn links with, the one we just came out of,' he said, pointing to the map. 'Like the one under Oxford Street. Bazalgette couldn't put this one beneath Parliament, which had only just been built, so it was located next to it, with a link to a pumping room. That's how Guy Fawkes would get in today.'

The thick red line ran very close to the Palace of Westminster.

'To get under the Palace?' Cassie asked. 'How?'

'There's an access point to the sewer in Boudicca's statue, the bronze chariot on the Victoria Embankment by the Bridge. The door's behind the ticket kiosk.'

So it was that simple.

'This is the course of the Tyburn which we followed,' George traced a line with his finger. 'Under Great College Street, remember? We got about so far then stopped, but it continues on by the Jewel Tower to meet the big intersectional as well. We came back and went down the other branch.'

Silently, Cassie cursed. Was there a useable access point from the Tyburn to the Tower? If they had continued they would have found out. There was one shown on George's map, which also showed accesses to the old WWII bunkers.

'Are those doors still usable?' Cassie asked, pointing. 'Would someone be able to go from the Tyburn to the bunkers?'

'Dunno,' George said. 'The map doesn't show them as blocked off, so maybe, yes.'

'Are the other underground rivers as accessible as this one?' the serjeant asked.

'They're more difficult to navigate,' George explained, enthusiasm increasing. 'The Fleet carries more sewage so would be more unpleasant and dangerous. The Walbrook meets the Thames at Dowgate, but its gradient is steep and the flow is strong, so not advisable. Now the Westbourne, it's Victorian in Belgravia and Chelsea, because of the developer Thomas Cubitt, so it's large and gated. There is access at various points and it's walkable, especially from Hyde Park onwards. South of the Thames-'

Rowlands interrupted as George paused for breath. 'We're concentrating on the north,' he said.

'Is access always through manholes?' Cassie asked.

'There are sewer manholes,' George replied. 'But you need a key to open them. The rivers are far older than normal sewers and will have had all sorts of entrances in the past: private side tunnels, cellars -- whatever. The water authority knows most of them but not all.'

'So,' Cassie summarised. 'We have a network of tunnels beneath London's streets, which can be entered in any number of ways--'

'I wouldn't say that,' George interjected. 'Most access points are plotted and secured. Only the old rivers might allow access that doesn't show up on modern maps and we know most of those.'

'OK, so only in certain areas and some of the old rivers aren't walkable anyway.'

'Exactly.'

'Which narrows it down to-?'

'North of the Thames, the Tyburn and the lower reaches of the Westbourne.'

'Thanks George,' Rowlands said as he shot a glance at the serjeant. 'You've been tremendously helpful.'

'I enjoyed it,' the sewerman said. 'I haven't been down there since I did that review for Tideway, the new super sewer. You aren't the first folk I've walked the sewers with you know.'

'Review?' Cassie asked.

'Yeah, before the project got the go ahead,' George grew loquacious. 'Got paid for that one and had some fun too. Very sociable some of those MPs.'

'Which MPs? Who led the review George? Can you recall?'

'Can't remember 'em all, but a junior minister headed it. Frank what's his name, Frank Cairns. Liked a dram he did,' George chuckled at the happy memory of sharing a drink.

'We've taken enough of your time,' the serjeant moved towards the door. 'Let me show you out.'

Once they had gone, Cassie turned back to the maps. 'So Frank Cairns has been in the sewers and seen plans of them too. He could be a person of interest.' She remembered his mischievous charm.

'Why?'

'Parliament and the river Tyburn are never far away from this case and Frank Cairns is linked to both. I think we should investigate him further.'

'You mean you have a hunch,' Rowlands cast an appraising look at her. 'Do you know him?'

I met him at the Thames Estates launch yesterday. And...' she hesitated.

'Yes?'

'There was a hedge fund manager there, a Lawrence Delahaye, who was also at Monday's reception on the Terrace. He lives in Barton Street, that's where I was looking when we were in the sewers.'

'He has access to the Tyburn?'

'Possibly, though there must be a lot of people who live close to the Tyburn,' Cassie said, chin raised. 'It's in Central London, after all.' She hoped that she hadn't flushed. Rowlands' eyes widened and eyebrows rose. She obviously had.

He waited, watching her.

Why don't you say something else?

It was important that she told Andrew about Delahaye, about his interest in her. So why was she so reluctant to do so?

'He seemed... interested in me, but, on reflection, it didn't feel right.'

'Interested in you? In what way?'

'Well – as a woman...'

'Cassie, you need to be careful. Do you understand?' Rowlands reached out, his hands hovering near her upper arms as if he would take hold of her. 'Has he asked to see you again?'

She bridled and glared at him.

Who is Andrew Rowlands to tell me what to do? It's my private life.

'So what if he has?'

Stop behaving like a schoolgirl. And don't jump down Andrew's throat.

The door opened and the serjeant returned. Rowlands' arms dropped to his sides.

Cassie realised that she had been holding her breath.

'We've got a lead,' the serjeant was smiling, oblivious to the tension between them. 'Silana's friend has left her flat without a forwarding address but we have the name of her employer: it's CSL. And that's not all. Tadeusz, the young Pole, was working for Union Buildings, but Union is a subsidiary of CSL.'

'So CSL is a link between all three of the victims,' Rowlands said. 'We need to talk to the company directors.'

'My Westminster contact will let us know when they're at the Palace; he's promised to phone me when they arrive,' Cassie said.

'Good,' Rowlands said, then he addressed the serjeant. 'Find out everything you can about that company. And check out Lord Frank Cairns, as a junior minister he was involved with the Tideway project. I also need you to go over the lists I gave you with the event attendees. Let me know which of them also have properties on or near the river Tyburn. What else do we have?'

'There's the plague pit angle,' the serjeant said. 'The press latched on to this and it meant we had to spend a lot of time on damage limitation.'

And Andrew was savaged. Perhaps that was deliberate too?

'The plague hysteria has taken hold,' Cassie said. 'There's a perma-demo going on in Parliament Square, so it's on the news every night. I haven't dared look at social media. The government isn't covering itself in glory when it comes to clear communications. By the way, Vicki Ngoni was told to write that article about me and not by the political editor either, the word came from much higher up.'

'Somehow, it doesn't surprise me,' Rowlands said.

'One other thing occurred to me,' Cassie said. 'I'm guessing that you never found three bodies in a matter of days before? So why are the criminals so active now?'

'Is something important happening that is forcing their hand?' Rowlands asked.

Surely it couldn't be the Prime Minister's pending resignation? No, not possible. Surely...

'There's Thames Estates,' Cassie said. 'That's worth billions. Vicki's heard that there's some dodgy dealing going on with it, though she wouldn't name her sources.'

'It could also be an opportunity to manipulate markets,' Rowlands said, holding his chin in his hand. 'For the likes of hedge fund managers, like Lawrence Delahaye.'

Of course, markets could be manipulated to make money.

I'm going to dinner with that man. Could he really be crooked?

But that's not rape and murder.

Cassie looked at the whiteboards, forcing herself to think about the case, not about Delahaye or about Andrew's reaction to what she had told him. Were they any closer to finding the murderers?

They had a number of leads. First, the shoeprint, and now the CSL connection between the three victims. Several bodies had been found in or near the site of plague pits, which couldn't be entirely coincidental. Yet time was running out. She only had five days left before she had to give Charles Morecombe, the Deputy Prime Minister, her report.

◊ THIRTY EIGHT

Jack Martineau kept his promise and contacted Cassie later that day. Martineau met her and Rowlands in New Palace Yard.

'Thanks, Jack,' Cassie said, as they entered the Palace and left the noisy demonstrators behind. 'This is--'

'Andrew Rowlands, Detective Inspector.' Rowlands offered his hand to Jack.

'Jack Martineau, Parliamentary Security,' the older man responded.

'Jack and I have worked together before,' Cassie said, to forestall any questions. 'And no, he won't tell you when and where.'

'I didn't imagine he would,' Rowlands said, without inflection. 'Though I might have got lucky.'

She glanced at him. He was laughing at her. She tried not to smile but couldn't help it.

Concentrate on the case.

'Are the CSL people here, Jack? It's important that we question them.'

'Karen's usually here on a Friday,' Jack glanced at his watch. 'Vic Woods, her husband, often comes to collect her at about half past eight. We should catch them both. Follow me.'

They walked briskly along wood panelled corridors towards the river. Occasionally, Jack diverted down a side corridor and, after five minutes, Cassie was hopelessly lost. He stopped outside a door marked 'River Cafeteria' and led them in.

The room had a counter at one end and was filled with tables and chairs. Low upholstered chairs with wooden arms lined the far wall, beneath windows looking on to the Thames. In one of them sat a stern faced woman, her fair hair scraped back into a pony tail. She was balancing a clipboard on her knees. A man in a suit stood next to her gazing out at the view, his back to them.

'Karen, Vic,' Jack said as they walked over. 'May I introduce Detective Inspector Andrew Rowlands of the Metropolitan Police and Cassandra Fortune of the Deputy Prime Minister's Office.'

The woman stood to shake hands and the man turned to scrutinize them. He held himself well, Cassie thought, someone confident in his ability to deal with whatever came along.

'We'd like to ask you about one of your contractor staff, José Ortega,' Rowlands began. 'You too Mr Woods,' he said as the man turned to leave.

'Very sad,' Karen Woods said, resuming her seat. 'And him about to become a father too.'

Jack drew up chairs for the rest of them.

'I believe that assignments for the following week's work are given out on Fridays,' the policeman stated. 'Did you tell José that he'd be working at the Palace this week?'

'Yes, I would have done.'

'Was he getting a different rate of pay?'

'No, everybody's on a flat rate per hour.'

'So why did José think he was getting more?'

'Er...did he? I don't know,' Karen looked surprised. 'He knew what his rate was.'

'A number of witnesses remember he was pleased to be getting more money,' Cassie said. 'A man who, his friends attest, had been anxious and worried until last week.'

'Maybe he had found more work elsewhere' she suggested. 'Some of our people have other jobs.'

'Do they?' Jack asked.

'It isn't something we encourage,' Karen was backtracking now. 'But we can't stop them.'

'Do you record the hours your people work, Ms Woods?' Rowlands asked.

'Yes.'

'We'd like to take a look at those records please.'

For the first time the woman looked uncertain.

'We don't carry them around,' her husband said. 'Several hundred people work for us.'

'Nonetheless, we would like to see them,' Rowlands said. 'And the records for your subsidiary companies. It seems another of the murder victims worked for Union Buildings.'

Husband and wife wore blank expressions. Something, Cassie reckoned, they knew how to assume at will. This couple was hiding something. Andrew obviously thought so too.

'We don't know all our staff personally,' Karen said, eventually. 'And we certainly don't know those of our subsidiary companies.'

'Perhaps your friend put some work José's way?' Jack was still concentrating on the Spaniard. 'He's ex-army too isn't he? I've seen him around, often on a Friday evening.'

Victor Woods flashed him a hostile look but it made no impression.

'Are you ex-military?' Cassie asked.

'Royal Green Jackets for twenty years,' Vic said to her. 'Who do you mean?' he addressed Jack.

'Short chap, crew cut, keeps himself in good shape.'

'He means Don,' Karen said. 'Don Harris.'

Vic began to speak then thought better of it and glowered at his wife.

'I don't see what Don's got to do with anything,' he eventually said.

'Is he involved with CSL?' Rowlands asked.

'He's a shareholder,' Karen said. 'And he sometimes does consultancy work for us on security.'

'Address please,' the inspector said, preparing to enter it into his notebook.

'90A, Tachbrook Street.'

The street under the southern spur of the Tyburn.

'Thank you,' Rowlands said, his voice mild, but he gave Vic Woods a steely stare.

'We have to go,' Karen stood. 'We've somewhere to be.' She picked up a briefcase and stuffed her clipboard into it.

'Before you leave,' Rowlands said. 'Do either of you know a Ms Francine Jalabert, a young French woman living in London? We understand she works, or worked, for CSL.'

Karen shook her head. Her husband did likewise.

'She would show up in your records?'

'Yes, if we've paid her any money,' the woman replied.

'Thank you for your help, Ms Woods.' The inspector also stood. 'Mr Woods.'

'Just one more thing,' Jack said. 'Why's the Chapel cordoned off? You're not doing any work down there, there's nothing scheduled.'

'It's the old kitchens,' Karen replied. 'The plumbing. The paperwork's been submitted.'

'I couldn't find it when I looked,' Jack said.

'I'll check,' she said. Her husband was looking impatient.

'Thanks,' Jack said, as they watched the couple leave.

'I'll bet that wasn't the first time they've been questioned by the police,' Rowlands said. 'They've just gone to the head of the suspect list, though I don't know what part they play in the murders.'

'We certainly need to keep an eye on them,' Jack said. 'By the way, I've got more information for you, if you've got five minutes?'

'For you, all the time in the world,' Cassie said, as she sat back down.

'First, the stolen passes haven't been used. Second, I've been nosing around,' Jack said, looking at the policeman. 'Anything I say will, of course, be completely off the record.'

Rowlands nodded acquiescence.

'There are rumours about two men when it comes to serious violence and sex, William, Lord Priess and Sir Percy Dugdale, MP.'

'What kind of rumours, Jack?' Cassie asked.

'The Priess family has a long history, sometimes illustrious, but the current Earl's father and grandfather were known to be abusive. There were even suspicious deaths, prostitutes for the most part. *Droit de seigneur* and all that, all hushed up.'

'Sins of the father, Jack,' Cassie said. 'Doesn't mean he's like that too, society's moved on. Is there anything about Priess himself?'

'Nothing specific I can find but one or two of the female staff find him creepy.'

Hmm... he didn't seem creepy to me. Probably gossip, but abusers often learned their behaviour from family members.

'What about Dugdale?' Rowlands asked.

'Where do I start? A finger in every pie, a very dodgy reputation, but too powerful to cross: he chairs the Oversight Committee. There's also a scandal in his past. A school servant died when he was at public school, possibly suicide. Percy was implicated but nothing could be proved. That's been a pattern ever since, nothing sticks.' Martineau shook his head. 'According to their diary secretaries, both Dugdale and Priess were in Westminster and didn't have any duties on Tuesday night. You will need to verify all of this, there may be personal alibis.'

'We will,' Rowlands said, writing again.

Dugdale's dodgy, but corruption doesn't equate to sexual violence. And a dead man from long ago? Not sure about that.

'Jack, what about Frank Cairns,' she asked. 'He's newly ennobled, are there any rumours about him? He had a promising career, why did he accept being shunted upwards?'

'He drinks – it's not unusual in this place – though I wonder if that isn't an affectation, he always seems in control to me. Too popular and clever to get rid of, but unreliable, so was put somewhere safe. He has been hawking himself about, for paid commissions, consultancies, that sort of thing. He'll have taken a substantial drop in earnings from being an MP and a minister, even a junior one, to being a peer and he doesn't have a private income. As to why he accepted the peerage when he could have stayed and fought to keep his seat... who knows?'

Interesting. There are unanswered questions about him and he is a lord.

'On the delay in making information available,' Jack continued, 'I think there was interference, probably from the Commons, so it must be by someone senior, though not the Speaker. Somebody here doesn't like this investigation.'

'Dugdale's in the Commons,' she said. She would have to include this in her report.

'Thanks Jack,' Rowlands said. 'We'll follow up your information on Cairns and Dugdale. Those seem the most obvious routes to go down. I'll have Priess checked out too, but he seems less likely.'

'No problem, I enjoyed doing it. It brought back the old days.' He smiled at Cassie.

Cassie touched his arm. 'We'll be over tomorrow morning for a tour of the basement when we come to meet the Craft Team. That's where they hang out isn't it?'

'It is. Right, I'll get back to my cubbyhole.' Jack rose, as did the others. 'A pleasure meeting you,' he said to the policeman. 'See you again tomorrow.'

'Likewise and thanks again.'

Outside dusk was falling. Lights twinkled on the opposite bank of the Thames, reflecting in the water as Cassie led the way out of New Palace Yard. She felt tired but also didn't want to let the case go.

'Fancy a drink before calling it a day?' the inspector asked.

'Yes. Though haven't you got someone waiting at home for you?'

'No. Nobody. I'm entirely free.'

He is on his own.

Suddenly she didn't feel so tired.

'OK. Where shall we go?'

'Somewhere quiet's hard to find on a Friday night.'

'Let's try St James's, the early evening drinkers will have gone home by now,' she suggested.

◊ THIRTY NINE

The pub was busy. Cassie left Rowlands at the crowded bar and went through to the garden where she found a free table and a couple of stools. A string of solar garden lights was looped around the small yard, augmenting the glow from metal wall lamps.

Not as fancy as last night, but much better, in a way.

Cassie ran over elements of the case in her head. It was beginning to come together. For her, each investigation was like a tapestry. As patient as the mythical Penelope, she wove, undid and rewove the strands, some of the threads feeding directly into the central pattern, others peripheral. She was confident of finding the central design.

The service company link between the three victims was the first thread, the shoeprint at North Audley Street might prove to be the second. A third seemed to be plague pits and a fourth the military. Silana had described her abductor as being like a soldier and Victor Woods, even if it wasn't him, had been a Royal Green Jacket. Jack thought Don Harris was ex-army too.

Their suspicions were solidifying around four main players: Percy Dugdale, Frank Cairns, William Priess and, more peripherally, Lawrence Delahaye. Running beneath it all there was the Tyburn, the dark river connecting all the places of power. It ran like a noxious strand through the weave, interlacing everything and everyone together, yet it was hidden from the view of the people who crossed it, unknowing, on the surface.

But now the clock was ticking. She had to report to Charles Morecombe on Tuesday and the overall design was not yet revealed.

'Phew, it's a scrum in there.'

Rowlands placed the tumblers of gin, ice and lemon and the two bottles of tonic on to the table.

'Thanks.'

'I like your friend, Jack,' he said as he sat.

'The feeling's obviously mutual,' Cassie said, smiling. 'He's a shrewd judge of character; you should consider yourself privileged.'

'My my, I do believe that's a compliment.'

There were laugh wrinkles at his eyes when he smiled, she noticed.

'Has Daljit reported back on the Woods pair yet?' The serjeant had been asked to check Karen Woods and her husband for any previous convictions or cautions.

'No, but I've added Harris to the list.'

'And the Royal Green Jackets?'

'Yes. I've also asked her to check on the lord Jack mentioned, she's already checking on Dugdale. Oh, and Lawrence Delahaye.'

Oh...

'Apparently, he's being investigated by the Serious Fraud Office.'

Cassie diverted her gaze away from Rowlands' hard stare. 'Hedge fund managers often are,' she added.

Well, maybe not every hedge fund manager. The SFO doesn't concern itself with small fry.

'I'd say we've made good progress today.' Rowlands raised his glass and clinked it against hers. 'It's about time we had a break, a little bit of luck.

'Andrew, if the Woods are involved in this, then why was José at London Road with my pass? If he was selling it to them he could have dealt with them at any time at the Palace.'

'I know, that occurred to me too.'

Suddenly she felt very cold.

'You're shivering. Here.'

Before she could refuse he had taken off his jacket and placed it around her shoulders.

She felt a glow of interior warmth at being cosseted and cared for. Then every feminist principle she'd ever held rose up against the idea of being treated like a weak and feeble woman. She was an adult professional, she wasn't the type to be mollycoddled. She didn't flirt and simper. Anyway, this was a kind man being gallant to a colleague, nothing more? How could it be?

'Really, you don't need to do this.' She rose abruptly and swung the jacket off her shoulders. 'We can go inside.'

One of the tumblers shattered as it was brushed off the table and hit the flagstones.

'Damn!'

Clumsy idiot. And ungrateful too.

Andrew retrieved his jacket as a man carrying a long-handled dustpan and brush emerged from the pub.

'My fault, sorry,' Cassie said to him as they headed back inside.

The crowd of drinkers had dispersed and there was a table free by the window.

'Look, I'm sorry for being so ungracious,' Cassie said when he joined her with a replacement drink. 'You were just being kind.'

'Kind?' he said. 'Listen Cassie, I was being practical. It wasn't cold out there but you were trembling like a leaf. Don't underestimate the effect this case is having on you.'

'I'm fine.'

'If you are, then you're very strange,' his voice was low and gentle but persistent. 'Within five days you have seen three corpses, followed hot on the trail of a ring of murderers and abusers and had your flat broken into – very likely by one of them. I don't know what you were used to in GCHQ but I'll bet it wasn't this. It would be very surprising if you didn't suffer some sort of reaction.'

He might be right. Of course he's right.

She shook her head.

'Cassie, I am *not* being patronising, I am *not* challenging your right or your ability to determine your own actions and I am most definitely not in competition with you...' he said, with an exasperated frown. 'Why are you set against me? What have I done wrong?'

But I'm not set against you. I want to help you, I...

'This is my case. I didn't complain when you were drafted in - at least not to you. I've let you run your side of things and even put up with you butting into mine. So why are you so antagonistic?'

Am I? I can be spiky, especially when someone's getting too close.

'I...' her throat constricted and she couldn't form words. She remembered her final days in Cheltenham when she was fighting for her career and her husband accused her of rejecting him, of pushing him away. She felt a prickling behind her eyes.

She would not weep. It was completely unprofessional, despicable, little girly. She didn't want him to see her like that. She blinked rapidly and drew a deep breath. 'I'm sorry. I'm not being very professional.'

'Professional.' There was a pause. 'No, Cassie, you're not. Come on, I'll take you home and don't bother to argue. It's happening.'

Cassie followed him out of the pub door and was blinded by flashlights.

'Any comment on the Plague Murders, Ms Fortune?'

'You and the inspector enjoying a quiet drink, are you, while murderers roam our streets?'

'Is it true that you were a secret agent?'

Blinking, she saw the mesh of the microphones thrust into her face.

'Cassie!' She heard Rowlands' voice and felt him grip her hand. 'Excuse me, excuse me please.' She was scooped forward into the crook of his arm as he shouldered his way through the crowd towards a taxi rank.

'Here.' He opened the cab door and pushed her inside, turning to face the scrum of reporters.

'Please address all your questions about the case to the Scotland Yard Press Office.'

So saying he got into the cab behind her.

'Clapham, please,' he said to the cabbie.

'You don't need to...' she protested weakly.

He ignored her.

She looked at the streets passing, the shops and hotels of Victoria, the wide thoroughfare to Vauxhall Bridge and the old brick railway arches.

She sneaked a glance at her companion.

He was staring out of the other window, face set and grim.

Should I say something? But what...?

They sped along in silence and it was only when they neared Clapham and the driver needed directions that Cassie spoke. As they pulled into her road, Rowlands told him where to stop and she got out while he paid.

'Thank you,' she said. 'And thanks for bringing me home though it really wasn't necessary. I can manage now.'

He was scanning the parked cars, not listening to her. A Ford Fiesta parked at the kerb about twenty feet away flashed its headlights and Rowlands acknowledged the signal with a wave. It was her shadow.

'I'd offer you a coffee but it's late and we'll have another long day tomorrow,' she said as the policeman opened the gate to the little front garden of her building. 'My alarm hasn't been tripped, I've been checking–'

'No coffee, thank you, but I'll check the place. Then go.'

'It's–'

'Going to happen. Then you'll be rid of me.'

She turned the key in the lock and switched on the hall light, clicking off the alarm and greeting a sleepy-looking Spiggott who was trundling into the hall. Rowlands closed the front door behind them and immediately went into the living room. Going through to the kitchen, legs entwined by the cat, she flicked on the lights. All was normal inside and outside the light showed an empty garden.

'Other bedroom.' Rowlands walked past and opened the furthest door, switching on the light. 'All OK,' his voice was without inflection. 'See you at the Yard tomorrow morning. Goodnight.'

'I'll let you out.' She hurried towards the front door but he was already there. 'Goodnight.'

With a slight wave towards the Fiesta he stalked away in the direction of the Common and the station.

Cassie closed the front door, locked and bolted it, then leaned back against it.

What just happened?

He was looking out for her. Making sure she was safe. He was a gentle, decent man.

It's my fault.

What had he said? That I was behaving as if he had done something wrong? But he's done everything right!

Her world was coming loose from its moorings. People who believed that the Black Death had returned to the streets were attacking ambulances, the young and vulnerable were being abused and killed, her own home wasn't a safe place anymore and the press was at her heels. But it was manageable, somehow, if Andrew Rowlands was at her side. She needed things to be right between them.

I need him to think well of me. I need... what do I need?

'Oh Spig,' she said, picking up the cat. 'I've put my foot in it. Again. You'd think I'd have learned by now.'

SATURDAY

◊ FORTY

She was still unsettled the following morning, her dreams haunted by Andrew's face, jaw tight and lips pressed thin, then the neutral professional expression she knew he adopted when he wanted to keep his thoughts and feelings hidden. This blended into visions of the Tyburn, the secret river with its clandestine entries and exits.

She went into New Scotland Yard determined to make things right with him.

When she found him he was subdued, perched on a desk and staring at the whiteboard in the empty incident room. Concentrate on the case. Maybe that was the way to cheer him up, to return to their easy camaraderie.

'Did we find anyone who saw the comings and goings in North Audley Street?

'No.'

'Silana was abducted in the early evening and woke up there later. It can't have been that late. So how could an unconscious woman have been carried inside without someone noticing?'

'But no one did.'

'And no one saw anyone entering or leaving the Woodstock Street entrance to where Tadeusz was found, either.'

'Cassie, I think I know where you're going. What if the way in is from the underground river?'

'Exactly. It runs beneath or close to both places, so don't you think it's possible that they are using the river as a means of moving around London? It might explain why no one sees them.'

'Maybe we don't have any eyewitnesses because they took care not to be seen.' He leaned back and folded his arms. 'You've been along the Tyburn, it's not an ideal way of getting around, especially if this is organised crime selling services. Their clients wouldn't relish a trip through the sewers. Also, we know they used the external entrance at North Audley Street, we found the footprint in the passageway leading to it.'

'OK, so, maybe they go in and out from street level,' Cassie said. 'But the Tyburn would still be useful when transporting a body, whether unconscious or dead.'

The inspector sighed.

'Two of our locations – London Road Depot and Golden Square – are nowhere near the Tyburn.'

'Yes, that stymied me for a while. But neither place was the site of one of the staged 'events'. Silana was placed in Golden Square deliberately and London Road is on José's way home. I think the Tyburn is linked to their regular activities, the 'events'. If I'm right and it is the Tyburn, we can discount large swathes of central London when trying to identify the next possible location they might use.'

'If you're right. We don't know that. We don't even know what José was doing at London Road.'

'And we don't know why he was carrying my pass.' Cassie drew breath.

'No, but we will find out.' Rowlands was watching her intently. 'Have you seen the newspapers this morning?'

'No, I avoided them.'

'Good,' he said, his face grim. 'Avoid looking at social media too.'

'Anyway, I've been thinking about the passes,' she said. 'They're useless to access the Palace but they could still allow freedom of movement once inside. Someone could enter with a visitor's pass, but those passes are distinctive, they would immediately identify their wearers as being in the wrong place if they strayed from the public rooms.'

The policeman hesitated, unfolding his arms.

'So you're saying that, once inside, they switch from the visitors' passes to those permanent access passes which were stolen. Then they can roam as freely as they wish in the private sections of the palace. Wouldn't the passes be checked?'

'In some parts of the palace, yes, and scanned too, but in other parts their passes would only be looked at from a distance. There's a reliance on self-policing, people spotting strangers and challenging them. '

'I'm glad I don't have to worry about the security of the place,' he said, eyebrows raised.

'So, I was thinking... the Palace might be a potential location for an 'event'. Think of how exotic and attractive that would be to these people.'

'Cassie, if your theory about the passes is correct, it's far more likely that they will be used to steal or spy. Think of how much money political secrets could be sold for.'

'Maybe,' Cassie said, temporarily deflated. 'Though most MPs are based in Portcullis House now not the old Palace building, so there are fewer to spy on and less to steal. But to stage an event in the Palace, what a demonstration of their power that would be. And power is what this is about.'

'Hm... rape and murder in the Palace of Westminster.' His lips crinkled and he frowned.

'We've already made the link between Westminster and rape and murder. That happened when we made the connection between Tadeusz' body and José's, killed in exactly the same way. Ordinarily, José's death would have been an isolated incident, a few missing passes wouldn't be linked to multiple rape and murder.' She paused for breath. 'Except that we found Tadeusz and made the link.'

'There is a logic to it, I'll admit,' Rowlands said. 'But there must be hundreds of other possible places they could use.'

'We need to identify other suitable sites close to the course of the Tyburn, which also have access from street level. There may not be as many as you think, I'll get Siobhan to do some more research.' She hesitated. 'But I'd like to talk to Jack about this idea.'

'*If* they're using the Tyburn,' he said. 'We can't be sure of that. And without more to go on involving Jack would be premature.'

Damn.

The inspector returned to scrutinizing the whiteboard in silence.

Don't get annoyed. Apologise. Do it now.

'Andrew, I'm sorry about last night,' Cassie said in a rush. She stepped nearer to him. 'It was my fault. I'm horrible sometimes, thoughtless and inconsiderate. Do you forgive me? Please.'

He looked at her unmoving.

'I – I feel awful about it.' She looked up at him, mock-pleading. She could win him round, she was sure. He wouldn't reject her appeal. 'Please forgive me?'

Then his mouth twitched. There were laugh lines in his skin.

'Andrew?'

His lazy smile appeared. She could smell the scent of him, clean and fresh.

'Though don't tell anyone about me batting my eyelashes.'

'Is that what you're doing? I wasn't at all sure.' His eyes were a smoky grey, the pupils wide as he looked down at her. He wasn't so much taller.

Cassie became acutely aware of how physically close to him she was and how much she wanted to touch him. She stepped away with an embarrassed laugh.

Then Rowlands' face grew serious. 'Cassie, have you agreed to meet Lawrence Delahaye?'

Instantly, her hackles rose.

Damn the man, just when things are getting better.

'Yes. What of it?'

'You mustn't go. It's not appropriate.'

'I'm going, Andrew, I'm going to have dinner with him tonight, in a public place. It's only dinner.'

'That's not what worries me.'

'So what does?'

'Can't you see that there's something strange in this sudden interest in you?'

'You mean how could a man like that possibly be interested in a woman like me.'

'That is not what I meant at all.' He stood. 'You're putting words into my mouth that I didn't, that I wouldn't ever, say, even if it was true, which it isn't.'

She was about to blaze at him, but she stopped herself.

You've asked yourself the same question.

And they were arguing again, the last thing she wanted.

There was a knock at the door.

'Detective Inspector Rowlands?' A young man poked his head inside. He wasn't wearing a police uniform.

'Yes,' the policeman snapped.

'I'm from Press Office. Mr Edgerley said that you'd help us prepare lines to take for the Sundays. Also, I understand that you and Ms Fortune were accosted by some press people yesterday. We might seek an advisory notice, for the civilian at least. But we need a statement.'

Rowlands pressed his lips together, his mouth became a thin line.

'When?'

'Um, now, sir, if you're free,' the young man suggested tentatively.

'Very well. I'll come down in a few minutes.'

'So I'm a civilian,' Cassie said after the young man had left.

'He just means not a police officer.'

'I know, Andrew, I'm fine with it, please.'

He looked so tired, the lazy smile had disappeared. Dealing with the press was obviously not something he enjoyed. How could she make things better for him? Not for the first time, she wanted to hold and comfort him.

'This is damned annoying, Cassie. Daljit has a lead on the shoeprint, a Jermyn Street cobblers – I was going to accompany her. Will you go instead?'

'Of course. Anything.'

Even accompanying the prickly serjeant.

For a moment he looked at her. She thought he was going to ask again that she not see Lawrence Delahaye, but he said nothing.

'See you later.'

◊ FORTY ONE

Rickerman's of Jermyn Street had an old-fashioned shop bell, which rang as they entered. It also had the unmistakable air of serving the privileged and wealthy. Elegant footwear was displayed on stands or within vitrines.

A man came from behind a deep purple curtain to stand behind the counter. Middle-aged, pink-cheeked and plump, he wore a waistcoat with his pinstriped suit. He held his hands together at his waist and smiled.

'How may I assist you?'

The serjeant produced her warrant card.

'Oh.' The hands fell to his sides.

'This is a cast of one of your shoes,' the serjeant said. 'We are trying to trace its owner in connection with a crime. Fortunately for us your shoes carry a distinctive maker's mark. I understand they are unique?'

'That's correct.' The man sniffed and took the plaster cast. 'But this cast isn't of a shoe, it's of a shoe sole.'

'So?'

'We keep records of all our shoes, many of our customers return again and again, but a sole...'

Not the lucky break then?

'Though our cobblers might be able to tell what type it is and how often that type is used. They might be able to link it to shoes made with it.'

'Can you ask them to look at it please?' the serjeant requested.

The man nodded but did not move.

'We'll wait.'

Pursing his lips, the man retreated behind the curtain.

Cassie looked around the shop. Gentlemen's shoes of shiny leather, with hand stitching and brass buckles, sat on stands. None had prices attached. If you had to ask the price, she thought, you probably couldn't afford them.

A door at the back of the shop opened and a round shouldered, bespectacled man entered. He looked long past retirement age and wore braces over a striped shirt with baggy trousers and a woollen cardigan.

'You're looking for the owner of the shoe with this sole?' he said. 'I can usually track down an owner, I've been making shoes since I was fourteen years old.' The man held up the cast. 'This is a sole from a right shoe.'

Cassie peered at the cast.

'See this rim, it's double overstitched, which means it's probably our Hunter range. The manager can look up the customers who have purchased them. We make about fifty pairs for each size,' he said. 'Many of those will be bespoke and sold to regular customers. The Hunter is a new range, only introduced six months ago, so it's not become established yet.'

'Thank you, that's really helpful,' the serjeant said, taking back the cast. 'If we could have a word with -'

The pink-cheeked man reappeared as if by magic.

'Yes?'

'Names and addresses of people who have bought shoes from your Hunter range, please.'

'I don't know if...'

'Or we can get a warrant and publicise the fact?'

'It'll take me time to fish out all the records. Where do I send them?'

The serjeant handed him a card. 'Fax through a list with names and addresses. Thank you.'

The bell jangled as they left the shop.

'Not enthusiastic to help,' Cassie said.

'They want to protect their clients but I'll have someone chase them if they don't comply. Are you coming back to the Yard?'

'Andrew and I are due at the Palace in an hour,' Cassie replied. 'I thought I'd walk across St James's Park, if that's OK with you.'

'Fine. But... Cassie, are you OK?'

'Yes, why do you ask?'

'You seem...distracted.' The serjeant compressed her lips and frowned. 'The boss is too.' She shot an anxious glance in Cassie's direction but said no more.

'I'm fine,' Cassie said.

Except that I'm not.

'See you later.' With a wave, she strode off southwards.

◊ FORTY TWO

Cassie wanted time to think. The park had always been a calm place for her, somewhere tranquil in the mornings before the tourists arrived, or at dusk. She would go there when she was up from Cheltenham, to watch the birds and get away from the world of Intelligence.

Into St James Square. This was formal club land, the Naval and Military, the East India, Chatham House, in their elegant classical stucco or black-bricked Georgian buildings. Much larger establishments than the one she had visited on Thursday and might visit again tonight.

Or not.

She could cancel, maybe she should. The Serious Fraud Office didn't pursue minor infringements, though they might find nothing.

Andrew's concern about her seeing Lawrence Delahaye was genuine, she had no doubt of that and she had come to trust his judgement. She wasn't sure her own was as dependable, especially in relation to Delahaye. Yet, as she had said to Andrew, they would be in a place with other people, what could happen and, anyway, who would know or care?

Then there were her feelings about Andrew.

Never get involved with colleagues.

But it was too late. She was much too attracted to him. And he was right, the date wasn't what she should do in the middle of a case.

I'll cancel.

Feeling better that she had made a decision, she walked down Waterloo Place. Across the Mall was the park, with its lakes and ponds once fed by the waters of the River Tyburn. There was no escaping that dark river.

Down the steps and into the park. But it wasn't quiet. Helicopter blades whirred overhead and there were distant sirens. She could hear the noise of large numbers of people, though she could see only a few tourists. What was going on?

Her phone rang.

'Hello.'

'It's me. Where are you? Daljit says she left you in Jermyn Street.'

'Yes, I walked down to the park.'

'There's a demonstration in Whitehall and there might be trouble. The plague truthers are in the Square and a rent-a-mob has shown up. Come back here. We'll go in the van with the riot police.'

'OK. I'll go through Admiralty House.'

Her phone went dead.

Cassie began crossing Horse Guards Parade to enter Admiralty House by the rear doors. Tourists wandered on the rectangular marching ground. Through the arches on the far side she saw chanting marchers slowly processing down Whitehall, shepherded by police, on horseback and on foot.

What the hell's that?

The high, whinnying sound of a horse in pain. People were edging towards the park, parents called their children, anxiety in their voices. There was shouting and yelling and a group of a dozen protesters ran on to the parade ground. For a moment, they halted.

'Eh, that's her! I seen her online, she's one of them. The plague pit woman.' A man shouted and the men hastened her way, their boots crunching the cinder surface underfoot.

Cassie quickened her stride. The creamy-yellow walls of Admiralty

House were fifty yards away and the men were between her and them. Two of them wore hi-vis jackets, but they didn't look like stewards. One was filming her on his phone. All had determined and angry expressions.

Keep walking.

'Why can't people get medicines, eh?' A heavy-set man yelled at her as he stepped into her path. His aggression was palpable, violence very close to the surface. She veered around him, saying 'excuse me.' The others surrounded her, shouting questions as they walked.

'How many are already dead?' She felt spittle fleck her arm and fought the urge to wipe it away.

'Why are you all lying? Fucking liar!' This straight into her face.

'No one is lying,' she said, fighting to keep her voice from quivering.

Twenty yards.

'What about the murders?' A younger man jostled forward, snarling. 'Why weren't we told?'

Don't antagonise them.

She cast her eyes down.

Ten.

'People like you should be strung up,' a man in a baseball cap sneered.

'I'd fuck 'er first,' another voice said and there was laughter.

She pushed through the doors, which swung closed behind her.

At last.

Chants of 'Scum! Scum! Scum!' followed her but the men didn't enter. She fumbled in her bag for a tissue and rubbed at her arm.

Through the turnstiles, along the wide corridor, up a couple of steps; she got as far as the front reception but her legs would carry her no further. She collapsed on to one of the reception sofas, trembling. Eyes closed, hot tears spilled on to her cheeks.

'Cassie, Cass.' A voice broke into her misery.

It was the inspector, he was crouching in front of her. He took her hands in his.

'Oh Andrew, it was so...'

'I'm sure it was. What happened?'

'A gang of thugs threatened me. It was horrible. I'm not hurt, just upset. I feel dirtied, besmirched. I've never been harassed like that before.'

Yet it must happen to women all the time in lots of places in the world.

She wiped away the tears and attempted a smile. 'I'll just need a minute.'

'Take as much time as you like.' He shifted position to perch next to her on the arm of the sofa but kept his hold of one of her hands. 'We'll identify them later.'

'One of them was filming, there might be something online.'

'Cassandra?' It was Sir Terence, the Permanent Secretary. He looked from Cassie to the inspector and back to Cassie. Rowlands' fingers tightened on hers, then let go.

What was he doing here? Of course, his office was here.

'Sir Terence.' She struggled to her feet.

'And you are?'

'Detective Inspector Andrew Rowlands.'

'Ah.' His glance flicked to Cassie. 'You look very pale. Are you OK?'

'Yes, I was on Horse Guards just now, when--.'

'She was accosted by some thugs,' the policeman said.

'I see,' Sir Terence's voice softened. 'Maybe you should stay here until you feel better.'

Don't show weakness.

'No,' she said, decisively. 'I'm OK now.' She gathered up her bag.

'As you wish,' the Permanent Secretary said and began to walk away. 'I'll leave you to get on with it. Goodbye Inspector.'

Cassie watched his retreating back. She took a deep breath and set her jaw. She had diazepam at home, left over from the end of her time at GCHQ, when life had been a waking nightmare. She would take some later. It would calm her down, do the trick.

'We can go now,' she said with icy calmness to Rowlands. He seemed about to demur. 'I'll be OK, really.'

She didn't wait for his response but walked out of the reception.

◊ FORTY THREE

'Good God, it goes on for... how long does it go on for?' Rowlands peered into the dimly lit expanse before them.

'Almost the length of the building,' Jack replied, smiling. 'Or Barry's new-build anyway.'

Rowlands looked at Cassie.

'Sir Charles Barry designed and built the current Palace of Westminster in 1836,' she said. 'The previous Houses of Parliament had burned down and there was a big architectural competition to build the new one. Think of it as the Thames Estates of its day.'

The inspector smiled. He seemed to enjoy her explanations now. Since the incident in Horse Guards, he had rarely left her side. She felt safe when he was there.

'And the pipes,' the policeman asked. 'What are they all for?'

Stretching away into the distance were pipes. Old, encrusted, heavy ceramic, flecked and mottled metal and even some made of plastic.

'I'm not sure anyone knows,' Jack chuckled.

'Are you serious?'

'Not really. The Craft Team knows about ninety per cent of it. The pipes carry water and heating, but the system has never been fully overhauled and replaced, only added to over the years. There are probably enough pipes for three heating and water systems.'

'What about links to the sewers?' Rowlands asked. 'We were told one runs close by.'

'Yes, but the connecting tunnel is micro-grilled, alarmed and checked regularly. There's no way into the Palace that way.'

'So, where does the Craft Team hang out?' Cassie asked.

'This way,' Jack reached for the light switch and striplights flickered into life all along the ceiling. It became apparent that the long space was irregularly intersected by bunker-like structures made of reinforced concrete and brick. 'Follow me and mind where you step.'

Cassie concentrated on navigating through the maze of puddles and pipes.

'They can be a touchy lot,' Jack said as they approached one bunker. 'Leave the introductions to me.' He rapped hard on a metal door, waited for several heartbeats then opened it.

'Anybody home?'

Wow.

Inside its concrete shell, the place resembled a Piccadilly clubroom. The walls were oak panelled, elaborate fretwork covered unsightly pipework and even the ceiling had plasterwork cornicing. Without natural daylight, brass hanging lamps lit the space and large armchairs and sofas, in worn but still fine leather, made it comfortable.

Two battered but elegant desks stood against one wall, pigeon hole wall racks above them. At a captain's chair an overall-wearing young man was using an antique PC. Cassie couldn't see any cabling and wondered if the Craft Team had even managed to fix the notoriously bad Palace wifi. Technology here always breaking down.

At the far end of the room a carved wooden screen hid what might have been a kitchen.

'Hello, Jack. Has it all settled down out there now?' An older man wearing a similar overall appeared from behind the screen. 'Brew?' He handed mugs to two colleagues sitting on the sofas.

'No thanks, Norm. I've brought you some visitors. This is Detective Inspector Andrew Rowlands. He's investigating the murder of José O.'

The men shifted in their seats murmuring and the young man at the PC came over to join them, attentive and alert. Cassie sensed that this was a canny group.

'How can we help?' the young man asked. 'José was a good mate.'

They would be about the same age.

'This is Gary,' Norm introduced him and indicated the others. 'Brian and Raj.'

'My friend Cassie,' Jack replied.

'Sit down, sit down,' Norm said. 'Can I get you anything?'

Cassie shook her head as she and Rowlands sat on one of the low sofas. Jack remained standing.

'What d'you want to know? It was a real tragedy, him being killed. What's Iñes going to do now?'

'She's going back to Spain,' Cassie replied.

'He had a real way with those old pipes,' said Brian, the man nearest to them. 'I'd hammer away at the valves to force them loose but José seemed to know how to make them turn.'

'Was José his usual self recently?' Rowlands sat forwards his elbows resting on his knees. 'Did he exhibit any signs that he was worried or frightened?'

The men exchanged looks.

'Aye, he was worried about money,' Norm said. 'What new father wouldn't be.'

Cassie observed them, they were watchful. This wasn't all there was to it.

'We heard that the police thought he'd been stealing,' Brian said. 'We didn't believe it.'

'Items went missing,' Cassie said. 'My own access pass amongst them.' *That's a surprise to them.*

'You understand that it raises the question of who wants Palace of Westminster passes, possibly terrorist involvement. So we have to find out what's going on.'

'As well as who killed José,' Rowlands added.

Raj grimaced and Norm took a sip from his mug.

'We wondered,' the older man said. 'Maybe he had been helping himself to some bits and pieces, old Palace furniture, that sort of thing. Stuff nobody wanted. Doing it up and flogging it as souvenirs.'

'I didn't think that,' Gary said. 'If you ask me, it's that old squaddie and the woman who come and dole out the work.'

'Why do you say that?' The inspector's voice was neutral.

'It was the woman José always dealt with until a couple of weeks ago,' Gary said. 'Then it was the man he had to see.'

'Do you know why?'

Gary shook his head. 'But they've got some sort of scam, those two.'

'Like what?' the inspector asked, but Gary shrugged.

'And your other theory,' he addressed the others. 'Did you ever find any old Palace items went missing?'

'No,' said Norm.

'What about the stuff in the old kitchens?' Raj asked Norm.

'Nothing left,' Norm replied.

'Kitchens?' Cassie asked.

'The kitchens off the old Speaker's Dining Room,' Norm explained. 'Jose had been working there, a few weeks ago, checking the old pipework.'

'There are so many leaks, we don't know where they all come from,' Raj chuckled.

'So José had been asked to check the old kitchen pipework?' Rowlands asked.

'No, actually,' Norm said. 'It was something he decided to do himself. He knew all the ins and outs of the Palace. He had to; there's old pipes everywhere. He was always checking things, to make sure the structure wasn't compromised by water. He was conscientious like that.'

'One of the CSL directors told us there *was* work scheduled for the Chapel and kitchens,' Jack said. 'Though I couldn't find any paperwork. Are you saying there isn't?'

'Not as I know,' Norm answered. 'Though there are barriers up. Perhaps CSL jumped the gun?'

'Hmm... maybe.' Jack pursed his lips.

'Where are the kitchens?' Cassie asked.

'Off the chapel. They're empty now, since the chapel's being used again,' said Norm.

'The only chapel I know of in the Palace is St Mary Undercroft,' Cassie said.

'That's right. It used to be the Speaker's Dining Room, back in the day.'

'That's partially underground,' Cassie said. 'And the kitchens are still there?'

'Yes, though nobody uses them. Why?'

'Just a thought.' She looked at Rowlands.

'Was José working extra shifts?' he asked.

'He was already working as many as he could,' Brian said, laughing. 'He'd be here long after we left. He always wanted the emergency shift so as to earn more. And he moonlighted as a magician at the weekends, you know, kid's parties, that sort of thing.'

'He was good at it, he did our Asha's eldest,' Raj said. 'Had the kids entranced, making things disappear before their eyes. Then ta-da! Reappear in their ears. Well worth the money.'

'There'll be a collection for Inés and the baby,' Norm said.

'I'll look out for it,' Jack said. 'Well, we've taken up enough of your time.'

Cassie rose, as did Andrew.

'Thanks for your help,' he said.

'Find who killed him,' Gary said. 'He was a good mate.'

'We'll try.'

As they walked back to the stairwell, Cassie's mind raced. José's magician's skills would have helped him steal the passes and other items, but, more importantly, he had knowledge about the Palace to sell. Maybe he was selling information, not passes? Or both?

'He was a popular chap, José,' Jack said as they emerged from the stairwell into the daylight of a corridor with windows. 'The Craft Team doesn't take to everyone; they're a law unto themselves.'

'José knew the nooks and crannies of this place,' Cassie said. 'That information might have been worth money, though it could have got him killed.'

'It's possible,' Rowlands said.

'Would you take us to the old kitchens now?'

She shot a meaningful look at Rowlands. His returning glance told her that he understood. Maybe now she could raise her theory with Jack?

'Sure, follow me,' Jack said. 'Then you can explain to me what you're both thinking.'

◊ FORTY FOUR

Cassie and Andrew followed Jack down the shallow stone steps from St Stephen's Porch into Westminster Hall. The oldest part of the Palace, the Hall had a grisly history and late at night it was an eerie place, but now it was airy and light filled. She could hear megaphones and shouts from Parliament Square; the police were still dispersing the demonstrators.

The entrance to St Mary Undercroft chapel was on the right, down another flight of stone steps. A red and white stretchable barrier stood at the top of the stairs, with a Works in Progress sign hanging from it. Muttering, Jack moved the whole thing aside. At the foot of the stairs he unlocked the heavy wooden door and switched on the lights as he entered. A dull sheen reflected from gilded surfaces, of the painted wooden ceiling vaulting and the elaborate altar reredos. Lines of chairs stood either side of a central aisle leading to an altar. They walked across a patterned tiled floor to a recessed door on the left.

'These are the old kitchens,' Jack said, as he ripped down the black and yellow safety tape which barred the entrance.

A ceiling striplight flickered into life to reveal a small room. Heavy black iron hooks hung down from a stone ceiling above a large stone butchers' block. An open fireplace in one wall held a mixture of rusting kitchen implements.

This place could be made to seem very scary indeed.

'The fittings were stripped out,' Jack said. 'No one comes here now.'

Cassie exchanged looks with Rowlands. He said nothing.

Assume silence means consent. He can always disagree with me.

'Jack,' she began. 'We think we're on the trail of the criminals who killed José. We believe it's a highly organised crime ring. They abduct young people, terrify, rape and then murder them to cover up the crimes.'

Jack's eyebrows rose. 'I see. But what has that got to do with me and the Palace?'

'They frequently operate underground using unusual locations as stages on which to perform their crimes. They like to use exotic or outré settings, so the Palace of Westminster would appeal, maximising the transgression. It's possible that José was selling information about hidden places in the Palace, like this one, as suitable sites for their activity. You see, I think that the stolen passes aren't for access at all, but to allow freedom of movement once inside the Palace, once beyond the public rooms.'

'So, if you're correct, the participants will access the Palace in the usual way?' Jack nodded slowly.

'Yes,' Cassie said. 'They could enter either as guests or as tourists.'

She paused to allow the security man to absorb all the information.

'We know they're especially active now, we've found three bodies in four days. Given that building works will close the Palace completely when Parliament rises, any crime would have to happen before then,' Cassie said.

Jack drew his brows together. 'If it's to happen here, do you know *when* exactly? Not tonight?' He led them from the room and locked the door, and that to the Chapel, behind them as they left.

'We don't know,' Cassie replied. 'But I doubt it. The Palace is too empty; there are as many doorkeepers and security people as MPs and visitors.'

'Are you sure about this?'

'No, at the moment, it's only a theory,' Rowlands said. 'But you need to know that we might request permission to observe and monitor.'

'The Speaker doesn't allow surveillance,' Jack said, then paused. 'That's not to say that it doesn't go on. But it's unofficial. Only the Speaker and Black Rod can officially call in the police.'

Cassie waited. They needed Jack's help. They couldn't do this without him. He began to walk back and forth, his footsteps ringing on the flagstones.

'I can't allow any external Metropolitan police surveillance,' he said, eventually. 'But I can put the Palace security team on high alert, checking all passes so as to expel people who shouldn't be here, or who are in the wrong place. I'll arrange to station a couple of police outside the control room door, ready to be sent to intercept or apprehend. Without more concrete evidence that's all I can do.'

'Thanks, Jack,' Cassie said.

'Members will return tomorrow and the Houses will sit on Monday,' he said. 'From Tuesday onwards the Palace will be closed. No visitors, no nothing. So that leaves Sunday and Monday nights for any crimes to be committed, assuming it's a night-time activity?'

The inspector nodded.

'This is probably our last chance to catch them, at least for a while,' Cassie said.

'There is no CCTV down there,' Jack said, as they walked back up to Westminster Hall. 'The nearest you'll get is here.' He pointed to a camera high on the wall.

'I know,' Cassie answered.

'I'll check the book, see who's hosting dinners and if there are any private events scheduled. Then I'll be in touch.'

'Thank you,' the inspector said. 'We're following up what leads we have...'

'And if our suspicions firm up we'll be in contact,' Cassie said. 'Thanks again, Jack.'

'Thank me if it all works out,' Jack said with a wry grin. 'Now I'd best get back to my desk.'

Cassie felt a surge of gratitude as Jack waved goodbye. He could get into a lot of trouble for helping them. She felt a flush of warmth, thankful that he trusted her and her judgement enough to do this.

'Well, if they do try to use the Palace at least we'll be waiting for them,' she said to the inspector. But Rowlands was studying her, a pinched expression on his face.

'Are you still set on meeting with Delahaye?' he said.

Damn you! I won't let you pressure me into refusing.

'You don't have to listen to me, maybe I can't be objective, but use your own brain. There is something not right about this, Cassie.'

'I'm going,' she found herself saying, despite her earlier decision to cancel. 'Andrew, you're worrying too much. It's dinner, that's all.'

'Wait, Cassie!'

She came to a halt.

'Think about this, please,' the policeman said. 'It's completely inappropriate. You need to decide what you want, Cassie. Do you really want your career back? This isn't the way to get it.'

What nonsense was this?

'Don't worry. It'll be fine.' She resumed her path, raising her hand in a perfunctory wave. 'I'll see you tomorrow.'

◊ FORTY FIVE

Cassie's heels beat a rhythm on the pavement of Queen Anne's Gate. However confident she had sounded when speaking with Andrew, she was much less so now. At least she no longer felt panicked, the pills had seen to that.

She had dressed with care. It had been a long time since she had been on a proper date. Her hair was twisted up into a chignon and she wore a closely fitted silk dress with a wide neckline, a pale wool wrap and heels. She checked her watch. It was almost eight. Just ahead was the door to the club; she wouldn't be late.

'Mr Delahaye is waiting in the garden room,' the doorman said as he let her in.

Thanking him, she walked through the hall, glancing into the bar room as she passed its open door. Frank Cairns stood at the bar, holding out a large tumbler full of golden liquid to a companion. His eyebrows rose as he spotted Cassie, a surprised expression quickly replaced by a very appreciative look and his lopsided smile. His companion turned to follow his gaze. It was William Priess.

What are they doing here?

But she was past the door and there was Lawrence Delahaye, sitting on the sofa in the room she had visited on Thursday, looking out into the dusk.

'Lawrence.'

He started and rose. She seemed to have interrupted his thoughts. The pale summer suit set off his dark looks, his louche elegance seemed effortless.

'You look stunning,' he said, coming towards her. 'I was worried that work might intrude again. Here, I ordered the champagne,' he said, as he ushered her to the sofa. 'You said you enjoyed it.'

'Thank you,' she said. 'You're spoiling me again.'

'Why not? I like doing it and if it gives you pleasure...' he shrugged and smiled.

Be careful, don't drink too much, remember the diazepam.

They sat.

'So tell me about your day.'

Mustn't speak about the case.

'I was caught up in the disturbances on Whitehall,' she said. 'It was unpleasant, horrible actually.'

'Oh Cassandra,' he sat forward. 'How distressing.'

'It was. They, the thugs, seemed to be targeting me.'

'What!' Lawrence looked horrified. 'How? No, don't think about it, please, you're safe here. I would never allow any harm to come to you.'

'Sir, Madam.' The headwaiter interrupted. 'Your table is ready.'

Lawrence led her, hand in the curve of her back, through double doors to a dining room containing a table set for two. Candlelight reflected from cutlery and glassware, and bottles of wine and decanters sat on the serving table opposite the garden terrace doors.

This isn't a public place.

She hesitated for a second.

'Could we have the lights up, please,' Lawrence instructed as he drew out a chair for her. 'I'd like to be able to see my dining companion.'

Good.

'Of course, sir,' the waiter replied. He altered the light setting and refilled their glasses with champagne. Shall I serve the first course, sir?'

Lawrence nodded. 'I've ordered the tasting menu, I hope that's OK? The chef here is very good.'

'I'm sure it'll be excellent.'

For a while they ate, discussing the food, the evening, the summer. Lawrence shared her love of opera, she discovered. He could afford to attend performances she could only dream of. He claimed not to have time to read much but seemed to know all the latest books, indeed, to have read many of those which she had read. Cassie warmed to him, more and more. The first course had been cleared and the burgundy poured for the next course when the subject of the police case arose.

'So are you working on the Plague Murders? I saw the media report.'

'Is that what they're calling them now?' she replied. 'Only peripherally, I have a watching brief from the parliamentary perspective.'

'I don't understand why Parliament is involved at all?'

'One of the victims worked at the Palace of Westminster,' she said.

'So,' he said, frowning. 'The victims' places of work. Where did the others work?'

'One worked on the Eurostar, one in the Norman Scott buildings next to the Thames.'

What harm can telling him do?

'Do you have any suspects?'

'There are a number of people of interest,' she said. 'Parliamentarians too.'

'It's intriguing. Who? I'm curious,' he said.

Change the subject, you've said too much already.

'People are. It's human nature I suppose and these days everyone who watches TV thinks they can be a detective,' she smiled. 'Not something that troubles hedge fund managers, I'd guess. They're recognised masters of dark financial arts which ordinary humans don't understand.'

'It isn't hard to understand,' he said. 'Though it's somewhat harder to do. But tell me, is it Lords or Commons?'

'Both actually.'

'Scandalous! Who?'

The conversation was interrupted as the waiter brought in the filet mignon and accompaniments.

You can't tell him!

'Tell me about your dark financial arts,' Cassie said.

Lawrence smiled and complied.

'One has to know the markets intimately. I make money on currency fluctuations, options, derivatives, any market that changes, anything mutable. And yes, that includes change following disasters - earthquakes, tsunamis, economic meltdowns – which is why we've been called disaster capitalists.'

'Making money from people's misery?' She looked at him across the rim of her glass.

'Making money from the markets, not misery,' he countered. 'I make a lot of it, but I reinvest a lot too. Look at the bigger picture. Politicians have been failing for years and corruption is rife, so it's the charitable foundations that pick up the slack, funded by people like Bill Gates, by people like me.'

'Big international corporations don't pay much tax despite making huge profits,' she said. 'If they paid more there would be less need for your charity.'

'Barton Investments doesn't either, but that's perfectly legal and it pays for all this.'

'I'm sorry, that was a very gentle – and just – rebuke,' she said. 'I am enjoying your hospitality, I shouldn't criticise.'

'I would not rebuke you, Cassandra,' he said, laying down his knife and fork and resting his hand half way across the table. He looked so earnest. It made her feel like she could ask for anything and, if he could, he would give it to her. She reached across and, for a brief moment, rested her hand on his.

'I meant what I said the other day about looking for someone to help with this, to make real change for the poorest and most disadvantaged. That's the great thing about being rich. It means I have the chance to make a positive difference in the world. I can make changes that governments struggle with. What if you had all that money? What would you do with it?'

Cassie considered. Once she had been able, in a small way, to make a difference. It had its frustrations – she wasn't the only person with an agenda – but it had been exciting to have that power. How much more exhilarating to have the freedom to do whatever she wanted.

'I'd buy influence and use it in all sorts of ways.' She ticked them off on her fingers. 'First, I'd silence the opposition, buying their support or encouraging them to change in other ways. I'd fund and promote those whose work I wanted to see more of and make sure people knew about their successes. I'd have the press trumpet all my aims to create a broad national consensus behind them.' She spread her palms. 'Then I wouldn't be needed. People would be elected to Parliament to do it. I'd have made myself redundant.' She stopped when she heard him quietly chuckling.

'Not ambitious then,' he said.

'Yes, but the end result would be worth it.'

It almost seemed as if he nodded in assent.

He understands.

'Any civil servant worth their salt wants to make a real impact,' she said.

'And when you really can, that feels amazing; important, powerful. It's exhilarating.'

He really understands.

Cheese and dessert followed and the conversation flowed, becoming lighter, even giddy. Cassie found herself relaxing as the evening wound on, her barriers lowered, as two like-minded people discovered more and more interests they had in common.

Lawrence did try to draw her out again about the case, but this time Cassie laughed off his questions saying, 'I'm just a civil servant, very boring. I'd much rather hear about you.'

And it was true. As Lawrence talked Cassie found she envied him, not just the big house in central London, the music, the money, but his entire life.

'Would you like coffee here?' Lawrence asked. 'Or at my place? It isn't far. Unless you want to go home, my chauffeur could take you?'

Yes. That's what I should do.

'I don't want to go home yet.' She wanted to see what his house was like.

'Would you ask Gordon to collect us please,' Lawrence asked the waiter. 'And bring the lady's wrap.'

They walked through the garden room as police sirens sounded from the direction of the park. There were still demonstrators about.

'Gordon can take you home after coffee. It's not safe. Ah, allow me.'

Lawrence took the fine wool wrap from the waiter and placed it around her shoulders. She felt his fingers brush her shoulder. His touch made her skin fizz.

'I'm glad you're coming to my home.' He smiled down at her, standing close. 'Very glad.'

◊ FORTY SIX

'Your car's here, sir,' the doorman said and opened the door.

A stately limousine stood at the curb. Lawrence offered his arm and she took it. Despite his talk of her going home, it was very clear that he hoped they would make love tonight and she wasn't at all sure that she didn't hope so too. Any qualms she had had earlier seemed far away now.

A stocky chauffeur in a grey uniform climbed from the vehicle and circled round, moving formally and precisely, to open the rear door. Just as he did so there was a flash from across the street.

'Paparazzi,' Lawrence said. 'I'm afraid it's something of a hazard if you're out with me.'

The journey was very short. Cassie had scarcely time to enjoy sinking into the soft leather seat.

'Such a beautiful car,' she said as they got out opposite Westminster School and it swished away.

'You must come to Arundel,' he said as he led her to the front door. 'I've a place on the Downs. I'm remodelling the gardens; you might enjoy helping. Gordon can drive us.'

She followed him into a hall almost as large as that of the club, with a black and white tiled floor. There were doors to right and left and a wide staircase curved upwards on the right hand wall.

'Lights,' he said and there was illumination.

Voice activated services, this house is more than it seems.

'Let me take this.' He slipped the wrap from her shoulders and draped it over the newel post, adding his jacket to it. 'Come, please.'

The sitting room had high backed chairs on either side of a marble fireplace and a long leather sofa in front of it. An elaborate brass chandelier hung from the ceiling, its light reflecting in a grand mirror set above the mantelpiece and a tall copper fireguard in the grate. It was a masculine room.

'Now, what can I get you?' Lawrence said. 'Coffee is coming. Would you like a brandy? I have some excellent Armagnac?'

'Just coffee for me, thank you,' she said. She felt too intoxicated already, with the whole evening, the champagne, the meal and, above all, with him.

There was a knock at the door and the chauffeur, now minus cap and coat, brought in a tray containing a coffee pot, cups and petit fours. He placed it on the low table.

'Thanks, you can retire now.'

Lawrence poured the coffee, bringing one of the delicate cups over, contents steaming, to place it on the mantelpiece behind her. He rested his right hand next to it and looked down into her face. 'I would rather we weren't interrupted,' he said.

She had no idea what to say in response. She expected him to lean in and kiss her but he turned away and poured himself a coffee. With his back to her he sipped it, though it was too hot to drink.

'Lawrence?'

'I am having great difficulty keeping my hands off you,' he said, turning around to look at her.

'Do you want me to go?'

'No.' He was emphatic. 'No. I most definitely don't want that. I don't want to drive you away.'

'Perhaps I had ought...' she began. He stepped very close. She could see faint six o'clock shadow on his chin and smell his skin, a dry, leathery smell. He stroked her throat and lifted her chin with his fingertips and she let him.

The kiss was slow and increasingly passionate. She felt powerful hands stroke and caress her neck and shoulders. She arched her back as his thumb raked down her spine and the reflex action made her bend into him, to feel his arousal.

Cassie was lost amid overwhelming physical sensations. It had been such a long time since she had allowed anyone to touch her at all. Now this man, who seemed to be the partner she had always imagined, was handling her body with a sureness she found undeniable. Her own astonishment immobilised her.

'So perfect,' she heard him murmur, as she felt his hand slide against the skin of her back.

She knew what it was to desire and be desired. She had loved her husband, with a natural and healthy appetite, but when her career demanded more from her she simply shifted her focus. Temporarily, she believed. But their sex life had withered and she hadn't really cared. Her libido had been tamped down, her energies redirected. Her own sensuality went unnoticed.

She was noticing it now.

If I don't stop now, this is only going to end one way.

Is this what I really want? With this man?

Then she heard her mobile ring and opened her eyes.

'Leave it.' Lawrence kissed her again, tilting her backwards as he tugged at her dress. She closed her eyes and the ringing stopped. The outside world receded. Her body had assented. She unbuckled his belt, opened his fly and slipped her hand inside to stroke and caress.

'If you do that again we won't even get to the bedroom,' he whispered into her ear.

So she did, this time watching his reaction. He gasped silently, his eyes closing, then opening full of determined desire.

'Sofa or floor?'

There was a sharp rap on the door.

'What the fuck!'

It opened a crack.

'It's the telephone sir,' said Gordon's voice. 'I'm sorry. It's the police.'

'Get rid of them, man.'

'He says he wants to speak with the lady, sir. She's not answering her mobile. He says there's a police car outside and if she doesn't answer, they'll be in here to find out why.'

'What!' He was incredulous. 'I'll sort that out...'

'No, no,' she said, grabbing his arm and clutching at her dress. 'Please, Lawrence. It'll be the case. Something's happened.'

He reeled away from her grasp, breathing heavily, from passion or anger or both she couldn't tell. But he didn't go over to the door.

'I'll come, Gordon,' she said. 'Lawrence, could you?'

He pulled up the zip on her dress. The manservant thrust a handset through the slightly open door and she took it.

'Hello.'

'We've found another crime scene. And we've got a witness.'

It was Andrew. Who else could it be?

'Who? Where?'

'Mayfair. Near the Tyburn again, maybe you were right. There's a car waiting on Great College Street. I thought you might end up there.'

How can I leave?

Lawrence was watching her closely, black eyes glittering.

'Well?'

How can I not?

'On my way.'

There was a metallic crash as the phone went dead.

'I'm sorry, Lawrence.'

He stood, arms outstretched against the mantelpiece, clenching and unclenching his right hand its knuckles bloodied. The heavy copper fireguard lay, dented, on its side.

'I'm sorry.' She went towards him. 'Something's happened, I have to go.'

'No.' He held out a raised palm to keep her away. 'Go.'

She grabbed her bag, straightened her dress and headed for the door.

He glowered at her in the mirror as she turned to say farewell. She managed an almost wordless goodbye and fled.

◊ FORTY SEVEN

There were no sirens or flashing lights from the police cars parked on Curzon Street. This wealthy neighbourhood was not to be awoken from sleep by a mere murder. Cassie stepped out of the cab outside a massive building of Portland stone, its name emblazoned around a deep niche supported by columns, the Third Church of Christ Scientist. Police tape was stretched from the railings at the side of the wide steps leading into the church across iron stairs which led down to a basement door.

She had pulled a comb through her hair and applied lipstick in the car, but she was hardly dressed for work and her shoes made her clumsy descending the stairs.

What the hell, it's a Saturday night. People go out.

Inside there was another door leading to a stone staircase which went down still further. Was she under the church now, she wondered, or the barber's shop next door? At the foot of the stairs she walked towards the usual well-lit tent, her heels tapping on the flagstone floor. The tent was set up against the wall at the far end of a subterranean room. Rowlands and DS Patel waited in front of it.

As she approached they turned. The serjeant raised an eyebrow as she looked Cassie up and down. Rowlands' face showed nothing at all.

'Is there another victim?' Cassie said.

'There was.' The inspector was curt.

Cassie followed him into the tent, which was already occupied by several other people.

'Evening.' One of them was Dr Pottinger, white coat pulled over jeans and a T-shirt. 'Out on the town, I see.'

'Thanks for coming out on a Saturday night, when we don't even have a body,' Rowlands said to the pathologist. 'But your lab is the only one likely to help. What have you got?'

'Blood, lots of it, though mostly dried. We'll test it but I'm betting it's human.'

'Why?' Cassie asked.

'Look.' The pathologist moved aside and she saw a set of heavy manacles fixed into the stone floor and another set high up in the wall. Both were encrusted with the same material.

Who had been placed in these shackles?

'Remember the Danish boy I told you about?' Rowlands mouth was pressed thin.

Cassie nodded. 'Found in the Thames?'

'That's the one. His wrists and ankles were heavily damaged.'

At least he's speaking to me in sentences now.

'I remember him too,' Pottinger said. 'This treatment would be consistent with the injuries we found. We have his DNA on record. I'll see if it's a match.'

'Thanks, Bill,' Rowlands said. 'We may have found the place he died. I'll be round tomorrow.'

The pathologist peeled off his gloves, packed up his equipment and left. Cassie and Rowlands followed him out of the tent.

'How did you find this place? You said there was a possible witness?' The inspector stepped away, ignoring her.

'Daljit,' he snapped, summoning the serjeant to his side. As he spoke quietly, she glanced in Cassie's direction.

'Cassie,' she said, coming over and drawing her beyond the lights into shadow.

'What?'

'Turn around and I'll zip you up.'

Her dress wasn't fastened properly. The tidied hair, the lipstick, had been pointless. It must have been clear to everyone what she'd been doing, including Andrew. Cassie felt her whole body flush. She put her hands to her flaming cheeks and turned her face to the wall.

'Come on, the boss is looking impatient,' the DS hissed.

There was nothing for it. She turned, raised her chin and walked back into the light.

'What is this place?' she asked. When there was no response she ploughed on. 'How did you find it? I'll bet it links with the Tyburn. Have we found any access to it?'

'Not yet. Forensics are still working,' Rowlands answered.

'Just over a week ago a rough sleeper tried to kip in the entry,' the serjeant said. 'He was rudely awoken by two people leaving the basement in the early hours of the morning. He ran away but has subsequently found that someone's after him. So now he's terrified. He told a local policeman.'

Could be useful. Just as well – I'm running out of time.

'Do we have a description?'

'Not one that tells us much: 'two men, one tall, one "Asian looking".' That's it. Our witness was half asleep and booze befuddled, though he did say one interesting thing. He thought he'd seen the tall man before.'

'We need to speak with him,' Rowlands said.

'He's in a holding cell at the Yard.'

'Sir.' It was the white-suited forensics man from the Roman baths. 'Nothing so far.'

'OK, but keep looking,' the inspector said. 'And see if you can find a way into the sewers from here.'

'I bet he won't find any evidence,' the serjeant said. 'Same as before.'

'You may be right but this time we have a witness, however confused. If he's local and has seen one of the perpetrators before that might narrow our search radius. Now, I want to check this place on our maps.'

◊ FORTY EIGHT

The incident room was empty, its warm shadows replaced by flat white light as Rowlands flicked a switch. He walked over to the whiteboard to look at George's map.

'There must be a way into the Tyburn,' Cassie said as she came to stand by his side.

'If forensics don't find anything we could ask George,' the serjeant suggested. 'He'd know.'

'Hmm.' Rowlands was tracing the Tyburn's route with his finger. It ran almost directly beneath the church in Curzon Street.

'You see,' Cassie said, vehemently. 'It *is* the Tyburn. That *has* to be the focus of our efforts.'

'OK. I'm convinced,' the inspector said. 'We should focus on the Tyburn.'

Finally.

'Our rough sleeper is a piece of luck,' the inspector continued. 'We'll speak with him tomorrow and with Bill Pottinger. It's going to be a busy Sunday. Daljit, go home and get some rest. Don't come in until tomorrow afternoon, earliest.'

'And you, boss,' the serjeant urged.

'Yes, I just want a word with Cassie first.'

Oh no, what's he going to say?

As the serjeant left she almost collided with the young man from the press office.

'Oh, you're here,' he said, as his startled gaze rested on Cassie.' I was going to leave these for you for tomorrow.' He waved a sheaf of newspapers in the inspector's direction. 'The Sundays.'

'I'll have them,' Rowlands said. The man handed them over and left.

'Didn't he want to take you through them?'

'They're hardly surprising, look.'

'Plague killer, killer plague', 'Black Death stalks the streets of London', 'Plague and corruption'. All carried headlines criticising the investigation, many focused on the police failure to protect the only witness, several called for Rowlands' dismissal. They spread them out on a desk. Cassie turned the pages over. Many papers had pictures of them both leaving the St James's pub on Friday night.

'I look like a startled rabbit,' Cassie said, pointing to a photograph in which Rowlands was sheltering her from the main pack of journalists, blocking them with his body. 'You look like my knight in shining armour.'

'Hmm,' he turned the page.

There stood Cassie in her silk dress and high heels, clinging to Lawrence Delahaye's arm in the doorway to the club.

'Plague pit civil servant with billionaire boyfriend.' The words underneath ran. 'While London echoes with the sounds of violence and the body count grows, the civil servant at the heart of the Plague Murders case dines out in an exclusive London club.'

'I...' Cassie shook her head in disbelief.

'So that was your public place,' Rowlands said. 'A private club. You know what some of those clubs are?' Hands on hips and at full height, he glared down at her.

'I expected that we would have dinner in the restaurant.' She stared forward.

'Christ, Cassie, for a clever woman you can be exceptionally stupid!'

'It's not how it looks,' she said, unconvincingly. But it was her private life. 'Anyway, what I do in my own time is my business. This is press harassment.'

'You can screw who you like, Cassie, but not a person of interest in the case you're working on, a major fraudster.'

She flinched. It was like a slap.

'I haven't – we didn't,' was all she could say, hiccupping. Her face flamed.

'Just as well, but I doubt that's enough to save you. Then you turn up half-dressed at the crime scene. Your bosses won't be happy and nor will mine. How long do you reckon you'll survive?'

What will Duncan say? And Sir Terence? Stupid, stupid, stupid!

She put her face into her hands.

I've blown it. My one chance to get my career back, to do what I love doing, to have some control.

'Go home,' his voice sounded tired. 'I'll arrange for a car to take you. I suggest that you lay low for a while. You've got a report to write.'

'I want to carry on with the case,' she said, looking up. 'To follow it through. We're getting closer.'

'Yes, we are, but I doubt either of us will see the end of it.'

'I intend to.' Her stubbornness was kicking in. 'One way or another.'

'You won't be allowed to, Cassie. Not if you want to keep your job. You were supposed to sniff out scandal, not create it.'

He was probably right. He was right. Why was he always so bloody right! But...what did he say?

'Fraudster,' she said.

'What?'

'You said Lawrence was a major fraudster. Why? What have you learned?'

'Lawrence?' An eyebrow was raised above eyes she now noticed were bloodshot.

'That's his name.'

'After you left Westminster I did some phoning around,' he said, folding his arms. 'I tracked down the man investigating Lawrence Delahaye at the Serious Fraud Office. On a Saturday night, it wasn't easy. He is of the firm opinion that your 'billionaire boyfriend' is up to his neck in fraud.'

She blinked. Her body temperature had dropped.

Somehow, this news didn't surprise her. Even at his most passionate and aroused she sensed that Lawrence was calculating. Beneath the charm, he was cold and manipulative, she understood that. She knew instinctively that part of his attraction for her was the power she had to make him stray outside his usual boundaries, to abandon his cold logic.

'I've arranged an appointment with the SFO man at nine on Monday morning,' Rowlands was saying. 'You can hear it from him, even if you don't believe me.'

'It'll be good to speak with him,' Cassie said in a contrite voice.

'Though I do believe you, Andrew, of course I do.'

But fraud wasn't rape and murder; it was white collar crime. Not that white collar crime was irrelevant; it just wasn't part of this case.

'I'll ring down for the car.'

'And Andrew, I'm sorry for turning up like that. I didn't realise...'

Again she put her hand to her flaming face. It was so embarrassing.

'OK, maybe I exaggerated,' he said. 'It wasn't that bad.'

Cassie shook her head. 'I'll go. I'll be back later, if I'm allowed.'

SUNDAY

◊ FORTY NINE

Cassie heard birdsong and the hum of traffic on the south circular by the Common. She had tossed and turned through what was left of the night, alternating between cringe-inducing shame, anger at her own stupidity and anxiety about her future.

The clock said half past nine. Feeling awful, her head fuzzy, she rose and padded through to the kitchen to feed Spiggott. On the front door mat, her Sunday newspaper carried "Plague" as its banner headline. She sat in the kitchen sipping coffee, stroking the cat and turning the pages over. Inside was the photograph of herself and Andrew beside an article on the plague scare: overextended doctors, crowded hospital Accident & Emergency departments, reduced school attendance.

Real life consequences of a media-inspired fiction.

There were the riots and demonstrations and not just in London, not just in Britain. A Belgian couple, lately returned from London, had fallen ill and were said to have contracted plague. The panic had reached Antwerp. Hysteria was spreading as surely as any virus, fuelled by social media.

She would go into the Yard later. There were things to do. The body count was rising, as the newspapers pointed out and so far, they had no idea how to stop it. But first she needed to think about her report. Parliament rose on Tuesday, it had to be completed before then and today was the obvious time to work on it. She opened her laptop.

It had been stupid to meet Lawrence in the middle of the case. Had she really only done so because Andrew had insisted otherwise, like some rebellious teenager? If the Serious Fraud Office was interested in him she should have steered well clear, regardless.

' ...then you turn up half-dressed.' She kept hearing Andrew's voice.

Stop thinking about Andrew. Try and salvage what's left of your career. Limit the damage.

She drafted an email to Sir Terence and copied it to Duncan, a report on the latest find. Sir Terence would, she assumed, summon them both, so she had to try and manage their reactions to what they would have seen in the press.

In her inbox were the results of Siobhan's research into potential locations, which lay close to the course of the Tyburn. As she scanned it she realised that there were fewer possibilities than she had thought. Cassie sent Siobhan her thanks and a jokey reminder that she shouldn't believe everything she read in the papers. Within minutes, the secretary had replied, telling Cassie not to look at social media.

Cassie resisted the urge to do so.

Now get dressed and go into New Scotland Yard.

As she rose her attention was caught by a hand waving above the garden fence. It was her neighbour's.

'Hello?' She called, going out into the small side return and garden. She stepped up on to the low wall of a raised bed and looked over the fence.

'Cassie, have you seen the people out front? The reporters and photographers?'

That's all I need.

'I haven't.'

'You can come out through here if you want.' There was a gate at the bottom of her neighbour's garden into the next street. 'Oh and this came.' She handed over a large bouquet of roses. 'The courier couldn't get through the crowd so he rang my doorbell.'

'Thank you.'

'You're a dark horse. Billionaire boyfriend, eh? And good looking. There was this too.' It was a long, slim leather box, emblazoned with a jeweller's insignia.

Uh oh.

'Thanks, I'd better go and put these in water.'

She opened the card accompanying the bouquet.

'I promised to keep you safe and I failed. I hope to make amends. L.xxx'

Apparently, he had forgiven her the abrupt departure.

The roses were beautiful, with a heady scent. Cassie opened the box and lifted out a bracelet, a band of gems caught in a silver filigree web. Sunlight was refracted through the translucent stones into a rainbow of colours on the kitchen wall.

How exquisite.

Diamonds. She had no doubt they were real. She fitted the bracelet on to her wrist and turned her hand this way and that. Diamonds and roses, more than a touch of old-fashioned romance. It was very traditional, like the sitting room, the car and the country house on the South Downs. Straight out of the how-to-be-a-millionaire manual, including Gordon the manservant, the love of opera and gardening.

Wasn't it all a little too scripted? Lawrence Delahaye was an interesting character but he would be more so, she suspected, if one could get to the real person beneath the facade. Why work so hard on the outward show of wealth when he was actually wealthy? Who was the performance for and why? She felt a shiver go up her spine.

Her telephone beeped.

A text from Lawrence.

'Have you got the flowers etc?'

Some etcetera.

'Yes, thanks,' She replied. 'Can't possibly accept bracelet.'

'Why not?' A text came back immediately. 'Disappointed if you don't.'

'Sorry, can't.'

'Damn. Why won't you let me spoil you?'

She waited but that seemed to be it. Then...

'Perhaps I should have sent a necklace? Diamonds would sit well around your lovely neck.'

She flushed, remembering the evening before, but his attentions were very flattering and the diamonds were very beautiful. It seemed so churlish to reject him.

'No. Really. Must go.'

She really couldn't accept the bracelet. It could be construed as a bribe. Reluctantly, she unclasped it and placed it back in the box. She would have to report receiving it. It would be interesting explaining that to Andrew.

Her mobile rang.

Speak of the devil.

'Cassie, I'm going to the mortuary. I thought you might want to come along,' he said.

'Yes.'

'I'll send –'

'Not to my flat, there are press people out front. Send him into Belleville Road, I'll come out through my neighbour's garden. Give me half an hour. I've only just got up.'

'OK.' There was a pause. 'Cassie, are you alright this morning? I'm afraid I didn't mince my words last night.'

'I behaved stupidly and made things more difficult with the case, so you were angry. I understand. Though you *were* horrible,' she was only half joking. 'I wasn't half dressed.'

There was silence at the other end of the telephone.

'I'm sorry. It wasn't easy, seeing you like that, looking like you were making a present of yourself to that man.'

Umpf. That was a blow to the solar plexus.

'I've just made things worse, haven't I?'

'Yep.'

'See you at the mortuary.'

◊ FIFTY

Cassie entered Westminster Mortuary for the second time within a week. She went searching for Bill Pottinger in the basement. The inspector was already there.

She had done some thinking while in the car. She would speak with Andrew Rowlands privately about the diamond bracelet before she reported receiving it. She also wanted to put him straight on a few things. Women in the 21st century wore whatever they chose and it was entirely normal to dress up to go out to dinner.

'Morning, Cassie,' the pathologist greeted her. 'Left the glad rags at home today.'

'Hello, Bill.'

'Cassie.' Rowlands nodded and thrust his hands into his trouser pockets, something she now recognised he did when he was on the defensive but didn't wish to show it.

He's waiting to feel my wrath. Good. Let him.

'I've found the DNA from the Danish boy,' Bill said. 'We'll try and match it with the blood taken from the manacles last night. But I've not been able to test yet. Our scientists have been co-opted to other diagnostic and research laboratories.' Seeing the inspector frown, the pathologist continued speaking. 'I hope I'll be able to tell you if that was where he died by tomorrow.'

Cassie felt her gorge rising. She swallowed heavily. Probably a toxic mixture of alcohol, diazepam and lack of sleep, along with her mental image of the murdered boy.

'I think I'm going to vomit.'

'There's a sink over there,' Pottinger said. 'Then use my office to have a sit down.'

Cassie hurried over to the sink but by the time she got there her nausea had passed. She went through to the small room used as the pathologist's basement office and sank, gratefully, onto a chair. Five minutes later he joined her.

'Still here,' he said. 'I thought you'd left with Andrew.'

'Has Andrew gone?'

'Yes,' the pathologist replied as she stood. 'Look Cassie, what's going on between you two? I've heard the gossip about how you treat him and I don't believe it, Andrew Rowlands is no fool. But I've never seen him look so miserable.'

'Going on...? Nothing's going on,' she said. 'I have to go, forgive me.'

How dare he leave without me?

She sped along the tiled corridor.

He always comes for me, he's always there. At St Mary's, in Clapham after the break-in, when the press hijacked us, in Admiralty House yesterday, refusing to take 'No' for an answer on the telephone when I almost.... He's always there when I need him.

How dare he leave?

She took the stairs two at a time. Perhaps she could catch him up; he couldn't have been gone long. She must catch him. She ran out of the Mortuary building almost skidding into the road as a bus drove past. Where was he?

'Cassie!'

He was leaning on the wall to the side of the building, mobile in hand.

'Andrew! I thought you'd gone. Bill said you'd gone. You'd gone without me!'

'Calm down. I came up to take a call, that's all. What's the problem?'

'Nothing.'

Everything.

'Let's walk, give you a chance to calm down,' he said, glancing sidelong at her. They turned in the direction of the river.

Act like the professional you are, not a demented idiot. Tell him about the bracelet.

'I must tell you - when you phoned this morning I'd just received a... communication from Lawrence Delahaye.'

Silence.

'He sent a gift, which I am going to report and return. I thought you ought to know about it.'

'What kind of gift?'

'A diamond bracelet.'

'Diamonds. He sent you diamonds?'

'With some roses.'

Silence.

'As you say, you have to report it.'

'I know, it could be construed as a bribe.'

'Or a payment for services rendered.'

'What?'

'We know someone is giving the press details about the investigation.'
I told Lawrence about the case.

'One of the team receiving jewellery from a person of interest doesn't look good, even if he isn't involved in the crimes. That's what I meant.'

'No, of course.'

She halted in the middle of the pavement. 'Andrew, we seem to do nothing but bicker and row and it's not as if it's about the case.'

Silence. She moved to let other pedestrians by, leading him into a side alleyway.

Oh well, here goes. Not sure if saying this is a good idea at all.

'Andrew, you seem to care about me more than just professionally.'

'Never get involved with a work colleague. It's a good rule.' His lips barely moved.

'Yes, I know I've had reason to remind myself of it recently. But you're exhibiting a degree of partiality –'

A scowl crossed his face and his grey eyes paled, pupils disappearing to pinprick black.

'So you're not going to leave me with even a vestige of pride,' he said, his voice bitter. 'Haven't you made your choice? You do exactly what you want to and I let you. Then you come back, apologetic, supplicant and I give in to you again. That's what really stings – I let you do it every time.'

'But, Andrew, you don't understand! You are one of the kindest, most considerate, most decent men I have ever met, with such dedication to what's just and right. The last thing I want to do is belittle or hurt you. I admire you. I – I can't function properly without you.'

'But I can't offer you diamonds. Friendship, honesty, care, maybe even love, but no diamonds.'

Time stopped. She realised that her mouth had dropped open and snapped it shut.

'You do care for me.'

'Cassie, I've cared for you since the moment we met. When you were covered in filth, when you were so furious that you were a suspect, when you took such joy at being able to do the job you loved again. I had hoped that – once this was all over…'

'Oh Andrew, so did I. But I thought you would be bound to have someone–'

'I told you I didn't.'

'Yes, but that was after –'

'– Lawrence Delahaye.'

Suddenly everything made sense. There might be plague, corruption and death in the streets but the world was no longer so terrifying. There was Andrew.

'Please, Andrew, would you hold me?'

He looked at her warily, as if he didn't quite believe what she had said.

Then she was wrapped in his embrace and felt him kiss the top of her forehead. She slid her arms around him beneath his jacket. This was how it should be.

'Oh no.' Gently, he pushed her away. 'Press.'

They'd been spotted by a gaggle of photographers on the other side of Horseferry Road.

'Come on.' She grabbed his hand and dashed away to her left. 'We're on my territory now.'

Cassie pulled him along to a door in the glass-walled office block and punched a security code into the keypad panel. The door opened.

'They won't be able to follow us here.'

She led him further into the building to the lifts, smiling over her shoulder at him. 'You had better stop grinning like that or you'll disappoint Siobhan,' she said. 'She's rather keen on you, you know.'

'Hmmm, I prefer her boss.'

She felt his hand stroke her behind.

'What is this? Plague pit civil servant goosed by Detective Inspector.'

'Get used to it.'

'I'll enjoy doing that,' she said, as she stopped walking and looked into his eyes.

He bent to kiss her, gently, on the lips and drew her close.

To be cared for and desired.

The ping of a lift arriving on the ground floor interrupted them and Andrew stepped back, though his eyes remained fixed on hers. The lift doors opened, but it was empty.

Concentrate! There's a case to solve and a career to restore.

'Actually, going up to my floor might not be a good idea,' she pulled out her phone and checked her messages. 'It's Sunday but someone might be about. I've had nothing from Sir Terence yet.'

'We need to get to the Yard anyway.' He straightened up, lifting his chin. 'That call I was taking was from Daljit, our rough sleeper is awake and relatively sober. But the press might be waiting.'

'Doesn't matter. We can go from government building to government building pretty much all the way to Broad Sanctuary.'

'Lead on.'

◊ FIFTY ONE

'He came round at about nine this morning, apparently,' the serjeant explained as she led them to the holding cells beneath New Scotland Yard. 'His name's Richard Fullman, commonly known as Spikey. He's been living rough since early spring, mainly in the Mayfair area when he's not being moved on; claims you get a better class of hand-out there.'

The door to the cell was ajar but its occupant showed no inclination to leave. A scrawny man dressed in a mismatched collection of clothes sat on the bed, an empty meal tray beside him. His hair was a red brown colour and stuck together into spikes protruding from his head. His skin was grey.

'The cell's not big enough for all of us.' The serjeant stood back.

'Mr Fullman,' Rowlands said, reaching for the single chair and handing it to Cassie. 'I'm Detective Inspector Rowlands. I understand that you were sleeping in the basement entry outside the Third Church of Christ Scientist on Curzon Street just over a week ago.'

'I was.' The man's eyes narrowed. ''bout then.'

'And that you were awoken in the early hours?'

'Yeah, I already told the other one, the sarge.'

'Can you tell us too, please,' Cassie said. 'It's important. We're trying to track down a murderer.'

'Don't I know you?'

From the newspapers. Even the homeless....

'No, I don't think so.'

'What happened, Mr Fullman?' The inspector asked.

'I was sleeping, then got shoved out of the way by the door opening. I swore blue murder. There were two men.'

'Did they say anything?'

'One of them was jabbering away, the other one was trying to calm him down, pushing him up the steps to the street. But I could 'ear them. Just as well for me.'

'Why was that, Mr Fullman?' Cassie leaned forward.

'You can call me Spikey.'

'Okay, Spikey. Why was it good that you heard their conversation?'

'The tall bloke said he'd send someone round to sort me out. So I scarpered. Went round to Shepherd Market, but you can't kip there comfortable any more, too many posh shops with studs and spikes outside. They clear you away with the rubbish in the mornings. Then I got the word. Somebody was looking for me and not to give me no hand-out neither. There were traveller's signs all over Mayfair - danger. It was that mob.'

'What mob?'

'Dunno, but there's word about a gang. Killers. I didn't feel safe so I talked to your lot.'

Julie Anderson

'Had you seen either of the men before?' Cassie asked.

'The tall bloke. I seen him before.'

'Would you recognise him if you saw him again?'

'Yeah, I reckon.'

'Can you describe him?'

'Tall.'

'What else, Spikey? Is he fat or slim? Does he have long hair or short?'

'Slim. Dunno 'bout his hair. I wasn't really with it. Being woken up and all.'

'Can you tell us anything else about him? Or the other man?'

'He sounded posh, that's all.' Spikey shook his head.

'Are they part of the mob you mentioned?'

'Dunno. Dunno nothing about any mob. What time's dinner time?'

Cassie stood. 'Bye, Spikey,' she said. 'Take care of yourself. Probably not a good idea to go back there.'

'I know.'

'Get him another meal, Daljit, and then have him taken to a proper cell. We can't lose this one,' Rowlands said as they headed back to the incident room.

'Boss.' It was a uniformed constable. 'The Deputy Commissioner wants to see you.'

'Edgerley,' the inspector said. 'Another dressing down.'

'Best of luck.' Cassie clasped his hand for a moment then let him go.

The serjeant watched Rowlands depart then swung her gaze back to Cassie.

'About time,' she said. 'I was beginning to think you were blind. Either that or you were a first class bitch.'

Did everyone realise but me?

'But we've only known each other for a week.'

'Cassie, it doesn't take long to fall for someone.'

'My phone.' She pulled her ringing mobile from her handbag. The number was Duncan's. 'Excuse me, I have to take this. See you back upstairs.'

She walked towards the front of the building as she returned Duncan's call.

'Duncan, you rang,' she said.

'Hello, Cassie. I've seen the newspapers. Can't say I've heard you mention this wealthy boyfriend at all.'

'He's not my boyfriend,' Cassie said. 'There's a lot to explain. Have you spoken with Sir Terence?'

'Yes, he wants to meet us both at two in Admiralty House.'

She looked at her watch. It was already one thirty.

'OK, see you there.'

'And Cassie, be prepared. It won't be pleasant.'

◊ FIFTY TWO

In Admiralty House she waited in the anteroom to Sir Terence's office until she heard Horse Guards' clock strike two.

Look confident, doesn't matter how you feel. You must salvage what you can.

She knocked on the door and opened it.

Duncan was already there, seated on one of the boxy sofas. Sir Terence was standing at the window, hands clasped behind his back, silhouetted against the light. Sundays' newspapers lay open on the coffee table.

'Cassandra,' he said in greeting, his tone dry.

'Cassie,' Duncan made as if to rise but she shook her head and took the seat next to him.

'First, has the situation changed since your report on Thursday?' Sir Terence asked.

'There are developments. As you've seen,' she indicated the newspapers. 'Journalist contacts have confirmed that there is interference at the highest levels of the press. You may remember I suggested this when –'

'Owners or editors?' Sir Terence cut her off.

'Unknown.'

'Hmm, perhaps I'll have a quiet word.'

'With great respect, Sir Terence, we don't know who is complicit. It might be unfortunate for the case and any of the journalists who have spoken with us if you speak to the wrong person.'

Sir Terence pursed his lips and said nothing.

'On possible terrorism: since we last spoke, the Intelligence Services have been consulted. They agree that the risk of a major incident in the Palace of Westminster is low. I met with David Hurst at that meeting and I subsequently spoke with the DPM, at his own request.'

He'd not been pleased the DPM excluded him. Not my fault but it won't stop him blaming me.

She waited for the Permanent Secretary to speak but he didn't, so she continued.

'There is more to learn at Westminster. CSL, the service company which the Spanish plumber worked for is linked with both the other victims. It seems to be the one unifying link between all the murders and it does the vast majority of its work for the Palace of Westminster.'

'CSL is one of the preferred bidders for some of the Thames Estate contracts,' Duncan said. 'Is the programme bound up with the deaths?'

'Possibly.'

'In terms of Parliament? Will there be reputational damage?' Sir Terence asked.

'It's possible, even likely. We are considering specific individuals. There were attempts made to obstruct the investigation which could only have come from a fairly senior MP.'

The Permanent Secretary stared at her. 'Have you told the DPM so?'

'Not yet.'

'Are you and the inspector any closer to apprehending anyone?' he demanded.

Not really.

'There are a number of concrete leads.'

'You'd better get your skates on. The Commissioner is not happy with DI Rowlands' performance.'

'His conduct of the case has been above reproach, Sir Terence.'

'But not very effective. You may find he will be replaced.'

Cassie tightened her jaw. 'I believe that would be counter-productive.'

'What is your connection with Lawrence Delahaye?'

Now it comes.

'I've seen him socially on two occasions. One of those occasions was after a professional event.'

'He is a major political donor,' Sir Terence continued. 'Not a man to cross.'

'That photograph is misleading, Sir Terence.'

'Is it?' The Permanent Secretary raised his chin and looked down his nose. 'I had to be persuaded that you should have this commission, Cassandra, against my better judgement. I wasn't convinced that you were up to it and I find my concerns are now vindicated. You don't know how to conduct yourself as a senior civil servant. You have gone over my head to speak with the DPM directly, you have offended the man likely to be our new Prime Minister and you have been instrumental in starting a major public panic. You also clearly have a very colourful private life. '

There's nothing I can say.

'I consider your behaviour grounds for dismissal. You have until Parliament rises on Tuesday. Write your report, but understand this, if there is no resolution to the case you will find that the civil service has no place for you.'

She hadn't been commissioned to solve the case. This was neither fair nor right. But then what had fairness to do with it?

It's happening again.

She hoped Duncan might interject but he said nothing.

So, this too.

Former allies and friends would distance themselves from her failure.

She could fight any dismissal proceedings. Some of what Sir Terence had claimed was nonsense. She hadn't gone over his head and she had tried to stop a panic, not help start one. But the enmity of a powerful Permanent Secretary would destroy her in Whitehall. It could prevent her getting any consultancy positions or similar jobs attached to government contracts too.

No career. No standing in the halls of power. No influence. No nothing.

Without a break in the case, she had no future as a civil servant and she might not have much of a professional future at all.

◊ FIFTY THREE

The incident room was busier when Cassie returned. The serjeant smiled at her as she entered and Cassie felt a stab of envy; she seemed impervious to stress and tiredness.

Rowlands saw her arrive from his desk and rose as she went in to see him.

'Daljit told me where you were. Was it bad?'

'Yes.'

'What about Edgerley?'

'I've got forty-eight hours or I'm off the case.'

'Oh Andrew, it's because of you that there is a case. Will they replace you?'

'They'll have to, given the press coverage. But who knows what my successor will make of it all.'

'There may be more victims then.'

'I fear so,' he said, his mouth turning down at the corners. There was despair in his eyes.

'I want to hold you,' she said.

That made him smile.

'I'd like that but it would get us both fired – assuming that you still have a job?'

'Not looking likely.'

'I'm sorry Cass, I wish –'

'I know. Look, I'm going back to Clapham, I've got to draft my report and write a covering note to go with the bracelet – that's going to take some explanation. Shall I give Jack a call?'

'I'll do it. Bring him up to date. He should keep his people on high alert.'

'Will you come round later?'

He smiled again. 'I'll phone first and see what the situation is with the press. If they're still camped on your doorstep, I won't come. It would be throwing away what credibility we have left if we appear in tomorrow's headlines as well.'

Let alone destroying my reputation completely, but then you've already thought of that.

She smiled at him faintly. She desperately wanted to spend time alone with him and it seemed from the intensity of his gaze, the same was true for him. But it was impossible.

'Speak later then.'

'Hang on, Cassie, you'll want to hear this,' the serjeant breezed in, an eager look on her face. 'I ran the checks you asked for, boss. Karen Woods was bound over for a drunk and disorderly, ten years ago. Victor was a person of interest in a number of cases but was never charged.'

'What kind of cases?' asked Rowlands.

'Two GBH and one case of stalking. The complainants retracted their claims before the cases went to trial.'

'Sounds like he's got a nasty temper. Any evidence of witness intimidation?'

'There's nothing on file but all three had a conveniently timed change of heart,' replied the serjeant.

'Unfortunately, that's not evidence of rape and murder.' Rowlands shook his head.

'No, but get this, both Woods and Harris are ex-Royal Green Jackets. They go way back.'

'Interesting, so either of them could be the military type Silana mentioned,' Cassie added.

'Let's not get ahead of ourselves,' said Rowlands. 'But the link is interesting. CSL ties all the victims and we suspect, given what the Craft team said, that Vic Woods was involved in something with José in the lead up to his death.' Rowlands turned to the DS. 'Could you find anything more on Don Harris?'

'Other than he lives in Tachbrook Street, which is on the Tyburn, no. He's an original shareholder in CSL and works for them as a security consultant. Aside from that, he seems to live off his investments.'

The serjeant picked up a pen and began writing on the white board. 'Sir Percy Dugdale.' She underlined the name with a flourish. 'According to the Register of Members' Financial Interests he has significant outside business interests and he chairs the Oversight Committee for the Thames Estates Programme. He was investigated over an unexplained death years ago, but never charged.'

'The school servant,' Rowlands nodded his head.

'A domestic assistant fell down two flights of stairs in the middle of the night,' the serjeant continued. 'The man had complained to another staff member that Dugdale was verbally and physically abusive. He implied it might be racially aggravated. It looks like the staff member was pressured by the school not to give evidence, and the death was eventually ruled a suicide.'

'It's horrible if there's any truth in it, but Dugdale isn't a lord, he's a baronet,' said Cassie.

'Yes, but 'lord' could still just be a nickname,' said Rowlands.

'Lord Cairns is also on the Oversight Committee,' the serjeant added his name to Sir Percy's on the whiteboard. 'He has a reputation for hard drinking but no record of violence. He hasn't been in the Lords long but already has lots of links with big business and touts himself around, so probably needs the money.'

'If this is a crime ring at work, organised crime, it could be lucrative,' Cassie said.

'Could we have a look at his financial records?'

'Without a warrant, not a chance,' Cassie said. 'Last time the Met searched an MP's computer without a warrant, the Serjeant at Arms nearly lost their job and a Cabinet Minister resigned.'

'We don't have enough to get a warrant,' the inspector said. 'Yet.'

'Lord Priess is another committee member,' the serjeant went on. 'He's a blue blood, inherited a fortune, nothing against him more serious than a speeding fine, aside from unsavoury rumours about his family. Though, interestingly, he lives in Mayfair, when he's in town, very near the course of the River Tyburn.'

'So, Priess, Harris and Delahaye all live on or near the course of the Tyburn?' Cassie said.

'Yes, something of a coincidence, though you could say the same of half of the homeowners in Mayfair and Pimlico,' the serjeant said, adding William Priess to the list of names. 'So, the dodgy Sir Percy Dugdale, newly-minted Lord Frank Cairns, hereditary peer Lord William Priess and worked-his-way-up Lawrence Delahaye. The first three have parliamentary power and, Cairns aside, money. Delahaye has plenty of that too and some influence in the City, but we can't establish a link between any of them and rape and murder.'

'Certainly not enough to pull them in for questioning. We've also got nothing to link the military man and the lord together.' Rowlands turned to his serjeant. 'Unless you've got anything more up your sleeve?'

She shook her head. 'Sorry, boss. Though I've got someone speaking with the street people around Mayfair, and the charities which offer them support, to try and track down the rumours of Spikey's so-called 'mob'.'

'Good. But as regards the rest, it's all too tenuous.' Rowlands said, turning back to the board. 'The shoeprint is still our only real lead, unless we can catch them red-handed.'

Everyone contemplated the list of names.

'I'm sorry,' Cassie said eventually. 'But I have to go. I need to write my report.'

When she turned the corner into her road, she was relieved to find only one acne-ridden reporter sitting on the wall opposite her flat. She smiled at him as he spoke into his phone but he scowled.

Spiggott was hungry and Cassie fed her before making herself a sandwich with week-old bread. In the study she switched on her laptop and, while she ate, began drafting a bland submission to be attached to the bracelet. Her report to Charles Morecombe, the DPM, was more difficult. She had to impress on him that she had fulfilled her original commission. Thereafter, it was a question of what to include and what to omit. The last section was unfinished. Perhaps she would be able to write the final chapter tomorrow, or early Tuesday morning, to include the names of those apprehended. She worked on it until the light began to go. It was half past eight.

She stood, stretching after sitting for so long. As she drew the sitting room curtains closed she saw the press outside. She would tell Andrew not to come, however much she wanted him there.

She fed Spiggott again and checked the contents of her fridge. When the phone rang she took the handset into the bedroom as she closed those curtains too.

'Hi, it's me.'

'I thought it would be.'

'Is the coast clear?'

'No. There's still an encampment, but come anyway. I want you here.'

'Sounds promising.' She could hear the smile in his voice. 'But it isn't sensible, Cassie. Your picture's already been splashed all over the Sundays. Imagine the headlines if--'

'Alright, alright. It's just...'

'I know.'
'I want to talk to you.'
'So, talk.'
'I think I'm falling for you, Andrew.'
'Only think?'
Too soon for anything more.
'I want to wrap myself around you and comfort you and –'
'Is this phone sex?'
'No.'
'Shame. I might like it.'
'Is this a senior police officer eliciting sexual favours over the phone?'
'Maybe, maybe not.' He was winding her up.
'What is it then? Don't you like Clapham?'

'Oh, I do... which is just as well, given that I intend to be spending a lot of my time there, preferably with you wrapped around me at every possible opportunity. Now, tell me just how you would do that, again. I want details.'

'That *would* be phone sex.'

'Hm, I think I'll hold out for the real thing.' There was a pause. 'I'll see you at nine tomorrow morning outside the Serious Fraud Office.'

'You say the sweetest things.'

'Night night.'

MONDAY

◊ FIFTY FOUR

So the police had found another of the locations. At least the clean-up had been comprehensive, Harris had assured him of that. Why hadn't he been told about the eye witness? Why? Harris had been searching for the tramp for almost a week before he'd confessed that a witness even existed. Fool!

He breathed deeply and felt the power flow through his body's core as he lifted the weights, sublimating his anger, channelling it into physical effort. Then he placed the weights back on to the rack and began the stretching exercises he did every morning.

Rigorous physical exertion was something he enjoyed. He understood the chemistry of endorphin release and increased serotonin levels, but it didn't stop him from feeling the pleasure. 'Runner's high' it was called, though exercise wasn't the only way of achieving it.

As soon as he had learned about the tramp he'd had all his agents scouring central London to find him before the police did. But it was too late. He had received word that the man was being held in the cells of Scotland Yard itself. It would be difficult to reach him there and he doubted that Rowlands would let him go.

Too close. The police were far too close.

This evening's entertainment should be cancelled, it was much too risky. Except the Russian had made it plain that he expected it to go ahead as planned and, for now, he needed Oleg's support. Without it, a number of his international ventures would fail and the intricate web of global alliances he had created would be threatened. If one wasn't hunting in the pack, one soon became the hunted.

He would have to attend himself, whatever he had told Percy. Oleg would expect nothing less. It was not something he looked forward to. However useful the participants in the entertainments might be to him, he had nothing but contempt for their inability to control their desires. He preferred to engage intelligently with women.

A companion who could match and surprise him was what he wanted, a willing partner. It amused him to contemplate offering Cassandra marriage; it would be convenient and legally useful, a wife not having to testify against her husband, and advantageous for her too. If she became tiresome, she could be dealt with. But he needed to expedite matters.

Percy was already glancing in her direction; the sooner he turned her to his purpose, the safer she would be.

In the meantime, there was this evening. Percy was convinced that he could pull it off, but he didn't enjoy relying on the MP, especially with Rowlands and Cassandra lying in wait at the Palace. He remembered seeing them together in Whitehall; he'd been told that they were becoming close. He dismissed the thought that the policeman could be a real rival. It was unimaginable.

At least this would be the last event for a time.

And, if all went as planned, Parliamentary Security would look incompetent and the Metropolitan Police would be seen as usurping parliamentary sovereignty, the ramifications of which he could exploit later. Cassandra would be made more vulnerable, more receptive.

Tonight was a gamble, but, if it came off, would yield plenty of rewards.

Good. He had set it in his mind. It had to happen. Now he just had to mitigate against the risk.

◊ FIFTY FIVE

The bells of St Martins-in-the-Fields rang nine as Cassie and Rowlands approached the doors to the Serious Fraud Office. Dimitri Remis had a miniscule office on the seventh floor, but it had a magnificent view over the rooftops of Whitehall and down to Big Ben, the Houses of Parliament and Westminster Abbey.

'Thank you for seeing us, Mr Remis,' the inspector said as they were seated. 'And apologies for bothering you on Saturday night.'

'No problem, I'm glad that the police are interested,' the young man replied. 'Do you have any useful information for me?'

'We were rather hoping that you had information useful to us,' Rowlands said.

'Hmm. Well, Lawrence Delahaye was first brought to my attention by a colleague at the Financial Conduct Authority.' He switched into explanatory mode. 'The FCA's responsible for, among other things, authorising hedge fund managers to operate in the UK. Most hedge funds are based in overseas territories for tax reasons but they need authorisation to carry out business in London.'

He stopped and opened a slim cardboard file.

'Delahaye was suspected of market abuse, insider dealing, market manipulation and failure to notify short selling positions. Market abuse includes using information acquired illegally in order to make money on the exchange; bribery, corruption, that type of thing. It also covers market manipulation, the deliberate creation of artificial expectation, saying that something is going to happen, or positioning a certain stock in a certain way, to drive up its value, so the wrongdoer makes more money when it falls.'

'We won't understand the complexities,' Rowlands said. 'In broad terms can you tell us what you believe Delahaye, or Barton Investments, is up to?'

'Delahaye abuses the market in a big way. First, by acquiring data illegally and misusing it; second, he directly influences the market outside of the trading floors. He seems to have contacts and partners across a range of sectors and professions and, if I'm right, in government too. That means a lot of influence and an ability to steer events, which he can then use to make money from by buying before a price or value rises or, if he chooses, by selling short.'

Were the politicians on their list the creatures, or willing associates, of Lawrence Delahaye, Cassie wondered? What about the businessmen? How far would this reach?

Power is just another way to gain money and money another way to gain power.

'Then there are the international aspects, not only the tax havens, but the links with other big beast capitalists: the Russian oligarchs, Mafia dons, Saudi oil princes,' Remis went on. 'This network is bigger than any one person, even someone like Delahaye, but he's part of it. Individuals like him, aligned with other business leaders and political decision-makers, can game the system. That's what's really frightening; a cabal of very wealthy people manipulating markets and events for their profit and to everyone else's cost.'

'But if the markets are consistently manipulated in favour of a few then everyone else loses,' Cassie spoke her thoughts aloud. 'That's unsustainable. Businesses are likely to go bust, pension funds become worthless, the City is undermined and there are knock-on economic impacts, eventually with global consequences. The 2008 financial crisis would be a blip in comparison.'

Not what Sir Terence had had in mind maybe but a massive scandal nonetheless.

'With respect,' Rowlands said, slowly. 'Do you have any evidence to support your hypothesis?'

'Nowhere near enough,' the investigator grimaced. 'My superiors would never take a case like this to court without copper-bottomed proof and right now I can't supply that. What do you have?'

'I can't share information,' Rowlands said. 'Doing so could prejudice any criminal trial.'

'At least tell me this: should I give up, or keep digging?'

'Don't give up,' Cassie said quickly.

'That's something, I suppose,' Remis said.

'Thanks for your help, Mr Remis,' Cassie shook his hand as she and Rowlands stood. 'I think that there might be some big fish in your net when you haul it in.'

They stepped on to Cockspur Street minutes later.

'So that's how Delahaye acquired his fortune,' the inspector said.

'He may be a crooked hedge fund manager but it doesn't make him a murderer.' Cassie spoke slowly.

'Correct.' Rowlands frowned. 'It doesn't link him to rape and murder. But Cassie, you don't go anywhere near him. I'm serious. You understand?'

Oh yes, I understand.

She nodded. In fact, she was relieved. What Delahaye was doing was illegal, immoral and destabilising to the economy but at least it wasn't worse. She glanced over at Andrew and felt a pang of guilt. How could she have been so dazzled by Lawrence?

Whitehall lay in front of them. At its far end, she saw the Palace of Westminster. The Elizabeth Tower was shrouded in scaffolding, obscuring the clock face. Green netting was wound around the west face of St Stephen's Porch. What else enmeshed the Palace and those within it? Had the corruption already taken hold, bringing its odour as surely as the subterranean Tyburn, flowing beneath it, brought the stench of putrefaction?

◊ FIFTY SIX

'Does this take us any further forward?' the serjeant asked.

They were sitting around the whiteboards in the incident room.

'We now know a lot more about Lawrence Delahaye and his financial schemes,' Rowlands said. 'But nothing on the murders. We still have to try and anticipate the gang's next move.'

Before time runs out.

'Our best chance is to catch them red-handed. If there is to be another murder, I think it's likely it will be tonight,' Cassie said.

'Why?'

'Because I think it's going to take place in the Palace of Westminster and the Palace closes down completely tomorrow,' Cassie replied.

'But won't it be easier for them when the Palace is shut down?' asked an officer. 'They'll be less likely to be caught.'

'Hardly,' countered Cassie. 'The only people in the Palace will be workmen and security. They'll be much easier to discover precisely because there are fewer people around. This evening the Palace will be fuller and they'll use that to their advantage.'

'We assume the gang is likely to operate somewhere close to the route of the Tyburn,' the serjeant said, looking unconvinced. 'So that excludes large parts of central London but it doesn't necessarily point to the Palace of Westminster.'

'Actually it does,' Cassie said. 'I asked Siobhan to do some more research into potential locations along the route of the Tyburn.'

She stood and pointed to the map.

'There are two source streams for the river in Hampstead, here and here. But Hampstead wasn't part of the city until the mid-nineteenth century and, while there are old cellars and crypts, these aren't near the Tyburn. It's only when the river enters the older parts of London, south of Baker Street, that we find likely locations for the crimes.'

'You're assuming that some individuals come in from street level,' Rowlands said.

'Yes. That's important. We know they accessed the Roman baths from the surface, we found the footprint in the passage and they used the basement stairs at Curzon Street. So there has to be an entrance from the surface. That helps us a lot.' She traced the course of the river on the street map. 'Possibilities are St Peter's on Vere Street and the Georgian buildings on Marylebone Lane, but Siobhan says access is controlled there, the church locked. Past Bond Street, the first plague pit discovery and the Roman baths and you come to Berkeley Square, that's another possible location, although most of the buildings are offices now.'

'We could patrol and monitor them,' the serjeant said.

'Exactly,' Cassie replied. 'Then into Curzon Street and the most recent discovery. Across Green Park and St James's, open parks where there's no access. Then we're into medieval London. There we can rule out very large areas: underground car parks, basements etc. Places which are not conducive to the crime ring's activities. We can also rule out access from government buildings, the Justice Department, the Education Department and so on. This is important. They're secure and there are a lot of them along the Tyburn's course.'

'So, assuming it's none of the sites you've just mentioned, where does this leave us?' the inspector asked.

'Thorney Island,' Cassie replied. 'Or close to it.'

'What about that labyrinth of offices you called Churchill's bunkers?' someone asked.

'I thought about that,' Cassie said. The maze of rooms where service personnel had worked, amassing data - on casualties, planes destroyed and food convoys - during the darkest days of the Second World War stretched from Downing Street to Horseferry Road and was partially open to tourists. 'George's map shows entry to the bunkers from the Tyburn but surface access is from government buildings only, which are tightly controlled. We know where those entry points are and can ensure that no one enters through them.'

'So that's ruled out too.'

'Which covers a lot of Thorney Island,' Rowlands said.

''When you have eliminated the impossible, whatever remains, however improbable, must be the truth'', Cassie quoted Conan Doyle's detective and pointed to the map. 'The Palace of Westminster.'

There was a pause as everyone contemplated the possibility.

'But would they be able to rape and kill unseen, unheard?' the serjeant asked.

'Jack Martineau, from Palace Security, took Cassie and I to an old subterranean room the other day,' Rowlands explained. 'It's unused and forgotten and could be the next location. CSL had it cordoned off.'

A police constable entered and handed the inspector a piece of paper.

'Tonight's the last night the Palace will be open,' Cassie said, reaching for her phone. 'We need to keep watch. I'll contact Jack. We should also watch the sewers entrance beneath Boudicca's statue on Westminster Bridge.'

'Agreed. Organise that straight away, Daljit,' Rowlands said, reading. He seemed distracted.

'Boss, have you cleared the extra resources for that?' the serjeant said, frowning.

Rowlands didn't respond, he was concentrating on whatever was on the paper. Gradually, his face was split by a broad grin.

'Boss?'

'We have a lead to follow up before then,' he said, cheerily. 'The footprint has yielded more information. Rickermans have identified the customers who bought those shoes.'

'Great!'

'Have they narrowed it down?'

'No, but we can,' Rowlands said, beaming at them and enjoying the suspense. 'There were twenty-five UK residents who bought that model and size of very expensive shoe, but only ten live in London or the south east. One of them is William, Lord Preiss.'

'Priess!' Cassie exclaimed in surprise. The aristocrat had inherited wealth. Why get involved with such a vile business as this? Cassie's skin began to crawl. Did he, could he, enjoy it? Just like his father and grandfather. Was it what he had been taught from childhood?

'And, as we know, he has a house in Mayfair. Spikey Fullman might recognise him. We have enough. It's time for an arrest.'

◊ FIFTY SEVEN

The police car wove through the warren of small Mayfair streets. Cassie could barely suppress her excitement as the elegant Georgian townhouses flowed past. Could this be it? Such a wealthy, establishment figure as Priess - could he really be the man behind these crimes?

By her side, Rowlands' manner was brisk but there was an eager tension in his every movement.

And Sir Terence won't be able to fire me!

The car stopped in Curzon Street, close to the scene of the last murder.

'There's Half Moon Street,' Cassie indicated a road running to the left. At its far end she could see the trees of Green Park. 'This is arrogance, Andrew, to carry out such a crime so close to home.'

'They are arrogant. But that's to our advantage; they're getting sloppy.'

Number 27, Half Moon Street was a black-bricked, five-storey town house sitting behind painted railings with a blue door and brass fittings. As they walked towards it the door opened and a man in a servant's livery hurried down the front steps, manhandling a large suitcase, with a travelling bag slung over his shoulder. He stacked them into a waiting taxi and returned to the house.

Moments later, Priess made his way down the steps, immaculately turned out in a cream summer suit with a wide-brimmed fedora and carrying a walking cane. Could this dandy have raped tiny, helpless Silana? Cassie recalled his salute to her on the Terrace and her insides grew cold.

'Looks like he's about to leave town,' said Rowlands as he increased his pace. 'Get the car.'

He strode along the pavement and drew out his warrant card. Cassie signalled the police car, then ran to catch up with him.

'Stay there until I tell you otherwise,' he said to the cabbie, showing him the card, before he turned to the man. 'Lord William Priess?'

'William, Lord Priess is my title,' the man replied, looking down his nose at the warrant card.

'Detective Inspector Andrew Rowlands and my associate, Ms Cassandra Fortune; we would like to speak with you, sir.' Rowlands positioned himself between the man and the taxi.

'Cassandra, this is as delightful as ever, but terribly inconvenient right now, I'm afraid,' Priess said, ignoring the inspector. He glanced back to the manservant standing at the top of the steps.

'We can talk inside or down at the station, whichever you prefer, sir,' Rowlands was polite but immovable. 'I suggest you might find the first option least embarrassing.'

'Oh, very well.' The aristocrat summoned the servant with a wave of his hand. 'Stanley, take the bags back inside and pay the cabbie for his time. Follow me.'

Cassie and Rowlands followed Lord Priess who led them into a drawing room off the grand hallway. They were not asked to sit.

'Now, what is this all about,' the aristocrat demanded. 'I have a train to catch.'

'We want to ask you about this.' From his jacket inside pocket Rowlands produced a plaster cast of part of a shoe. 'This cast is taken from a shoeprint found at the scene of a serious crime.'

'What has that to do with me?'

'Rickermans of Jermyn Street identified the shoe as one made by them,' the inspector said.

'Their Hunter range,' Cassie added.

'I am indifferent to the names they give their shoes,' the man looked disdainfully at the cast.

'You purchased such a pair of shoes, Lord Priess.'

'Rickermans has been making my shoes for decades, so if they say I did, I must have done. But that doesn't mean I still have them.'

'What do you mean by that, sir?'

'Old clothes and shoes are donated to the needy, rather than discarded. My man can verify.'

He made a movement towards the door.

'We will interview your valet, Lord Priess and ask him to make a formal statement down at the police station,' the inspector interjected.

'And disrupt my household further? Why are you doing this, Inspector?' his voice was haughty. 'What is this all about?'

'We are investigating a series of very serious crimes, sir, multiple rapes and murders. So we need to find the person who wore the shoe. Your assistance would be appreciated.'

The aristocrat pressed his lips together. He stood very still.

'The shoemaker's records show that you purchased a pair of Hunter shoes from Rickermans four months ago. Are you saying that you have already thrown them out?'

'I doubt that, but it's possible. As I say, I am a longstanding customer of Rickermans, I have probably bought those shoes before.'

'Not that range of shoes,' Cassie said. 'They're a new model.'

'Look, this has nothing to do with me,' his voice became harder.

'We spoke with the young victim before she died, sir,' Rowlands said softly. 'We have a very specific description of her abusers. We await DNA from the most recent murder, which took place underneath Curzon Street, just along the road from here. There was a witness. He's currently in custody.'

A little misleading...

The man's eyes narrowed. His glance flicked from the policeman to Cassie, then back again. The hauteur had disappeared, along with the old world charm. Lord Priess was no foolish fop or aristocratic antique, however he chose to present himself to the world. A wave of intense dislike swept over her.

It's him, he's our guy alright.

'I refuse to speak with you without the presence of my lawyer.'

'Then I'm arresting you, sir, on suspicion of the rape of Ms Silana Tabriki on the tenth of September. You do not have to say anything but it may harm your defence if you do not mention something which you later rely on in court. Anything you do say may be given in evidence. You will now accompany us to the station where you may contact your lawyer.'

'I... I,' Lord Priess gaped. 'This is insupportable.'

Cassie checked out of the window. 'The car is here,' she said.

'I refuse... I completely refuse to go.'

'You have been arrested, sir, you don't have a choice,' Rowlands said. He gave the aristocrat a cold glance. 'You can leave with us or be forcibly removed by the Police Constables.'

'Very well,' Lord Priess said after a moment. 'But I will say nothing more without my lawyer.'

'This way, sir.' Rowlands led him out to the waiting police car.

Priess did not speak again until they reached New Scotland Yard, where he demanded that his lawyer be contacted. The valet Stanley was already making a statement in an interview room.

'He'll be charged, though not right away,' Andrew told Cassie. 'For the moment we'll keep him and his man on ice, let them stew for a while. I don't want a lawyer tipping anyone off that we've made an arrest before this evening's stake-out.'

'Then?'

'We'll set up an identity parade after he's charged. If Spikey Fullman ID's him, that could send him down and, even without Spikey, the shoeprint at the Roman baths gives us a strong case. I'm prepared to bet he'll implicate his accomplices in return for a reduced sentence or a more lenient prison regime; he's not the type to forego his comforts.'

'What about those individuals who take part in the crimes?'

'Same goes for them. It's in Priess's interest to sell them out.'

This is going to be a scandal of mammoth proportions.

'The scandal, Andrew.'

'He'll be kept in protective custody. We don't want an unexplained death before we get the names, like Epstein. '

'But he'll still go to jail? At the end of it?'

'I think so. Even the most persuasive lawyer will find it difficult to convince a judge that his Lordship should avoid a custodial sentence,' he replied. 'But if he cooperates he'll probably get off more lightly than he would otherwise have done.'

'When I think of poor Silana.'

'I know,' he gave her a sympathetic look. 'But it's the way the system works.'

Cassie wanted him to take her in his arms.

'Cheer up,' he said. 'He'll go down and he'll take the others with him.'

So that's it? It's over? Case solved?

'The arrest will take the heat off you?'

'Yes. Will it help you?'

'I don't know but it'll make my report look more positive.'

'There's every possibility that we'll catch the others later.'

Can we still save my career?

'Assuming that there will be an event going ahead this evening, even without Priess?'

'Why else were the passes stolen? And we know something's driving their activity right now. If they are going to use the Palace, this is their last chance. Maybe they'll abort, but maybe not, if they don't know Priess is in custody. In any case we have to proceed as planned, just in case - there may be another young life at stake.'

Of course, that's much more important.

'But let's go for some supper first. Fancy a pizza? I realize it's not exactly what you've been used to.'

'Andrew, will you stop doing that, please.'

He smiled at her in that way that he had. Her insides did gymnastics. The urge to touch him almost overwhelmed her and she clasped her hands behind her back.

'I know a place,' he said.

◊ FIFTY EIGHT

It was a tiny trattoria behind a small shop that served lunchtime sandwiches and rolls. Deep within were Formica-topped tables in little booths, each with a small vase of fresh flowers. They chose a table hidden from the street and a waitress brought red-checked place settings, napkins and cutlery with a small dish of plump olives and a short menu. Glasses and a carafe of water were delivered as they ordered.

Andrew sat across from her, a half-smile on his face as he reached for her hand. It filled her with quiet joy.

How did I fail to see what was in front of me? This is the man for me, whatever happens. It might not always be easy, with his job and mine, but it'll be worth it.

'Bruschetta to share.'

They both drew back to allow the waitress to serve. As she walked back into the kitchen Cassie heard her remark in Italian. 'Have you seen those two lovebirds? They can't stop smiling at each other.'

'I take it that we're the topic of conversation,' Andrew said.

'He's been in here before,' someone in the kitchen continued. 'He's police. Working on the Plague Murders, saw him in the paper.'

Cassie nodded as she reached for a piece of bread. 'She thinks we're lovely.'

'Good.'

Andrew rested his chin on his hand as he watched her lick tomato juice from her fingers.

She felt her cheeks burn. 'Andrew!'

'What? I like watching you.'

She hadn't blushed when Lawrence Delahaye had studied her so much more frankly. So why was she blushing now? She knew the answer – because this wasn't a game. It was real.

'Quattro stagioni?' The waitress was back.

'Me,' Andrew said, looking up at her,

'Parmesan?' She raised an eyebrow.

The waitress was being flirtatious and Andrew, Cassie noted, was taking it as his due. She thought of Siobhan. Women liked Andrew, especially young women. It was partly the clean-cut good looks, but also his reserve, the physical presence, the very maleness of him. He looked like a man to make a woman feel safe and cared for. It would be interesting being with such a man. No. It would be amazing.

'Fiorentina for you. Parmesan?' She got no special smile as the pizza was placed before her.

Cassie caught Andrew's eye as he picked up a pizza slice.

'Aren't you the popular one,' she said.

He hung his head in mock contrition, then grinned. 'Jealous?'

'No.'

Never admit it, even if you are.

'Oh.' He pouted, self-mockingly. 'You don't need to be, Cassie.' There was a smile in his grey eyes. 'You won't ever need to be.'

'Good.' She bit into her pizza.

He's mine now.

From the kitchen came a trill of Italian.

'It's her – the one with the billionaire boyfriend. So what's she doing with this guy?'

'Greedy. What a tart.'

'What?' Andrew frowned. 'What did they say?'

'Nothing.'

'Don't.'

'It seems I'm not as popular as you,' she responded. 'It'll take a while to live down that photo.'

'Not once the case is cracked,' Andrew said. 'You'll be a heroine then, that's the way it works.'

'You're assuming it will be cracked.'

'Now we have Priess, yes. Even better if we can catch them tonight.'

'You're not a hundred per cent convinced that it's the Palace of Westminster, are you?'

If it wasn't my theory would you even go along with it?

'I wish we were more certain about the precise location, it's a big place. But, it's a good theory. So we're acting on it.'

There's so much riding on it.

'What if I've got this whole thing wrong? What if—if it's a failure, then you get fired and I get fired, and—'

'Cassie.' Andrew took both her hands in his. 'Stop. Stop it. Whatever happens, if either of us lose our jobs, we'll make it work.'

'Even if I'm unemployable?'

'I'd still want to be with you.'

She smiled weakly and squeezed his hand. 'I'm sorry. I'm just getting twitchy.'

'Bit early for that,' he finished off the last piece of pizza. 'It could be a long night, Cass. What's that?'

There was noise and a commotion out in the street. Andrew took out his wallet and drew several notes from it, casting them on to the table as he stood. The first waitress appeared at their table.

'It's the press,' she said. 'Do you want to go out the back way?'

'Yes.'

Cassie hurried after the waitress through the kitchen.

'Here.' The woman opened a fire door. 'It wasn't me who tipped them off,' she added. 'Good luck.'

'Thanks.' Cassie said, descending the steps into the ill-lit yard of the restaurant, as the waitress stood, backlit in the doorway. Andrew brushed past to a gate in the wall. He slid back the long bolt and peered into the alleyway beyond.

'It's empty. Come on.' He took Cassie's hand. Together they hastened along the alley.

'If we can get to St Martin's Lane, we'll be able to get a cab,' Cassie said.

'It's where I'm headed.'

As they reached the narrow lane, a shout came from behind them. They had been followed through the restaurant. Andrew's hand tightened around Cassie's and they ran, weaving between the early evening pre-theatre diners. A black cab drew up in response to Andrew's hail and they climbed in. It pulled away from the kerb and their pursuers.

Cassie flopped back into the deep black seat, panting slightly and laughing. She smiled at Andrew, who reached out and folded her in his arms. She laid her head against his chest and closed her eyes, sliding her hands around his body.

Hmmm. I want this man.

'Come to Clapham tonight, whatever happens,' she said.

'I would like to...'

'I'll phone my neighbour. She can let us in through her garden. The reptiles won't catch on.'

She kissed him softly on the lips and felt his arms tighten around her as she snuggled closer, stroking his face, wanting to stroke other parts of him.

'You know perfectly well that I can't say no to you,' he said, looking down into her eyes.

They kissed as the taxi threaded its way through the early evening commuters to Trafalgar Square and then to the Embankment.

'I don't want to let you go,' Andrew said. 'But I'm going to now. It might not be a good idea to arrive at the Yard in a clinch.'

'Sorry.' She sat up abruptly.

'Hey, don't apologise.' He still held her hand. 'Thanks, here'll be fine,' he said to the cabby.

◊ FIFTY NINE

The atmosphere in the small control room was tense. The arrest of William Priess had raised spirits but everyone was now focused on the next stage, of catching the whole ring. There might, as the inspector pointed out, be another life at stake.

Light flickered as Tim, a young member of palace security staff, and the serjeant switched from one camera to another on the TV screens. They were tracking through those areas of the Palace where CCTV existed, especially the route to Westminster Hall and St Mary Undercroft. The black-and-white screens showed empty public spaces, tourists and day visitors having left long ago. The last Commons debate had concluded at just after eight o'clock and many MPs were leaving, but there were still Parliamentarians about.

Cassie glanced at her watch. It was nine thirty.

Several dinners were taking place in the Palace that evening, but attention centred on Sir Percy Dugdale's party in a dining room next to the Strangers' Bar. Sir Percy's guests had been signed in and allocated visitor passes. None of them had attended the reception on the Terrace a week ago. So Frank Cairns wasn't among the diners and neither was Lawrence Delahaye, which was something of a relief to Cassie. Not that she had any lingering admiration for the hedge fund manager, the SFO visit had cured her of that, but it could have confused matters if he had been involved and things were confusing enough.

She watched Andrew, who was leaning on the corner of a desk, mug of tea in hand. Jack was regaling him with stories about his time in intelligence, well-practiced tales, many of which she had heard before. The policeman caught her eye and smiled. Both men looked more relaxed than she felt and she had a nagging suspicion that they were conspiring against her, but she couldn't work out how.

Focus on the task in hand.

A plain-clothed officer was watching the sewer entrance at Boudicca's statue on the bridge, despite Jack's assurances about access from that quarter. The Abbey crypt had been reconnoitered and deemed secure. There was no entry to or from the Tyburn that way. All the bases were covered.

'There they go,' Tim said, breaking into her reverie.

It's happening!

Everyone stared at the screens.

They showed the dapper MP with his head of white hair exiting from the dining room, followed by a group of people. All walked away from the camera, Sir Percy leading and speaking silently to those behind. It was ten o'clock.

'Can you zoom in?' Rowlands asked. 'So that we can see the passes they're wearing?'

Tim shook his head. 'Not from here, though the pictures can be enhanced later.'

The group kept disappearing, the stragglers leaving the range of one camera before Sir Percy came into that of another. Every so often the group halted as a feature of the Palace was pointed out to them.

'They're heading towards Central Lobby,' the serjeant spoke into a walkie-talkie to alert her Palace police colleagues, stationed outside. 'On the way to Westminster Hall, perhaps.'

The CCTV picked up the group in the dimly lit St Stephen's Hall, admiring the murals as best they could. Then they entered St Stephen's Porch and the cavernous medieval hall. Here the magnificent hammer beam roof and buttresses were brightly lit, through the high arched windows, by the floodlights on the lawn outside. At each side of the top of the wide stone staircase which led from the Porch into the hall proper, chandeliers cast pools of light, but the floor of the hall beyond was shrouded in darkness. The stairs to the Undercroft were on the right of the stone steps.

But the group didn't walk in that direction. Sir Percy was addressing them, pointing to various specific places as he led them into the shadows of the hall proper.

'Are you certain about this Cassie?' Jack asked, frowning. 'This looks like any private tour.'

'I'm not certain at all, Jack,' she replied. 'It's just – what!'

First one, then another of the TV screens lost connection, showing only grainy snow.

'What's going on?'

Tim was trying to restore the images. 'This shouldn't be happening.'

The inspector crossed to the door in two strides and pulled it open.

'Get down to St Mary Undercroft, quick as you can,' he ordered.

The two Palace policemen set off at a run, swiftly followed by Rowlands, Cassie and Jack.

As they strode along the corridor the inspector spoke into a walkie-talkie. 'What's happening, Daljit? Have you got pictures back?'

'Yes,' she heard the serjeant's voice. 'But there's no sign of our group.'

'There must be,' he snapped. 'They can't vanish into thin air.'

At a run they passed through a silent Central Lobby, into St Stephen's Hall, their footsteps echoing.

'Daljit? Anything?' Rowlands rasped.

'No, boss, nothing.'

Through the double doors into the porch. The huge dark space of Westminster Hall lay before them. It was empty. The two Palace policemen were emerging from the steps to St Mary Undercroft, the beams of their torches preceding them.

'It's locked, sir.' One of them called up to Jack, his voice reverberating in the vast space.

Jack fished inside his pockets for a key as he hurried down the stairs, followed by Cassie and Rowlands using their phones as torches. At the foot of the staircase he opened the heavy chapel door.

The chapel too was empty.

Where are they?

Cassie slipped past Jack to the door to the kitchen and opened it. All was silence. She felt along the wall for the light switch. The room was as empty now as it had been a couple of hours ago. It was impossible to tell if anyone had been there since.

But everything pointed to this.

'Nothing and no one,' she said as she returned to the chapel where the inspector and Jack waited. The former was tight-lipped, the latter looked anxious.

'OK, back to your usual posts,' he said to the PCs.

'Daljit – hello? Hello?'

'It won't work down here,' Jack said. 'Let's go back up top.'

'The dining room Sir Percy's dinner was in, take us there please,' the inspector said, climbing the stairs. 'Daljit –'

'Boss?'

'Any other movement?'

'Not that we've seen.'

What was going on? The analysis of the possible locations was logical, the Palace of Westminster was the most likely. Add in the theft of the passes and José's interest in the kitchens and it became obvious. But...

At the dining room, Rowlands made to rap on the door but Jack raised his hand to pre-empt him. He opened the door after the lightest of taps.

'Sorry to bother you, sir,' Jack pushed his head around the open door. Cassie briefly caught sight of a single white-haired figure sitting at the dining table. 'Can the staff clear away now?'

'Yes,' Sir Percy answered. 'My guests have left.'

'And their passes, sir?'

'Handed in at the desk.'

'Thank you, sir. Just checking that they are accounted for. Goodnight, sir.'

He closed the door and pointed down the corridor, leading them back to the control room.

'Did we get any more footage of them, Tim?' Jack asked his colleague when they arrived there.

'Not as is obvious,' Tim replied. 'But I'd have to go through the lot to be sure. That'll take hours.'

'We can give you someone to help,' Cassie said. 'Tomorrow.'

She looked around for the inspector and serjeant. They were still in the corridor.

'Stand everyone down.' She heard him say through the open door. He was trying hard to hide his frustration and disappointment. When he came back into the room their eyes met.

'Not quite as we'd hoped,' he said, sounding tired. 'Maybe they got wind of Priess being detained and aborted. Someone could have seen us at Half Moon Street. It was always a possibility.'

'I'm so sorry,' she said.

She wanted to go home, to slink away from the embarrassment of being wrong. This had been her idea. Andrew had been sceptical but she had persuaded him. Already Jack had gone to speak with the Palace police to try, she assumed, to minimise any damage done by the failed stake-out. If there was anything going on tonight, it was happening elsewhere. It was a complete and utter disaster.

'There's still his Lordship,' Rowlands said. 'He'll turn Queen's evidence, I'd put money on it. We're not beaten.'

'Are you coming back with me?'

'Oh, I would like that, Cassie, very much.'

'Boss.' It was the serjeant. 'Edgerley wants to speak with you.' She handed him her walkie-talkie.

She watched him walked away. Another tongue lashing from the deputy commissioner. At least she would be able to comfort him later, make him feel that not all the world was against him.

'I've got to go into the Yard,' he said as he returned.

'I'll come wi–'

'No. Go home, Cass. I'll speak with you in the morning.' He squeezed her fingers in his own.

'Andrew, you said–'

'I know but I can't and you look wrecked. Get a good night's sleep, we can start again tomorrow.'

Bugger.

'There's nothing happening here tonight. I'm going to have to send the car back, Cassie. Make sure you take a cab home.'

'Yes, I just need a moment.'

'OK, but stay safe.'

'I will. See you tomorrow.'

He turned away.

She looked out into the dark courtyard. She had hoped to catch the crime ring, to give the DPM the culprits, get Sir Terence off her back and vindicate Andrew's long, hard slog to track them down. Instead, her career was over, her job gone and her future uncertain.

The Houses of Parliament were in recess for conference season tomorrow. Time had finally run out.

◊ SIXTY

Cassie plodded across New Palace Yard. Her limbs felt heavy with tiredness and the release of tension, but she squirmed with embarrassment when she recalled her certainty that the defunct kitchens would be the gang's next location. José's interest in the kitchens had seemed an obvious pointer and then to find that CSL had cordoned off the entrance seemed only to confirm it. She had been so sure that the passes were to be used to enable visitors to roam around the building. It had all made sense. Yet she had been wrong.

The Speaker didn't allow surveillance and if tonight's activities were brought to his attention, heads might have to roll. Jack's could be one of them. She didn't like to think of her friend at the mercy of someone like Sir Percy Dugdale.

She tried not to think how Andrew would justify the resources used that evening. DC Edgerley was probably removing him from the case at this very minute and she couldn't even offer comfort. He had trusted her judgement and she had let him down. And neither he, nor Jack, had uttered one word of blame.

Unbearable.

Don't give way to despair, she told herself as she walked out on to St Margaret's Street. Priess would talk and the case would break, Andrew certainly thought so. But tonight was her deadline. She had to submit her report tomorrow and, however she dressed things up, the case hadn't yet been solved. Tonight she had lost her career, her position and probably her means of making a decent living. She had wanted the influence and power to shape the course of events but now she wouldn't even be able to pay her mortgage.

Damn. Damn. Damn.

She began walking westwards. Parliament Square was still brightly lit but there were few people around at the late hour. The occasional black cab arrived via Whitehall, the 'For Hire' light dimmed. She would flag one down in a moment and go home.

It was then that she saw it: a light in the lower storey of the Jewel Tower across the road.

The four-storey rough-stone tower stood on the other side of Abingdon Street, completely separate from Barry's Victorian Gothic palace. It was medieval, built on land once belonging to the Abbey, but was still part of the Palace of Westminster. Around it the Abbey moat had run to join the river, with its mill and a jetty into the Thames. The Tyburn had fed into that moat.

It was the one place that they - that she - hadn't even considered. And there seemed to be something taking place in its cellar very late at night. Was some poor innocent becoming the latest victim? Was there still a chance to catch the gang?

Cassie reached for her phone and called Andrew's number. After a few rings it went to voicemail.

She crossed over the road. To her left Abingdon, or 'College', Green was covered with the detritus left behind by demonstrators. It stretched away until it reached the wall of Westminster School. She could see the branches of the trees which lined Old College Street beyond.

At the railings she looked down to the lawn below. The base of the

Tower lay below street level. To one side of it there was a deep trench, the last remnant of the Abbey moat, but otherwise it was surrounded by mown grass. All seemed dark. Could she have seen a reflection of car headlights in the casement windows?

Again she tried Andrew but got voicemail.

'Ring me,' she left a message. 'I think I might be on to something.'

If she descended the steps from the pavement to the lawn, she would no longer be visible from the road. Alarm bells rang in her head. Don't put yourself in danger. Never go it alone. Stay safe.

She looked back towards the lights of New Palace Yard where there was a police security point. She could get back-up. That's what she should do but the shame of the evening lay heavily on her.

How can I? How can I convince them again?

After the earlier debacle she couldn't do it. It was too humiliating. She took out her phone, this time calling the serjeant's number. There was no reply. The policewoman must be on her way home, probably on the tube speeding through tunnels beneath the ground. Cassie left a message.

I'll have to do it myself. It's my last chance. I don't have a choice.

Gripping her handbag shoulder strap more tightly, she began to descend the steps, giving only one glance back at the road. It was darker here and the noise of any passing cars was deadened. There were no lights in the windows of the Tower.

Perhaps she had been mistaken? But she knew she hadn't been. One last time she tried Andrew. Again she left a message, in hushed tones.

The lawn was springy underfoot as she crossed to the Tower, going around to the left where the former moat exposed more of the lowest storey.

There! A light. Just a sliver, but it was there. No one should be in there at this time of night.

Quick, now get the police.

Fumbling for her phone, she began to dial the emergency number.

A figure loomed in front of her. She opened her mouth to call out but a blow to her head set her ears ringing. Then something was being held over her face, it smelled of chemicals. She couldn't breathe.

TUESDAY

◊ SIXTY ONE

There was a pounding noise, reverberating, thumping over and over.

Cassie frowned and a shard of pain twisted in her skull. She put a hand to the side of her head, opened her eyes and examined her fingertips. In the half-light she saw that they were flecked with black – blood, dried blood. Her own.

The memories came rushing back: the failed stake-out, the disappointment, Abingdon Green, the Jewel Tower and then... nothing.

Her hand flopped back to the bed.

The embroidered coverlet was white, but there were no stains, not on the bed linen nor the oversized grey silk pyjama top she wore. So she must have come here after the wound on her head had stopped bleeding.

She looked around the spacious room with its high ceiling and plaster ceiling rose. Daylight peeped through floor-length curtains and muted light came from brass wall sconces. The furniture was modern, the very best in pared-back, expensive design. An array of electronic controls lay on the bedside table and a TV hung on the wall. It could have been an expensive hotel or a smart apartment but Cassie thought she knew where she was, a Georgian townhouse on the corner of Barton Street.

How did I get here?

And what had Lawrence Delahaye to do with all this? He was a money man – crooked, if the SFO was correct – but not a killer. What connection, if any, did he have with whatever was taking place in the Jewel Tower?

On the chair between the windows opposite was her handbag. There was no sign of her clothes. Cassie swung herself upright and around until her legs hung over the side of the bed. Her vision swam and the pain washed over her again. She blinked. The pain receded to a dull thudding.

Get your phone. Contact Andrew.

She pushed herself up and stood, head reeling.

Concentrate. Place one foot in front of the other.

She reached the chair.

Everything was there, except for her purse and her phone. A glance around the room told her that it didn't have a telephone, or, if it did, it wasn't on display. There were no clocks either. She pulled back a curtain and peered out.

Sunlight and shade dappled an old stone wall beneath plane trees. The wall stretched away to the right to meet the Embankment. The cars there were nose to tail. It was rush hour.

Then she heard footsteps beyond the door.

She stumbled back to the bed and fell upon the pillows.

A key turned and in three long strides Lawrence was at the bedside, leaning over her. She opened her eyes as he stroked her hair back behind her ear, examining the cut on the side of her forehead.

'Hmm, it's fine. You've been out for almost seven hours. I was getting worried. How do you feel?'

'Bloody awful! What's going on, Lawrence?' Cassie raised herself on to her elbows.

'You were found on Abingdon Green,' he said, sitting on the bed. 'You'd been attacked, mugged. One of my elderly neighbours came across you when walking his dog early this morning. He called me for help and I brought you here. I've sent for a doctor.'

'I want to go home, Lawrence.'

'I'm afraid I can't let you. You're unwell. You can't go home and be alone.'

'But –'

'It's for your own good.' He cast his eyes down. 'I confess, this wasn't how I had envisaged you being in my bed, Cassandra. After the other night I rather thought you might want to be here.'

'Lawrence, circumstances are different now and –'

'You haven't eaten for hours. You must be hungry.'

Delahaye rose and called an order from the door. Gordon entered carrying a heavily laden table covered by a linen cloth. Taking great care, he set down his burden and unfolded the cloth to reveal a table set for two, with silver spoons, glass and china.

Cassie said nothing but suddenly she felt famished. Her head was still pounding and she was struggling to make sense of anything. Had the muggers stolen her telephone? How did she come to be wearing pyjamas? It didn't add up.

The manservant returned to place a deep, lidded dish in the centre of the table. The aroma of smoked fish filled the room as the lid was removed. Cassie salivated, her stomach grumbled. Delahaye spooned out food into dishes and placed one on a dining tray.

'Please, eat.' His voice was silky and reasonable. His dark eyes met hers, anxious to persuade.

There was little to be gained by starving herself, Cassie decided. She should eat something; it might make her head feel clearer.

'I am hungry,' she said in as neutral a voice as she could muster.

'Kedgeree,' he said. 'It's important to keep your strength up. Let me help you.'

He spooned up the soft egg, rice and fish and proffered the spoon. Cassie took it from him; she had no intention of allowing him to feed her like a child. He gave her the tray with a rueful smile, one eyebrow raised.

He's still sexy, even if he is crooked.

Delahaye sat back, watching her eat.

'I was hoping that, by now, I might have persuaded you that we have a future together,' he said, 'We obviously enjoy each others' company and the physical attraction is certainly mutual. If it hadn't been for your precipitate departure on Saturday...'

Cassie concentrated on the food. On Saturday, she had made plain her desire for him, something she now regretted.

'Think how interesting life with me would be,' he said. 'You could have or do almost anything you wanted. We would make a fine couple and think how much good you could do with the sort of wealth and power I have. I know you want to. We could make such a difference to so many lives.'

Very clever. He knows me well.

'Actually, I am far more powerful than you know. It's not socially acceptable to say so, but if I'm asking you to commit to life with me, I have to be honest with you. Power today lies with the super-rich, the uber-capitalists, the invisible backers and donors. Not in governments and politicians.'

'We still have a parliament.'

He smiled.

Like an adult being patient with a slow child.

'Democracy is so easy to pervert, why replace it? Money, Cassandra. Money can buy anything. If a government gets difficult another can be sponsored. Sometimes it takes time, sometimes it's easier, but there are always people willing to take over. When national or global institutions fail to serve the purpose they are destroyed, distorted or hollowed out from the inside. Connect money with the newest technology and public opinion is easy to sway.'

Terrifying.

'Haven't you considered that you might be found out, get caught?'

His laughter sounded genuine.

'Most of what I do is perfectly legal. I have sufficient influence to determine events and I make an awful lot of money because of that. I have every intention of increasing my reach still further.'

'Market manipulation is against the law, I believe.'

'Laws are inadequate and there are powerful people making sure they stay that way. Regulators and the financial authorities in the UK are toothless and the whole system is stacked against them. The general public – pfft.' He gave a flourish of his hand. 'Has no idea.'

'If it's as wide-ranging as you say, you'll eventually bring down the City, which will end your schemes.'

'Oh no, one doesn't kill the goose which lays the golden eggs. One has to be careful. The Stock Exchange and the financial services industry are set to continue for quite a while yet.'

'And you really think I'll go along with this?'

'Mmm,' he had a speculative look in his eyes. 'Maybe I'll have to forego the more illicit elements of my career to persuade you. I don't really need them anyway. Would that please you? If I give you my word, I won't break it.'

Cassie thought of Dimitri Remis and his patient casebuilding. She put down her spoon. Delahaye was a criminal, Remis was clear about that and Andrew thought so too. But what exactly did that mean?

She suspected that many financiers found themselves, at some point, on the path leading to insider trading and market manipulation. People talked to each other, especially those who were rich and well-informed. Trade secrets were shared within networks of friends and family out of mutual self-interest. It might all be not quite legal but who was to know. This was how the wealthy had always maintained their privileged positions and fortunes, it went with the territory.

But this was different. This wasn't a fund manager seeking an edge over the competition, but a man intent on destroying the whole system while leaving only its facade in place. As with the City, so with Parliament. Delahaye would hollow that out too, until he controlled everything.

He has to be stopped.

'I'll leave you to rest now.' Delahaye stood. 'Consider your answer. I'll be back in a while.'

Cassie watched him leave as Gordon removed everything. The door closed and the key turned. In her head a small voice continued to argue Delahaye's case.

Just think what he's offering you.

At last. After the years in the wilderness, after being blocked by so many people in so many ways, she could finally make a genuine difference. What could she do with such money and power, with this man and his influence? To make real change, to do what she knew needed to be done.

Stop it! Stop even considering this.

Delahaye would never forego control. Nothing would be allowed to interfere with his ability to game the system and amass more wealth and power, including her. And she would never be content to be part of such schemes, however much good she could do. She would constantly be at war with herself. She belonged on the other side.

Besides, she loved someone else, someone who would never countenance such an alliance, someone who would never give up the fight for justice for those abused and murdered. The voice was stilled. The curdled self-loathing and frustration that had created it fell away.

Concentrate on getting out of here.

She needed to plan her next move. He wasn't going to let her go, he'd confessed too much, though she didn't think he would harm her either, at least not while she played along. Andrew and Daljit would have picked up her messages and the police would be searching for her. Andrew would move heaven and earth if he thought she was in danger. She had to stay alive and he would find her.

Do whatever's necessary and, if the chance to escape arises, take it.
In the meanwhile, think!

Cassie settled back against the pillows and began to do so.

◊ SIXTY TWO

Footsteps – there was a noise outside the door. Someone was unlocking it.

Delahaye might want her but he also wanted the game. Like Scheherazade in the old tale she would entertain him; her life might depend on it.

'Cassandra.' Delahaye entered and sat on the bed as before. 'I trust you're feeling better?'

'I am,' she replied. 'Thank you for breakfast by the way.'

'My pleasure.'

'But I want to know exactly what you want from me?' she asked, pulling her knees up against her chest under the sheet.

The meaning of the look he gave her was unmistakable.

'You know what I mean.'

'Oh, very well,' he brought a chair over to the bedside and sat, right ankle over left knee. 'You are the only woman I've met who might really understand me and what I do. You're accustomed to knowing secrets and are familiar with power. After all, you're deep in the Deputy Prime Minister's confidence.'

What?

Is that why he found her so attractive – a relationship with Charles Morecombe which didn't exist? Nothing to do with her then!

Perhaps I can use his assumption against him?

'As someone close to him, you have information which would be of considerable use to me. You also have influence. You can ensure that information is expedited through to him or blocked. Plus, you bring expertise, your knowledge of Whitehall is comprehensive and you know the Intelligence community from the inside.'

He thought she had power.

Control your reactions; don't let him see what you're thinking.

'I am also, I must confess, intrigued why someone of your calibre from GCHQ is, apparently, doing low profile procurement in the DPM's department.'

His misunderstanding surprised her but it gave her a way in.

'My line manager is Duncan Macfarlane but on certain issues I answer direct to Charles,' she said.

Delahaye leaned forward then sat back. He pursed his lips.

'Certain issues?'

'Mostly political,' she said. 'I have access to the government whips and their information. You have contacts you can check with, I'm sure. Robert Partington has been told to accommodate me.'

She hoped that the DPM had indeed spoken with Partington as he had promised he would. She had no doubt that Delahaye would check.

'Why would Charles Morecombe want your assistance?'

She lowered her voice, making Delahaye lean forward as she dangled her bait.

'Because Charles wants to be Prime Minister.'

There was no hiding his enthusiasm now. His eyes gleamed with anticipation.

'And will he be?'

'I think so.'

'With your help?'

'I do what I am commissioned to do.'

'And what, right now, is that?'

'Investigate David Hurst, whether he or the Home Office can be tainted with scandal, particularly with reference to the latest series of crimes. Hurst has ambitions; they are well documented.'

Delahaye shook with silent laughter. 'And the police too? So Rowlands is part of your investigation?'

She nodded.

'And I was beginning to think you had developed a certain *tendresse* for the inspector.' His voice hardened. 'He certainly seems to have an alarming amount of influence over you.'

Delahaye sprang to his feet. He placed a hand on the bed either side of her, his face inches from hers. She kept her face very still, expressionless, though her heart was beating rapidly.

'If you are lying, my beloved Cassandra...' he said, calmly and without passion.

She swallowed. She didn't need to feign fear. This was the true face of Lawrence Delahaye, cold and ruthless.

'You must be able to check what I am saying, or at least some of it. I met with Hurst recently at the Home Office. Sir John Sparrow was there and Peter Bradley from Special Intelligence. Surely you know someone at the Home Office who can confirm?'

He pushed himself upright and returned to his chair.

For a while he said nothing, scrutinizing her over the steeple of his long fingers. She stared back at him. He would never admit, she knew, if he didn't have the contacts to check and corroborate her story. Now she should press forward.

'When you have confirmed the truth, I want to be able to get up, get dressed, walk around,' she said. Then escape might be possible.

'You're in no position to make demands.'

Hold your nerve, she told herself. You can do this. They <u>were</u> alike, he was right about that – they both knew how to play the game.

'I will check.' He rose, uncoiling. At the door he stopped and looked back. 'I do hope you're not lying. I have such plans for us.'

The door slammed closed behind him.

She had bought herself more time. He would have to track down his contacts to confirm her story. The longer she stayed alive, the more likely she would be found. Her information would run out eventually but, for the time being, it didn't matter. Like Scheherazade, she lived to fight another day.

◊ SIXTY THREE

The key turned in the lock and the door opened.

'You wanted clothes.' Lawrence crossed the room to a door in the far wall, took a key from his trouser pocket and opened it. 'Come,' he said. 'Look.'

She slid out of bed and walked over, pulling the pyjama top down as far as she could. The door led to a dressing room, lined with cupboards with a bathroom beyond.

'Mine,' he said, indicating the cupboards nearest to the window. 'Yours.' He pointed at those furthest away from the door.

He retreated into the bedroom and Cassie explored the furthermost wardrobe. It was full of women's clothes, very good clothes and all in her size. There was lingerie in the drawers too, again in exactly her size.

These clothes had been bought for her. It reminded her of Silana and the costume. Her flesh began to creep.

He's crazy.

'Don't you like them?'

The voice came from right behind her.

She spun round and found herself in his naked embrace. His skin was warm. Last Saturday...

Things are different now.

She struggled but he was much stronger. The muscles of his arms, shoulders and chest were hard and defined under her palms.

'Cassandra,' he said, voice speaking into her ear. 'You can't win. You may as well acknowledge that now. It will make things easier. I know you want me, remember Saturday.'

'Just because I did then, doesn't mean I do now. Things change.'

Enraged, Cassie pressed her knees together and pushed him away. But Lawrence began stroking her, kissing and caressing her in all the right places. The kisses lingered. Despite herself, she felt a shiver of desire. Gently, he nibbled the soft skin on the side of her throat and then in the scoop near her collarbone. He forced his hand between her thighs.

'You're lying.' Withdrawing his hand, he smiled and licked his fingers. 'Fight me if you like. If that's what you need, I don't mind. The end will be the same.'

The light had changed when she awoke, alone in the bed. The sun was no longer on the front of the house. She was exhausted, the muscles in her arms ached and her thighs felt bruised, but her skin still tingled. How unexpected and how unfair – it had been so very good. And how deeply disturbing to find she wanted more of him.

The door opened and he returned, leaping on to the bed and wrapping her up in his arms. He nuzzled her neck, then kissed her tenderly.

'Cassandra, you taste wonderful. I can't get enough of you. I intend to taste every inch of you.' He began to nibble her neck. 'Oh by the way, Percy has confirmed that the Whips' Office has been told to cooperate with you.'

Cassie wriggled aside and he raised his face to hers. His eyes were bright, almost feverish.

The odious Sir Percy is one of his contacts?

It brought her back to reality.

What am I doing?

Lawrence traced the outline of her lips with his index finger and tugged at the lower before briefly slipping his finger into her mouth.

'I will write your name in diamonds on a mountainside,' he declared.

Play along.

'What is it with you and diamonds?'

'Hmm.' He kissed her nose. 'I have South African mining interests.'

She levered herself up on to her right elbow, facing him.

'You cheapskate!' She poked him in the chest. 'You sent me stock-in-trade! Wholesale!'

Lawrence collapsed backwards, laughing, and she pressed her advantage, her fingers jabbing.

Then she was flipped over on to her back and he was on top of her.

'Marry me, Cassandra.'

What?

'You're proposing to me?'

Why?

'Yes. I hadn't intended to, not so soon, but... circumstances.' He gave a small shrug. 'It would be good for both of us. You could have such a golden future. I can help you in ways you couldn't imagine. I'll clean up my act, I swear it,' he said, looking intently into her eyes. 'Say the word and I'll stop the fix. I've enough money now for us to do whatever we want and I can easily make more.'

He can't wipe out the past. He can't wipe the slate clean. He isn't going to change.

'Besides,' he said, gently parting her legs. 'We don't need all that when we have the new Prime Minister in our pocket, do we, my love.'

◊ SIXTY FOUR

She woke but Lawrence was no longer there. She stretched her hand across the bed to touch any warmth he had left behind.

'You're awake.'

He was sitting, still naked, in the chair by the windows, looking at her as he had done that first time at the club, taking in each part of her body.

'My contacts tell me that you met with Hurst, Sparrow and Bradley. You didn't tell me that Rowlands was in attendance too.'

'It was unavoidable. Anyway, you seemed rather prickly about the inspector, so I didn't mention him.' She mumbled, sleepily. It was true.

He drew in a breath but said nothing.

'I have something to show you,' he said, crossing to the bed and reaching into a drawer in the bedside cabinet for a remote control. The television on the wall burst into life as he knelt beside her.

She blinked. It was the midday news and a reporter was standing in front of a green space, Christchurch Gardens, off Victoria Street. There was a tent, like at Golden Square and Curzon Street, and scene of crime officers came and went. There was Bill Pottinger, the pathologist, grey-faced and sad.

'The discovery of the body earlier today has shocked the public and the police service. Detective Inspector Andrew Rowlands was an experienced and valued member of the force.'

'No!'

Cassie sat up, horrified. Delahaye held her tightly against his chest as she fought to be let free.

No, no, no, no.

'Inspector Rowlands was killed in the course of his duties,' the reporter said. 'Viewers may recall that he was working on the series of murders known as the Plague Murders. Christchurch Gardens is on the site of a burial ground for St Margaret's Church, also used to bury plague victims, and police are treating this death as linked to that case.'

This couldn't be true. It couldn't be.

There was a ringing in her ears, as she howled.

'Stop it!' Lawrence shook her. 'Did you really think I didn't know?'

He was staring intently down at her face, his own registering a mixture of contempt and exultation.

She hated him. He had had Andrew killed and then made love to her. She wanted to scream at him, to scratch out his eyes. Her fingers became claws.

'Andrew? How?' Her voice cracked.

'The usual. It was quick, you'll be pleased to know.' He looked sullen, almost sulky.

'His throat...?'

He didn't deny it.

She turned her head away from his triumphant face and began to weep, heaving great sobs.

He swept her up into an embrace. 'Shh, there, there.'

She pushed and pummelled his chest. 'This is your doing! Don't you try and comfort me! You did this! You!'

He wouldn't let her go, but his endearments had ceased and his grip hardened. Breathing heavily, she looked up into his face.

'It doesn't work like this, Lawrence,' she said, her voice tremulous and angry. 'You can't make me love you. And you can't own me. Brutalise, damage, kill, force me to pretend, but not own.'

'You only knew him for a week. What sort of future do you think you would have had with him?' he said, incredulous. 'Life in a shabby suburb, two holidays a year, early retirement on a police pension. And he would have betrayed you, had some sordid sexual affair while you focused on what's really important to you, your work. You're made for better than that. I've been waiting a long time for you.'

'I can't give you diamonds.'

'It's my choice, mine, not yours.'

'You assume that you have a choice about anything.' His voice was flat and remote.

Coldness swept over her. She had to survive and the icy stillness would help her. The ability to operate without emotion brought its own problems but now it might save her.

This is more than fraud, more than City fixing, more even than undermining Parliament. It's all linked – the murders too.

Inexorably, the pieces began to fall into place. Finally, she understood all the missed steps, the wrong assumptions. She began to see what was really going on and why. And exactly what she was up against.

'I wasn't mugged on Abingdon Green,' she said.

'Of course not. Gordon was keeping watch, he saw you. If Percy had found you, you'd have had a very unpleasant time and a painful death. I could not allow that.'

So Sir Percy had been in the Jewel Tower. Were the kitchens just a diversion then?

'You didn't need the passes in the Jewel Tower,' she said. 'I thought the stolen passes were to allow freedom of movement inside the Palace. But I was wrong.'

'Actually, you were right, just not for last night.'

So there's something else he's planning.

'Tell me, I was puzzled by how quickly you made the link between the Spaniard's death and the passes.'

'His wallet was found near where he was killed,' she replied. 'With his ID. So it wasn't difficult to make the link with Parliament. And he had my access pass hidden in the lining of his coat.'

'Hah! I knew something was missed.' His voice was dispassionate but he bared his teeth. 'He must have kept your pass as a bargaining counter to extort more money from my associates. He was stupidly greedy.'

As we guessed.

She steadied herself and he loosened his hold slightly.

She took a deep breath. 'It's all linked, isn't it, the rapes and murders, corruption and graft. It's a network and the killers are part of it, they help further your schemes and you help them get what they want. You manipulate everything. You're the spider at the centre of the web.'

His eyes glittered with amusement as she continued.

'Tadeusz died because someone had a fancy for a fit young fighter. You didn't intend for the body to be found but it was when the cavern collapsed. José needed money, so he stole the passes and tried to sell them to your associates, not knowing they were part of something larger. Silana was the favourite flavour of an influential American. And whoever was killed in the Jewel Tower was someone else's.'

'A Russian's, as it happens,' he said. 'He appreciated the setting, in the world's oldest democracy. Not that he's fond of democracy, in fact he loathes it. But he's very fond of redheads. The two together were irresistible.'

'What do you get from these men of power in return for enabling them to fulfil their darkest desires?' Cassie asked, already knowing the answer but wanting him to say it aloud.

'Favours, inside information, preferential treatment, with which I make myself wealthier and more powerful still. Ideally, any national or international law or governmental policy should align with my own interest. As you yourself pointed out, if I can create a consensus, using the mainstream and online media, the ideas and policies I and my agents advocate will receive the support I need and I can leave it to elected representatives to carry things out. I'll have made myself redundant.'

Cassie heard her own words echoing back at her.

Don't react.

'You're fixing the Thames Estates Programme too aren't you? Dugdale's helping with that and probably other contracts as well. You're ensuring the contracts go to the right companies so you can reward your friends and allies while you make money on the markets.'

'Of course.' Delahaye grinned proudly.

'You scratch their backs and they scratch yours.'

'They don't need much encouragement from me,' he answered. 'Power already has them in its grip; its contagion is as strong as any disease. All I do is organise. I ensure their specific needs are met.' He smiled.

'And you've got people to do that for you.' Cassie pointed out. 'Sir Percy and others, I don't doubt.'

'You would be surprised how many are happy, even enthusiastic, to help.'

'Parliament hollowed out, how many people there do you control? Did it even worry you when I told you that the police were looking at some Parliamentarians?'

'Not really, though I'd have liked to have known who,' he said, shrugging. 'Now you can tell me.'

'What about the victims, the young people? That was CSL's role, wasn't it, to find the victims for you. Then CSL get a share of the Thames Estates contracts. But what about the youngsters?'

'Flotsam. I would not have hurt them if I'd a choice but they met a need. Sex can be paid for but not the thrill of real power and dominance, the inspiring of terror, the power of life and death. It is what so many people crave.'

'They weren't "flotsam". They're individual human beings, like you or I.'

'Oh no, Cassandra, not like us. We are made of different stuff. And we are very alike, we are two sides of the same coin. You want power as much as I do, you're as fixated on it as me, though you call it 'influence' and clothe your desire and ambition in virtuous phrases like 'public service' and 'integrity'. Why do you think the sex is so good? We match each other perfectly.'

Her ambition had driven her into this in the first place. Her pride meant she had investigated alone. And she had been so focused on the chance to get her career back that she didn't see Andrew falling in love with her until it was almost too late. Now it was.

What if he's right? I'm just as bad, in my own way?

'What do you have to set against what I can offer you? Your career? A misplaced loyalty to those who treat you badly and pay you a pittance? A solitary life in Clapham with a cat?'

Cassie stared into space, numb and hollow, seeing nothing. She understood it all, but it provided no solace. Andrew killed, taken from her forever. Her career in ruins, an enemy made of a powerful Whitehall figure and hardly a shred of reputation remaining. She was alone and, without Andrew, more alone than ever. She had nothing left to cling to, she was floating, directionless. Useless. Complicit. Guilty.

What else is there for me now?

She turned towards Delahaye and, very gently, he laid her on her back.

◊ SIXTY FIVE

She opened her eyes. It was darker. Almost a whole day had gone by since she had first awoken in the bedroom in Barton Street. The day Andrew had died.

She lay entwined with Lawrence. Her nostrils were full of the scent of him, her mouth full of his taste. On the edge of her consciousness, black pain was crouching, ready to spring, but constant arousal kept it away and the physical ache she felt consumed her. She existed in a world of the senses. She wasn't powerless there.

Pain was patient. She knew it would wait.

'You're awake, my love,' he said.

She didn't reply but reached out to him.

'Again,' he said as he rolled her over on to her side and ran his hand over her breast and stomach. It came to rest between her legs. She felt him between her buttocks and she arched her back. 'Good girl,' he murmured into her ear.

There was a knock on the bedroom door and a voice she hadn't heard before.

'Sir?'

'What!' Delahaye hissed, as the door opened a crack.

'Sorry, but the police are outside, sir.'

In an instant he was sitting up. 'Find Harris,' he said to the servant. 'Send him to me.'

A loud knocking echoed through the house.

'Then let them in. Say I am out but due back at any moment. Show them into the front drawing room, give them coffee while they wait. I'll come and speak with them.'

The knocking sounded again.

As soon as the servant had shut the door, Delahaye grabbed her by the throat, his hands cold and dry, pressing her into the bed.

'How did they know? How did you do it?'

'I did nothing.' The pressure on her throat increased. 'I swear.' She could barely speak now. 'How could I contact them? I've been with you all day.'

'Yes,' he released her, casually. She stroked the tender skin around her throat, it was already swelling. 'Get dressed.'

She scrambled away into the dressing room where she pulled on a pair of jeans and a shirt from the rack and pushed her feet into a pair of loafers. She returned to the bedroom to see Gordon enter. He had a black eye and one side of his face was heavily bruised.

So this was Harris – Gordon was Harris, who lived above the Tyburn's course, who had been a soldier and was referred to by his old friends, like the Woods, as 'Don'. Harris was the killer, of Andrew, of Silana, José, Tadeusz and who knows how many others. Her stomach turned and she could hardly stand.

At least Andrew had gone down fighting. He'd done some damage.

'Take her to the cellar and wait for me there,' Delahaye said. 'I'll deflect the police.'

'That might not be so easy,' Harris answered. 'Priess has been arrested. His barrister phoned. He's selling us out to save his own neck.'

'What! When?'

'Yesterday. If you hadn't been so busy with her, you'd have known.'

Delahaye glared at Harris but he said nothing. Cassie could see him gauging how best to react to the changing situation. He would realise that the game was up. What was he going to do next?

'Prepare to evacuate,' he said as he crossed to a cabinet, pulled out a keyboard and plugged it into the TV. He set a computer programme running and Cassie saw the little icons of files on the TV screen winking out one by one. The programme was destroying his computer records.

Harris's gaze slid sideways to rest on Cassie.

'You heard me. Get on with it.'

Harris didn't move.

'We can go, sir, regroup, take on new identities, maybe return when things die down,' he began to argue. 'But she's a witness, she has to be dealt with.'

He drew a large sheathed knife from the inside pocket of his jacket.

Cassie stared, transfixed, as he took the knife from its case.

'I'll do it if you don't care to,' he said, and moved towards her steadily, a determined look on his face.

'No,' her voice croaked. She shrank back, but Harris advanced. He was almost upon her and she had nowhere else to go.

There was a dull snapping sound and he toppled sideways to the floor. He lay, clutching his thigh, teeth bared in a rictus of pain. Delahaye stood over the prone man, a silenced pistol in his hand. The drawer of the bedside table was open.

Cassie tried to stifle a sob. Blood had spattered her face and shirt. She was shaking as she wiped her face, her fingers red.

'Sir?' Harris looked dumbfounded, staring up at Delahaye as he lay in a widening puddle of his own blood.

'I'm taking her,' Delahaye said in a matter-of-fact voice. 'She's mine now. Can you make it to the river?'

'No.' Harris's face was pale.

'You'll have to stay here then. Keep your mouth shut. I will make arrangements to get you,' Delahaye said. 'Wherever they put you.'

He dragged Cassie through the dressing room and into the bathroom beyond.

'Here.' He moistened a towel and began to wipe the blood from her face. 'You'll feel better if you're not covered in blood. Wipe it off.' He gave her the towel and went to dress. 'I'll bring you a clean shirt.'

She looked at her reflection in the mirror. Her hair was messy, her lips looked bruised and already her neck showed livid blotches. She removed the blood-spattered shirt, revealing the marks of fingers on her breast. The blood she wiped away and the hair she combed, even the bruises would fade, but there were other, deeper hurts, hidden and beyond repair.

Then he was back, clothed and shod and helping her into a new shirt. As he began to button it up, he paused, catching sight of the finger marks. 'I'm sorry, Cassandra,' he said, stroking her cheek and running his hand along her jawline. 'I truly didn't intend... being with you is unlike anything I have experienced before. I wasn't prepared. I will make amends.'

She returned his gaze, saying nothing.

'We're going.' He seized her wrist, his fingers digging into her flesh. There would be another set of bruises. If she survived. 'To a new life.'

Delahaye led her past Harris. The man was grey with pain but now held a wad of cloth over his wound. He stared up at her resentfully.

They descended the stairs into the black and white tiled hall. The police were in the front room, all she had to do was shout. She felt the muzzle of the pistol in her back.

'No noise,' he whispered into her ear. It was as if he could read her thoughts.

Through a door to the cellar, down further into the bowels of the house, then along a passage to a heavy metal door. He swung the door closed behind them, slipping bolts across. Police, servants and Harris were now all shut off in the house above. The two of them were completely isolated. A large rucksack lay propped against the wall beside the skeleton of an inflatable dinghy.

'Take this,' he instructed, handing her the rucksack. 'And put those on.' He indicated wellington boots. 'I'll bring the inflatable, though we may not need it. Quickly. Don't stand there gawping.'

Cassie was pushed in front of him towards brick steps going downwards into the dark.

'It's not far,' he said. 'And it's something which I think will interest you.'

In the darkness at the bottom of the stairs she hesitated and

Delahaye walked into her, slipping his arm around her waist for a brief moment.

'Remember,' he said. 'We're together now, Cassandra.' His voice was sibilant as he said her name. 'Whatever happens.'

Then he turned, holding her at his hip, to draw back the bolts of a metal door. Already Cassie could smell the tang of the sewer ahead. The smell grew stronger as the door swung open.

'Here,' he said, 'is our escape route. The lost River Tyburn.'

◊ SIXTY SIX

The smell of ooze and decay was familiar, as was the cloying warmth of the atmosphere.

'One of London's lost rivers,' said Delahaye. 'Here.' He handed her a torch and she switched it on. Lit from below, his face took on a demonic look. Shooting his faithful retainer didn't seem to have affected him at all. He even expected the man to remain loyal to him. She would be treated similarly, no matter what he said he felt for her.

She shone her torch ahead and grimaced with genuine distaste. Its beam reflected in the sludgy liquid flowing through the base of the brick-lined tunnel. This time she would be walking through it without oilskins and waders. She remembered the last time.

'What are you up to?'

It was Andrew's voice she heard, the wry intonation, the droll humour. Her eyes widened.

'Don't worry,' Delahaye said, grasping her wrist again. 'The flow isn't strong. My you're cold. Stay in front of me.'

Think! Engage brain!

They went upstream, against the current. Her feet sank into the ooze and the suction made walking difficult. Water reached to just below her knees, slopping over the rims of the wellington boots. At least they kept out the solids suspended in the flow, which she tried not to notice.

They were going westward, Delahaye forcing the pace. They passed other doors, which she remembered as belonging to Westminster School and soon the brick roof changed to stone. This was the Abbey wall. An eerie sound echoed dully in the tunnel.

'Organ recital at the Abbey,' he said as she looked back at him. In the light of her torch he looked, carrying the inflatable, like some giant beetle-backed sewer creature.

There was the stone arch and the passageway on the right which led to the Abbey Crypt.

Now the sides of the tunnel were brickwork again. If she recalled correctly, it wouldn't be far until the buttresses began and there was a major step down in floor level, immediately as the tunnel dog-legged around. Then there would be street gratings and every twenty yards or so columns of grey light would illuminate the moving water. A series of small tunnels would branch off to the right.

'Where do they go, George?'

'WWII bunkers. Disused, shut up decades ago. I'd always meant to explore them but never got the chance.'

Now she knew where she was going to run to. As long as no one had bricked up the entrances. Or barred the doors. And if she could escape him in the first place.

Up ahead she saw the curving wall of the tunnel in the torchlight, turning away to the right. This was where the floor level changed. It was her chance. Her only chance. She looped the torch around her wrist and prepared to slough off the rucksack.

Don't underestimate him. He still has the pistol.

As the floor dropped away she screamed and pretended to fall. Delahaye stepped forward to catch her and she grabbed him, swinging around so that the weight of the rucksack hit him and shielded her.

'Be careful here, it's--ooof--Cassan--.' His head ducked below the surface.

They were almost in full darkness. His torch, knocked from his grasp, glowed from beneath the water showing where it lay, back down the tunnel. She felt him struggle to rise, gasping and splashing, but she rammed the rucksack across his body pinning his right hand above his head.

She pushed herself upright using the rucksack for leverage and ran on into the tunnel.

It was pitch black. She risked a flash of the torch. Here was the dog-leg turn. She flicked the torch off again and stretched out her hand towards the right-hand wall. The bricks were slimy to the touch but, if she followed the wall with her hand, she'd take the right-hand tunnel.

Behind her Delahaye was swearing and shouting. She had only a little time while he went back to find his torch. Then he would be after her.

Hurry.

The tunnel grew lighter, there was a street grating up ahead. He would be able to see her as she passed beneath it.

Where were the side tunnels? They couldn't be far.

Yes, her right hand had reached a corner. This was the first.

She ducked into it.

'You won't escape, Cassandra!' His shout echoed and behind her, in the main tunnel, the beam of his torch ricocheted from the walls.

She stumbled forwards, the floor was rising, the water growing shallower. Now she stretched her left hand out in front of her, the other holding the torch ready in case she needed to switch it on for a second.

Her left hand hit a solid object. She snatched it back, then put her hand forward again. It felt like a door. She risked a flash of the light.

'There! I see you!'

Quick!

The second or two of light had shown her a metal door with a recessed circular handle. She grabbed the handle, turned it and pulled.

The door didn't budge. She pushed and it moved a tiny way. The sound of splashing feet was growing closer. This time she put all her weight behind it.

She fell through the door as it burst open, then flung it closed behind her. Damn, she should have taken more care and closed it quietly. There was no key.

Block the door now. Block the door.

Cassie snapped on the torch, shining its beam around her. She was in a wide corridor, its walls of cream-painted brick, leading to a set of stairs. There was no furniture, although there were planks of wood on the floor, the remains of shelves or bookcases. Quickly, she gathered them, ramming them beneath the foot of the door and adding a folded wellington boot.

Better than nothing. Now go!

In five strides, Cassie was up the stairs.

At the top, she went through a doorway and stopped, shining her torch in a wide arc.

She was halfway down a long and narrow room, its brick walls painted cream with large pipes running a foot above floor level. Cobwebs hung in gauzy curtains covering metal furniture, library ladders and chair frames, the fabric chair backs and seats having long since perished. The walls held notice boards on which large sheets of faded paper were pinned. A map room, she guessed.

No one had been here since it had been closed up all those years ago. Behind her she heard a thumping noise. Delahaye had found the entrance. Her barrier wouldn't delay him for long.

She dragged the heavy door closed. It had no bolts, so she jammed a metal chair frame under the door handle and slid clipboards and the other boot under the door's foot. That might occupy him for a little while.

Now which way?

Left was north, she thought. It should lead her to the public rooms and the way out. If she kept reorienting and going left.

There was a crash from below. He was in the first corridor.

Shining her torch on the floor ahead of her, Cassie hurried to the far end of the room, pulling over furniture behind her as she went, the ladders, chairs, anything that would slow him down. The floor was dirty and cold to her bare, wet feet. She ducked through a door on the right.

The torchlight picked out serried ranks of wooden desks, their metal feet bolted to the floor, old-fashioned typewriters on top of some of them. A typing pool. Nothing she could use as a barricade here.

Move on.

Behind her came the muted sounds of Delahaye's cursing as he blundered through the debris of the map room. She was now several rooms ahead but her breath was coming in short gasps. Her head ached as if the running pained it. She was beginning to tire. Adrenalin had carried her so far but the cumulative impact of recent days was beginning to show.

She spotted a heavy security door up ahead with a wheel handle to secure it shut. This might hold him back if the mechanism still worked. She closed the door and tried to turn the handle – to no avail.

She tried again but it failed to turn.

Forget it: you don't have time. Go on.

Her torch's beam wove patterns on the floors and walls of room after room. Set out in a grid with interlinking corridors, it was a labyrinth, but she was leaving a trail for her pursuer to follow, the prints of her bare feet through the dust and detritus of decades were clear for anyone to see.

Delahaye would not be too far behind.

There was nothing for it but to press onwards.

◊ SIXTY SEVEN

His blood pounded in his ears and he shook with rage. He would catch her and when he did, he would kill her.

His foot caught in something and he sprawled on to his hands and knees, palms smarting, as he lost hold of his torch and it clattered forward. He could see scattered furniture and other debris in its rolling beam. Her doing.

He pushed himself upright and gathered his torch, wiping the dust from his wet hands on his shirt. He was dripping foul-smelling water and worse.

How could he have let her escape?

Back in the tunnel he had been taken completely by surprise, unable to do anything other than struggle to keep his head out of the filth. Bitch. She must have known the step was there and waited for her chance.

But that was impossible. It meant that she knew about the Tyburn. It meant that she'd been playing him all along. He'd been convinced that she was broken and that he had won.

He had offered her everything, to forego so much. He had allowed her her grief, her hysteria, had distracted her from her pain. He had loved her. He had risked it all for her and this was her response!

Did that mean that she knew her way around these rooms? No. No one had been here for decades, the cobwebs and dust attested to that. So they were even in that respect. And he had the pistol, tucked into his belt. She was unarmed. He had the advantage. All he had to do was follow and catch her. And then he would kill her, deciding exactly the moment of her death.

He directed his torch on to the floor of the room, her barefoot tracks were plain enough. She'd tire soon; the drug was still in her system. She couldn't keep going on adrenalin forever. When she did, he would find her. It wouldn't be long.

◊ SIXTY EIGHT

Cassie could hear her own laboured breathing in the silence. How much further was there to go?

At each doorway or junction, she recalibrated her direction, always trying to head north. She was passing through a series of small offices, linked by narrow corridors, with big central desks bolted into the floor like those in the typing room.

She no longer overturned pieces of furniture to impede pursuit. It cost too much effort.

At least it meant that Delahaye couldn't hear her progress and follow the sound. Yet, if he could no longer hear her, neither could she hear him, pushing away her barriers. The silence was unnerving. She had no idea how far behind he was. He might, at any time, catch sight of her and she would she get a bullet in the back.

The total darkness beyond her torch's slim wand of light was a suffocating thing, a passive creature, watching and waiting. Surely the bright beam was growing dimmer, the dark eating up its light? How many more of these rooms could there be? Then –

What the hell's that?

A concrete wall rose up in front of her, barring her way. No doors or corridors, only a wall.

Was it the basement of the Treasury building? No, that was the stratum above. The car park, maybe it was the underground car park? Somehow she must have gone wrong, taken a wrong turn. Now she had to double back and go around.

But how close behind was Delahaye?

She retreated towards the door and switched off her torch. In the darkness she couldn't see any other light approaching, so she slipped out, turned right and hurried along next to the wall, using her torch only sporadically. Through the door, across to another in the far wall, but it was slow going without the light to help her avoid obstacles.

'Ow!'

Her hands hit the floor just in time to break her fall. Her torch rolled away.

There was a shout from deeper in the complex behind her.

The torch? Where is it?

She fumbled around on the floor. There. She grabbed it, scrambled up and ran, passing through one doorway after another, shining the torchlight on to the floor ahead of her.

A shaft of light lit the wall in front of her, etching her shadow upon it. A splinter of wood leapt from the door frame.

He's shooting at me!

Through the door she veered left. She couldn't keep running in a straight line, it made it too easy for him. She looked back but the light had gone. What was he doing? Waiting for her to show herself again?

No time to think. Get going. Feel along the wall to find a door.

In the next room she risked a light. Her torch shone on stacks of chairs, desks and book cases. She edged past, turning north again, but anxious not to give her position away. Surely it was less dusty here? People had been here since the complex was closed down. Did that mean she was nearing the way out?

Please let it be close.

She couldn't carry on much longer.

Like the previous room the next was piled high with furniture, of more recent design as well as older, but it was taking her longer to get through these rooms. He would be catching up.

There!

In the opposite wall. A modern door.

I've made it!

Cassie wanted to weep with relief.

There was a clatter close behind her. He must have eyes like a cat.

Turn off the torch, quick.

She had seen enough to move silently between the stacks of chairs towards a large pile of desks beyond. She dropped to her knees and crawled beneath hoping that she hadn't left too obvious a trail.

If she could get to the door she would have a chance. She held the image of it in her mind, fixing its position relative to her own. The police would be looking for her, they might be nearby. Daljit knew about the bunkers, had she stationed some men at their entrance? In the silence she could hear the thrumming of her own blood.

Where was Delahaye? Had he seen the door?

'Cassandra.'

She almost leapt out of her skin. The voice came from the other side of the chairs. A yellow-white beam of light moved slowly over the furniture around her. She ducked lower.

'I know you're there, Cassandra.' His voice was seductive, smooth. 'Look, it doesn't have to be like this. You bested me. I acknowledge it. But it's part of our game.'

The voice was coming closer.

She slid her hand along the floor to her right. There were more stacks of chairs. If he came too close she could push them over at him, but then he might fire the pistol. At such close range he could hardly miss.

'You can still join me. I promise. I still want you, still love you.'

Closer still.

She would have to move soon. Push the stack of chairs, run for the door and pray that it wasn't locked. Cassie tensed, ready to heave.

'Whiskey, alpha, tango.'

A police radio!

Cassie shoved the closest stack of chairs with all her might. She vaulted over them as they fell and ran for the door. There was a flash as the gun fired and she shrieked in panic, but the bullet missed her.

In the blackness she felt for the door. There it was. As the door opened, she flung herself through it.

The light was fierce and bright. Blinded, she raised her hands to shield her eyes, seeing nothing. She stumbled forwards, blinking. A muffled sound deep in the room she'd just left signalled Delahaye's retreat.

Cassie smiled, wearily, her chest still heaving. She'd made it. She'd escaped. Her vision gradually returned.

Four semi-automatic rifles pointed directly at her.

She thrust her hands over her head.

'My name is Cassandra Fortune,' she said. 'I'm –'

The rifles were lowered.

'We know who you are,' the first policeman said. 'You're a high priority search.'

There is nothing else I would rather be.

Cassie's shoulders slumped as she lowered her arms, her next breath a sob.

'His name is Lawrence Delahaye,' she said, gesturing towards the doorway. 'The man trying to kill me – he has a pistol.'

'Leave him to us. You'd better come this way, miss.'

◊ SIXTY NINE

Sheer exhaustion - it swamped every other emotion.

Put one foot in front of the other. Just keep going.

Flanked by two policemen she walked through the Cabinet Office War Rooms as late tourists gawped. What a sight: a woman covered in filth and blood. Zombie-like, she passed through reception, by the ticket desk and up the stairs, out on to Horse Guards Road.

Blue lights flashed. There seemed to be masses of police, all wearing armoured vests. A small crowd of curious onlookers were kept back by a cordon. Over their heads, she saw the trees of St James's Park.

Then Daljit was there, hurrying towards her. Andrew wasn't.

He never would be now.

Warm tears ran down her cheeks.

'Cassie, Cass,' the detective serjeant grabbed her. 'You're safe now, you're safe. Thank God you're alright. My God, we've had half the force looking for you.'

'Andrew...'

'On here, please. Now.' A paramedic said, patting the padded stretcher trolley, which he'd wheeled alongside her.

She noticed his hi-vis vest. It was only just over a week ago, at Bond Street tube station, that everyone was wearing them. Before all this began. Her legs gave way and she sank down, only to be caught by a second paramedic who held her upright.

'Lie down before you fall down,' he said, helping her climb on to the trolley.

The silver blanket they covered her with felt crinkly to the touch. The sky was beginning to darken. Turning her head, she saw Daljit walking alongside the trolley.

'Who should I call?' the DS asked.

'My boss.' She really wanted Andrew but there was a gaping hole where he should be. Duncan was the first person she thought of. He was the only person.

Too late she realised as the trolley was lifted into the ambulance, Daljit may have thought she meant Charles Morecombe. Not so long ago the confusion about whom she worked for had probably saved her life.

The paramedics climbed in, as did a young uniformed policeman with a serious face. His short-sleeved shirt was blazing white, she noticed, against his black vest and semi-automatic rifle.

'Don't be alarmed. I'm here to protect you,' he said when he noticed her look.

The ambulance doors were closed and the vehicle began to move, its siren wailing.

'Where...?'

'St Thomas's,' the older paramedic replied. 'Not far. But we need to check you over, the blood...'

'Isn't mine. Or at least, not most of it,' she said. 'It belongs to one Gordon Harris, who you will find at 2 Barton Street.'

'Think we already have, ma'am,' the young officer said. 'And we've got men in the sewers after Delahaye.'

Maybe, Cassie thought, but there are plenty of exits and Lawrence Delahaye will know all of them.

'Can you move all of your limbs normally?' The other paramedic asked.

'Yes, but I'm so tired,' she closed her eyes. 'I was unconscious, probably drugged, I don't know with what.'

'For how long, can you remember? It might be important?'

'Monday night to the early hours of Tuesday morning. I was out for about seven hours.'

Tears were streaming now, her nose was clogged. She tried to sit up.

'Here.' One of the paramedics pushed another pillow beneath her head. 'You're in shock.'

He was probably right. But that wasn't the only reason she was weeping.

'Detective Inspector Rowlands...'

'Didn't make it, ma'am.' The young policeman's expression became stern.

'So it's true?'

'Yes ma'am.' He shut his mouth like a steel trap. 'But we'll get the bastards who did it – we've got most of the gang already. Delahaye won't get away.'

'Don't be so sure, Constable.' She heard Andrew's dry voice say.

The ambulance swung hard right.

'Here we are, miss,' the older ambulance man said as his colleague opened the doors. 'Let's get you looked at.'

WEDNESDAY

◊ SEVENTY

'Bloody hell, Cassie. You still look awful.'

It was Daljit.

She crossed to the bed and gave Cassie a hug, then made herself comfortable in the bedside chair. 'How are you?'

'I'm OK. Bumps and bruises mostly.'

'We were so worried. I picked up your voicemail early Tuesday morning. Andrew already had. Then there was no sign of you. We were tearing our hair out. Andrew assigned as many officers as he could to look for you, uniformed and CID. He was sure Lawrence Delahaye had found you.'

'He was right.'

'But we had to wait for a search warrant. The legal processes took much longer than usual, Delahaye had friends in high places. Cassie?' Daljit hesitated. 'He didn't?'

'I'd rather not talk about it.'

What was there to say? I had sex with him, voluntarily and with enthusiasm?

I was his prisoner, I was coerced. I did what I had to do to stay alive.

'We were worried about that too. Andrew...'

'How did it happen?'

'A tip off in the early hours. He took the call. Everyone was out looking already.'

'Were they waiting for him?'

Daljit nodded, her eyes moistening.

'Why did he go alone?'

'He was frantic, Cassie. He blamed himself.'

'Why? It wasn't his fault.'

'He left you alone, unprotected. He didn't keep you safe.'

I got myself captured and he came to find me. I caused his death.

The policewoman took a tissue from her handbag. Her tears were flowing freely now.

'They found him in Christchurch Gardens?'

'Yes, did they tell you?' Daljit sniffed.

'No, Delahaye made me watch the news. I saw the report.'

'Oh, Cassie, how awful. You must have felt so desolate and alone.'

'That was the idea,' she said. 'For a while I wondered if it was true, or if it was a report fabricated somehow by Delahaye, but I knew it was true, really. I was just hoping it wasn't.'

'He adored you Cassie.' Daljit's eyes filled with tears again.

'He loved me.'

And I would have loved him.

'Once we found Andrew's body, the proverbial really hit the fan. The Home Secretary was on the case, half the Met out looking for you, no problem getting warrants then. I went straight to Barton Street.'

'So it was you who prompted our flight into the Tyburn,' Cassie said. 'When the police arrived, Delahaye decided to make a run for it, taking me with him.'

'Were you there then? When we called?'

I was naked in bed with the man who ordered Andrew's death. How can I say that?

'Yes, I heard you knocking at the door.'

'So close...' Daljit filled the silence. 'You were right about Westminster but it was the Jewel Tower not the kitchens. There's no CCTV there and someone could have come up from the Tyburn and let the others in.'

'Probably Harris.'

'We were just looking in the wrong part of the palace,' Daljit smiled, sadly. 'Anyway, the good news is that Priess has turned Queen's evidence, just like Andrew said he would. We've arrested the criminals, including the husband and wife from CSL and Sir Percy Dugdale and we've got Harris. He was Delahaye's assigned orderly In the London Regiment, the Territorial Army equivalent of the Green Jackets.'

'So there *was* a military connection. What about Delahaye himself? Has he been found?' Cassie hesitated to ask; she thought she knew the answer.

'Unfortunately, no, but we're still searching. Ports and airports are on the alert. He won't get away.'

He already has.

'Cassie, you'll receive round-the-clock protection until he's found,' Daljit assured her. 'And we will find him. It's only a matter of time.'

Maybe, but will it be soon enough to stop him from having his revenge?

'Oh, what about Frank Cairns? He needed money, knew the sewers? Was he involved?'

'No, completely clean, the only thing he did wrong was join the same members' club as Delahaye, Priess and Dugdale.' The policewoman stood. 'Look, I'd best get back, there's a mountain of paperwork still to do. Are you coming next Friday?'

The funeral.

'If they let me out of here, yes.'

'So I'll see you then, if not before. We can catch up some more.'

'Yes, I'd like that. Thanks for coming.'

Cassie lay back on the pillows and stared at the blue sky and the stonework facade across the river with its glinting casement windows. Her room overlooked the Thames and the Palace of Westminster. One of the finest views in London, that's what he'd said, as they had stood on the Terrace last week.

The arrests were good news but Lawrence Delahaye had escaped. He had misdirected them all along and she, more than anyone, had been fooled. He'd planned to use her supposed access to Charles Morecombe and other politicians. With hindsight, it was easy to see that the break-in at her flat had enabled him to make himself appear her perfect match. The books she read, the music she liked, the food in her kitchen, it would all have been suggestive of her personal tastes and choices.

She had been duped. Andrew had sensed it, but she had ignored him. Cassie turned her face from the window and let the tears flow.

◊ SEVENTY ONE

The door to her room opened. This time, an armed policeman entered.

She heaved herself upright in the bed as Charles Morecombe's head peered around the door and he came in. The policeman took up position outside.

'Cassandra.'

'Deputy Prime Minister, forgive my –'

Morecombe waved her protestations away.

'Don't apologise, you have nothing to apologise for. Quite the contrary.'

Morecombe folded himself into the bedside chair and dropped a glossy gift bag into his lap, which he then seemed to forget was there.

'I'm told that you should make a full recovery.'

'Yes. Aside from a bump on the head, there's nothing physically wrong with me. I can come back to work.'

'I'm also told that you were kept prisoner,' he said. 'Have you spoken with a psychiatrist? There may be psychological scars.'

Cassie shook her head forcibly, then winced and stopped. She didn't want a professional inside her head; there was too much in there she didn't want anyone to know about, too much she was ashamed of.

'You'll need to recuperate.' The DPM pursed his lips and gave her a look that suggested she make no immediate plans.

Still out on my ear? After all I've endured?

'Let me bring you up to date before we touch on the matter of your return,' he said. 'You uncovered a remarkable network of influence, a dark mirror of the networks of the above-the-surface world. The participants were important people from all walks of life – universities, the judiciary, Parliament – not only the commercial world. The powerful have always shared certain personality traits with the psychopathic. We have details but they will remain undisclosed, at least for the moment. It will all come out in the end but we will manage it.'

'There may have been other victims. What about them?'

'The case isn't going to be closed. Someone will be assigned to follow all the loose ends, find any others who suffered or died, track down the families of those formerly unknown. There was data in Delahaye's computer files, which will help with that.'

But... she had seen Delahaye delete his computer files.

'And Cassandra, the police also found information about you.' He handed over a memory stick. 'They've gone through it. He did quite a lot of research. This is the only remaining copy.'

So it wasn't just the break-in which gave him his ammunition. She tightened her fist around the device. This would make interesting reading later.

'Sir, there needs to be a full review of security at Westminster and far more checks imposed. I believe that Delahaye had plans to use stolen passes for something else, something major. This episode in the Jewel Tower was merely a dry run.'

'It's already underway.'

'And the Tyburn?'

'Will continue to be part of the sewage system but we'll ensure it's not used for any other purpose, or attempted attack. Thanks, not least, to you and the Detective Inspector.'

During the silence which followed Cassie could hear booming music from a pleasure cruiser sailing down the Thames.

'DI Rowlands will be interred with full honours in just over a week from now. I have endorsed the commissioner's recommendation granting the Queen's Medal for Gallantry,' the DPM said.

It couldn't bring him back. Cassie felt the tears welling again.

Think about something else.

'What about the plague scare?'

'That will take time to subdue but it will be extinguished,' Morecombe said. 'The Chief Medical Officer and Chief Scientific Advisor have issued statements and are speaking to TV and the press. Number 10 has got a new communications strategy in place. The media barons will be anxious to gain the favour of our incoming Prime Minister. After all, he has a reputation for getting his way. Oh, this is for you.' He handed her the gift bag. 'Bev chose it, I hope it's alright.'

'Thank you,' Cassie said, setting the bag aside. 'So the PM's announcement will go ahead?'

'Yes. He'll announce his resignation in just under a week's time, next Wednesday. I will then become acting party leader while a leadership contest, a very swift leadership contest, takes place. Unless something unforeseen happens, David Hurst will assume the premiership.'

What about you? Wouldn't you like the job?

'It wouldn't be for me, Cassandra,' he said, divining her thought. 'I'm too uncomfortable in the limelight. David handles it better; he'll do a good job.'

Her heart sank. There would be no patronage from the man she had clashed with; the best she could hope for was that Morecombe could shield her from any negative impacts.

Maybe press my case now, he owes me something?

'Deputy Prime Minister, about my coming back to work? I was under the impression from Sir Terence –'

'You won't be coming back to work for me, which I regret. I don't expect you would work for Sir Terence again and I don't blame you. No, I think David Hurst has a post for you. He's really not bad to work for, you know.'

The man who is about to become Prime Minister?

'I'm not entirely sure what, I don't think he's worked it out yet,' the DPM said. 'But there will definitely be something. Concentrate on getting better for now. Rest. Take as much time as you need, Cassandra.'

The DPM was on his feet ready to leave.

After he had gone she pinched herself to make sure that she was awake. The Palace of Westminster still glinted in the sunshine, she could still hear the sounds of the hospital, but her place in the world might, it seemed, have changed. She had what she had wanted so desperately, she had her career back. She had a place of power.

She closed her eyes and lay back as the gift bag slid on to the floor. It was all too much.

Now she just wanted to sleep.

FRIDAY

(one week later)

◊ SEVENTY TWO

'I'm home!' Cassie called as Spiggott trotted into the hall to greet her.

She scooped up the cat and went into the bedroom. As she opened the doors to the garden she smelled the fresh-green scent of recent rain on foliage. Somewhere, someone was playing a radio.

She had survived but not unchanged. Right now, she was clinging on and she would keep doing so, at least until she had carried out her first commission for David Hurst. The diazepam helped.

Next door a window slammed. The cat meowed.

'What do you want, lovely?' said Cassie. 'I'll have to think what to do with you when I'm away.'

She couldn't ask her neighbour to feed and water the cat for a fortnight or more and Spiggott wouldn't enjoy a cattery. She would have to resolve this problem.

Andrew's funeral had been almost unbearably painful. The coffin was flag-draped with the Queen's Medal for Gallantry sitting atop it, but the family had foregone all other regalia. There was no formal salute, only the sliding of the casket behind the curtain.

Grief for what she had lost was very near the surface. Andrew Rowlands had been the man for her but she hadn't realised until it was too late. Her own obsession had got in the way. In that regard, Lawrence Delahaye had been right. It was her folly and ambition which had drawn her into Delahaye's clutches and drawn Andrew in after her.

The pain of that is something I'll have to learn to live with.

If Delahaye let her. He was still at large and, while he might be weakened, she knew she shouldn't underestimate his reach or power. He had kept her alive, saved her from Sir Percy and from Gordon Harris, and in his eyes, she had betrayed him. He would not forget.

I won't forget him either. He ordered Andrew's death.

She vowed to see him caught and pay the price. Delahaye said that they were alike and in some ways they were, not least in sheer obduracy.

After the funeral service, David Hurst had approached her.

'Walk with me,' he'd said and started out towards the cemetery entrance.

'Charles has told you that I want you to work for me?'

'Yes.'

'To undertake specific commissions,' Hurst had said. 'Oh, I know I have an army of public servants, all ready to give me what I want and can call on whatever experts I choose. But all will have their own agenda. I want one or two people whom I trust to find things out for me, often on sensitive issues.'

And you think you can trust me. Why? Because I wouldn't be bullied? Or because I delivered regardless of risk?

'You'll report to the Cabinet Secretary but work directly for me.'

It would be exciting and interesting and was a chance to become indispensable to the Prime Minister, the most powerful man in Britain. This was far beyond anything she could have hoped for when she agreed to Sir Terence's proposition but quite a lot had happened since then.

'When would I start?'

'Right away. I have a task for you in Greece. Have you ever been to Delphi?'

'Delphi? The Temple of Apollo Delphi?'

'So I believe,' Hurst had replied in a dry tone.

Things were moving so fast.

'Speak with the FCO and the Treasury. Honor, who manages my office, will give you the relevant names. The conference you'll be attending takes place this autumn. You'll be away at least a fortnight. Once you're fully briefed come and see me.'

At the cemetery gates the driver of Hurst's car had opened the rear door for his passenger. Hurst hadn't looked back as the car pulled away.

Carrying the cat, Cassie walked through to the kitchen. However saddened and scarred, deep down she also felt a sense of satisfaction.

Whatever Lawrence Delahaye claimed, Parliament and the law still counted. His schemes had been thwarted and those who helped him had been caught and would be punished. The corruption he had fostered had been, if not eradicated completely, then severely diminished. New laws were proposed governing MPs and other officials, their private sources of income and the ways in which they could use influence to benefit themselves personally. The City would be more closely regulated with private equity and hedge fund activities subject to punitive taxation and loopholes closed.

No one was going to argue. If they did, it would be assumed they were tarnished by the same corruption as the criminals. Even the media were chastened. There were battles yet to come, but for the moment, its moguls had been forced into retreat.

The good guys are winning!

And Cassie was the special envoy of the Prime Minister of the United Kingdom. She was where she wanted to be, at the centre of things, where the power lay, as a servant of state and people, not as an autocrat. She had been well and truly inoculated against the plague-like contagion of that sort of power. She sniffed, dry eyed.

Best to stop moping and make a start.

AFTERWORD

Plague is fiction, a work of the imagination, although some of what features in it is real. The 'lost river' Tyburn, the delta of which created Thorney Island, now known as Westminster, still runs beneath London's streets as part of Sir Joseph Bazalgette's remarkable Victorian sewer system. There are a number of accounts of walking along it. I have used those of John Hollingshead (1860) and Richard Trench & Ellis Hillman (1996).

The Palace of Westminster is beset by watery leakages and power outages, as it is in the novel and is under constant repair by the real Palace of Westminster Craft Team. The Craft Team's subterranean clubroom is my invention but I rather hope they have something like it down there. The Security Control Room is entirely fictitious but visitors to the Palace can see the Doorkeepers, in their antique uniforms, in the Lobbies at the entrances to the Houses of Commons and Lords.

At the apex of British democracy Parliament, not the government of the day, nor the judiciary (nor the police), is sovereign. It is not subject to the laws it makes, something which Cassie explains to Andrew and Daljit when she first meets them. There are, therefore, unusual policing arrangements in the Palace of Westminster, which is a unique, and passing strange, place in itself.

The Second World War bunkers beneath Whitehall are real though much of them has been replaced by later subterranean construction works, eg of the parliamentary car park. The Cabinet Office War Rooms are open to the public if readers wish to see what those underground offices look like.

The scientific studies quoted by Cassandra, of power and the chemical changes it prompts in the human body and brain, are real. Power is, indeed, a 'drug'. Researchers have concluded that those individuals who strive most for power are probably those most unsuited to wield it and that its corruption increases over time. Strong institutions, an independent civil service, transparency and accountability are therefore absolutely necessary to weigh against this tendency. Together with a limit on the power any individual may hold.

I have never worked at GCHQ nor in the security and intelligence services, though I know people who were part of that world. I have worked in Whitehall at a senior level, in various government departments, including the Office of the Deputy Prime Minister, which is where any comparison between myself and Cassandra ends.

Originally a quotation from Michel Foucault adorned the front of 'Plague' but was removed as being too pretentious. Nonetheless it is his conception of power, as being everywhere and within every relationship, creating a shifting balance of power between two or more participants that, I hope, pervades this book.

Cassandra will return, as the new Prime Minister says, in Delphi, Greece in *Oracle*, the second book in the series and then come back to London in *Opera*, the third.

To follow Cassie's adventures and learn more about her next book, follow me on **Instragram at @JulieAndersonAuthor** or on **Twitter at @jjulieanderson.**

Or follow **Claret Press** on **Twitter** at **@ClaretPress** or subscribe to the Claret Press website on **www.claretpress.com.**

I'd love to hear what you think of the book.

A C K N O W L E D G E M E N T S

I would like to thank a number of people with expert knowledge who were very generous with their time and expertise.

Thank you to Mike Naworynsky, former Deputy Serjeant at Arms of the Palace of Westminster for his invaluable insight into the workings of that august, if collapsing, place (and his great stories). Thank you also to retired Devon & Cornwall policeman, Graham Herbert, for his advice on police procedure and practicalities and to Dr Danielle Carson, microbiologist, for her excellent advice on *yersinia pestis* and other pathogens. I was also hugely fortunate to have Parliamentarians read the text, so thanks to Baron Collins of Highbury, current Opposition Spokesperson on International Development in the House of Lords and to Baroness Prosser of Battersea, current Chair of Trustees of the Parliament and Industry Trust.

A very big thank you must go to Gina Marsh and Katie Isbester of Claret Press for all their hard work and without whom this book would not be what it is.

The members of a number of book clubs across the country were kind enough to read earlier versions of 'Plague' including the Ivydene Bookworms in Somerset. Thanks to them and to Anne Carroll and Jenny Hollier of The Reading Den, an online support hub for book clubs, who helped organise some of this. Also to my neighbour and friend, Elizabeth Buchan, who was kind enough to listen to my ideas and read an early draft and who was unfailingly positive, even while saying what needed to be said. Thanks to David, John and others, the members of a local Clapham writing circle to which I belong, who took the trouble to read and comment on various iterations of the tale.

As ever, thanks to Myfanwy Garth and Annette Souter who have been tirelessly encouraging of my efforts and to Helen Hughes and Sue Pither for all their interest, help and support. Finally, thanks to Mark, my husband - long-suffering in the way spouses of writers have to be - a brilliant cook and a mean spotter of plot holes.

Lightning Source UK Ltd.
Milton Keynes UK
UKHW041130300620
365804UK00001B/47

9 781910 461464